"Hear the big news?" someone said.
"Sam Rivers is back in town."

Liza Courtland stilled in shock. The one man who could turn her whole world upside down was back. Why? Why now?

And how could this be, that the thought of having Sam back in Port Henry could make her knees weak and her heart pound?

He'd once had incredible power over her. But she'd been nineteen then. Eight years was a long time. She'd changed. Grown up. She'd had to....

Still, Liza remembered everything about Sam Rivers, down to the finest detail. She'd loved him with the fierce joy of youth. Then hated him for the pain he'd caused her. But always, always, she'd thought of him. Dreamed of him. Wanted him.

Liza trembled. Oh, God, she'd have to be careful.

And, above all, she had to protect her child....

Dear Reader,

In celebration of Valentine's Day, we have a Special Edition lineup filled with love and romance!

Cupid reignites passion between two former lovebirds in this month's THAT'S MY BABY! title. *Valentine Baby* by Gina Wilkins is about a fallen firefighter who returns home on Valentine's Day to find a baby—and his former sweetheart offering a shocking marriage proposal!

Since so many of you adored Silhouette's MONTANA MAVERICKS series, we have a special treat in store for you over the next few months in Special Edition. Jackie Merritt launches the MONTANA MAVERICKS: RETURN TO WHITEHORN series with a memorable story about a lovelorn cowboy and the woman who makes his life complete, in *Letter to a Lonesome Cowboy*. And coming up are three more books in the series as well as a delightful collection of short stories and an enthralling Harlequin Historical title.

These next three books showcase how children can bond people together in the most miraculous ways. In *Wildcatter's Kid*, by Penny Richards, a young lad reunites his parents. This is the final installment of the SWITCHED AT BIRTH miniseries. Next, *Natural Born Trouble*, by veteran author Sherryl Woods—the second book in her AND BABY MAKES THREE: THE NEXT GENERATION miniseries—is an uplifting story about a reserved heroine who falls for the charms of rambunctious twin boys…and their sexy father! And a sweet seven-year-old inspires a former rebel to reclaim his family, in *Daddy's Home*, by Pat Warren.

Finally, Celeste Hamilton unfolds an endearing tale about two childhood pals who make all their romantic dreams come true, in *Honeymoon Ranch*.

I hope you enjoy this book and each and every title to come!

Sincerely,

Tara Gavin,
Senior Editor and Editorial Coordinator

Please address questions and book requests to:
Silhouette Reader Service
U.S.: 3010 Walden Ave., P.O. Box 1325, Buffalo, NY 14269
Canadian: P.O. Box 609, Fort Erie, Ont. L2A 5X3

PAT WARREN
DADDY'S HOME

Silhouette®

SPECIAL ▼ EDITION®

Published by Silhouette Books
America's Publisher of Contemporary Romance

This book is dedicated to Gail Chasan, who has grace
and panache and a terrific sense of humor.

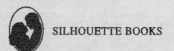 SILHOUETTE BOOKS

ISBN 0-373-24157-7

DADDY'S HOME

Copyright © 1998 by Pat Warren

Printed in U.S.A.

Books by Pat Warren

PAT WARREN,

mother of four, lives in Arizona with her travel agent husband and a lazy white cat. She's a former newspaper columnist whose lifetime dream was to become a novelist. A strong romantic streak, a sense of humor and a keen interest in developing relationships led her to try romance novels, with which she feels very much at home.

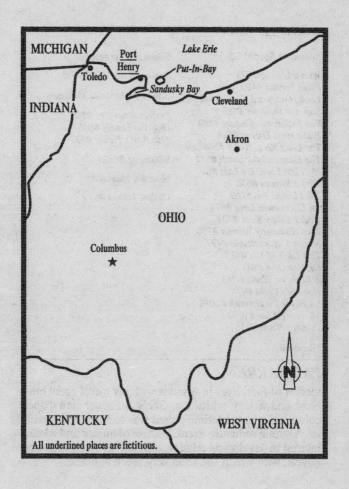

MICHIGAN

Port
Henry

Toledo

Lake Erie

Put-In-Bay

Sandusky Bay

INDIANA

Cleveland

Akron

OHIO

Columbus

★

N

KENTUCKY

WEST VIRGINIA

All underlined places are fictitious.

Prologue

Liza Courtland smiled at the delicate ivory-and-gold angel she held in the palm of her hand. Sam had given it to her just this morning when she'd stopped at the building site where he was working. It was the first, the only gift he'd ever given her, and she loved it almost as much as she loved him.

Leaning back in the old-fashioned swing on the wrap-around porch of her parents' cottage on Crane Lake, she closed her eyes and pictured Sam Rivers. He was tall and lean and very tanned from working outdoors in construction all summer. How she loved to run her hands over the hard muscles of his arms and solid chest, then let her fingers roam through his coal black hair as she watched those devastating blue eyes turn hazy with hunger. Hunger for her.

Liza shifted, stretching her long legs, her thoughts causing her body to respond. It'd been like that from the moment she'd laid eyes on Sam Rivers. And for him, too, she knew. As if they were meant for each other, though it had taken her a while to break through Sam's reserve. He was from the wrong side of the tracks, he'd told her repeatedly, and way out of her league. As if that mattered, Liza thought.

Still, she had to admit it might matter to her father.

Will Courtland owned nearly everything worth owning in the small town of Port Henry, situated on Ohio's Sandusky Bay. But he hadn't always, for the family holdings traced back to Liza's mother's family. Will had had intelligence and ambition, but very little cash, when he'd married into Elizabeth's wealthy clan. He'd cleverly tripled their vast holdings in short order—a poor boy who'd made good. That was why Liza had reason to hope her father would one day relate to Sam.

If only Sam's father wasn't the town drunk, a man who housed his family in what was little more than a shack at the edge of the woods. Joe Rivers, loud and boorish, was rumored to beat his wife. She'd have introduced Sam to her family sooner if not for his father's unsavory reputation. So she'd waited, biding her time until this Labor Day weekend at the lake cottage and the end-of-summer picnic that her parents always hosted, inviting family and friends from miles around. Surely, in this pleasant setting, surrounded by familiar faces, Will would see Sam for what he was and not judge the son by the father's mistakes.

Listening to the gentle squeaking of the swing, Liza prayed things would work out. Because next week she'd have to go back to Ohio State to begin her sophomore year, when all she really wanted was to stay home and be with Sam. He was five years older, working full-time and taking evening courses because he couldn't afford to go away to college. He'd finish though, she knew he would, because

Sam badly wanted to prove himself, to overcome the shameful legacy of his father.

Liza hugged the angel to her breast, her heart bursting with love. Everything would work out. It had to. Dad would realize Sam's potential, maybe even offer him a job at Courtland Enterprises. Mom would see through Sam's tough facade to the sensitive man beneath, the one Liza had discovered. Then one day, they'd get married and life would be wonderful. She'd never really wanted to work in the family business, nor be anything but a wife and mother. She felt a twinge of conscience, for she knew she'd be just another disappointment to her father, like the loss of her brother and the wild antics of her sister. But being with Sam was all that mattered, all she could think of.

A distant rumbling caught her attention. Looking across the lake, Liza noticed a lightning bolt split the evening sky. She glanced at her watch and saw that it was after eight. What could be keeping Sam?

The cottage was their favorite meeting place, one they'd visited every chance they'd had during the long, hot summer. The weekend festivities wouldn't begin till Saturday, so they'd arranged to spend Friday night here alone. Earlier, when she'd stopped to reconfirm with Sam, he'd seemed distracted, but he'd given her the angel, kissed her thoroughly and promised to meet her at the cottage around seven. It wasn't like Sam to be late.

Liza watched the first raindrops begin and felt a quick jolt of apprehension. Surely he hadn't gotten cold feet about meeting her folks and decided not to come. No, he wouldn't stand her up; he'd tell her face-to-face if there was a problem. A loud clap of thunder had her shuddering. Surely he hadn't had an accident. No, Sam was a careful driver.

The heat of summer drifted away. It grew cooler on the deep, shadowy porch with only the glow of the lamp coming through the window to add a little light. She glanced at the silent phone next to the lamp. Everything was all right, Liza told herself. She was just being a worrywart.

Giving in to a yawn, she set the angel on the three-legged table alongside the swing and curled up under a light afghan. She'd just close her eyes for a short time, and the next thing she'd be aware of would be Sam taking her into his strong arms and kissing her awake. On that delicious thought, she settled down.

Sam was on his way, Liza assured herself as she felt her limbs grow heavy. He'd have a perfectly reasonable explanation for being late. He knew she was waiting for him, and he'd never disappoint her.

The rain gradually became heavier and the wind picked up. Liza wasn't sure if it was the misty moisture that sprayed onto her face or the sound of something breaking that startled her awake. With a shake of her head, she sat up, blinking. While she'd slept, the storm had drifted in from the lake and was now blowing and gusting its fury at the cottage. Feeling foggy from her nap, she disentangled herself from the afghan and swung her legs over the side of the swing.

It was then that she spotted her angel on the wood floor of the porch. Apparently the wind had sent it flying. Slowly she picked up the two perfect halves and felt tears fill her eyes. How could she have been so careless with her beautiful gift? What would Sam think?

Sam! She checked her watch and was shocked to find that it was past ten. He should have been here long ago, or should have called. What could have delayed him? Frissons of fear suddenly raced up her spine. Something terrible had to have happened.

Where was Sam?

Chapter One

Home. A four-letter word as far as Sam Rivers was concerned. That's how he'd felt about his home for years, back when being Joe Rivers's son meant you'd better know how to use your fists. And even later when he'd had to use those same fists on the father he'd caught beating on his mother. Hell of a way to grow up.

Sam put on his right blinker and exited the Ohio Turnpike at Sandusky, deciding to leisurely circle around the bay instead of rushing along the highway. He was in no hurry to return to Port Henry, the town where he'd been born.

A bright April morning sun shone through the windshield and turned the bay waters a brilliant blue. He wondered just how much had changed, really changed. Eight years was a long time to be away. For most of those years, he'd been determined never to go back to the town that had stuck labels on him since before he'd started first grade.

Mean, cruel, degrading labels like white trash, no-account lazy loser and worse. Then the final accusation: murder suspect.

For too long, he'd avoided the past, but a man needed to be able to look in the mirror and be comfortable with what he saw there. So he'd decided it was time, time to face the ''good'' people of Port Henry and clear his name. He'd committed no crime, yet he'd been behaving like a man on the run from the law. Now, seated in his new Ford Explorer with plenty of money in his wallet and much more in his bank account, Sam rolled down the window and felt the warm breeze on his face. Quite a contrast to the rainy September evening when he'd left town in a broken-down pickup with less than fifty dollars in his pocket.

Those long, lonely years had matured him, and the hard work had paid off. By anyone's standards, he was a successful, self-made man who should be content to get on with his life and not give another thought to Port Henry and his painful past. He no longer felt he had to prove he was good enough to anyone. Yet he couldn't let go of the nagging need to return and discover the truth, even if in doing so, he'd have to face people he'd hurt.

Like his mother. Sam ran his strong workman's hand over his bearded chin, just one change in him that Ann Rivers would have to adjust to. Outward differences were quickly spotted, but inner transformations might not be so readily discernible. He was stronger these days, more confident and less able to be intimidated at thirty-two than he'd been at twenty-four.

Surviving had hardened him, but success had mellowed him somewhat. His mother had pleaded and begged him to come home in recent years, but he hadn't, not until he'd felt the time was right. She wouldn't be happy with his reasons for returning, because Ann Rivers preferred keeping her head in the sand. She'd lived her whole life believing that if she didn't think about things or draw attention to herself, the problems would go away. He'd have to convince her that only by digging for the truth could he remove the cloud they'd all lived under. He'd give it his best shot, if not for her sake, then for the sake of her younger son, Jim.

Sam eased the Explorer along the road that hugged the bay and glanced at a sailboat heading out toward Lake Erie as he thought about his brother. Jim had been eleven when Sam had left town, a skinny kid made afraid of his own shadow by the father who'd taken out his drunken rages even on a young boy. Jim was a freshman at Ohio State now and apparently giving their mother some problems lately, according to her recent letters, though she hadn't been specific. That had been another deciding factor in Sam's return. He hadn't been much of a big brother to Jim up to now, and wondered if he'd know the right things to do and say.

The outskirts of Port Henry hadn't changed much, Sam thought, gazing at the narrow streets that spoked off the main bay road. The building housing Hanley Pharmacy where he'd worked his first job seemed a shade more weather-beaten, but the high school looked as if it had recently been sandblasted. A new supermarket now occupied the corner that had been the vacant lot where neighborhood kids had played baseball.

Not that Sam had ever had time to join them, even if he'd been asked. As far back as he could remember, he'd worked after school—delivering newspapers, stocking grocery shelves, cutting grass. Anything to make a buck to replace the money Joe Rivers tossed down his throat in the form of cheap whiskey. It wasn't until his high school years that he'd found the time to try out for sports while carrying a B average and working evenings and most weekends.

Off to the right was a middle-income housing development he'd helped build when he'd joined Westbrook Construction after graduation. Neat, tidy homes he'd been proud to work on, learning from the ground up under the watchful eye of Mac Forrest, the foreman. Sam had put a lot of store in Mac's opinion of him, in the way the gruff older man had taken him under his wing. Maybe that's why it had hurt so much when Mac had fired him the very day his troubles had begun.

That day still haunted him. He'd gone over the events often enough to have memorized each tiny detail. The first hint of trouble occurred Thursday night, just before the long Labor Day weekend. His mother had awakened him about midnight to say that Joe hadn't come home, something that rarely happened despite his father's heavy drinking. So Sam had gotten up and cruised Joe's usual haunts, but he was nowhere to be found. Convinced that his father had gone somewhere to sleep it off, Sam had persuaded his mother to wait awhile before reporting him missing.

As soon as Sam had left the house the next morning, he'd begun to hear the rumors. Joe Rivers hadn't shown up for work on that Friday, and he never missed payday. Witnesses said Joe had been in a barroom brawl the night before, had left drunk and cursing. The sheriff's deputy was launching an investigation. Sam had tried his best to ignore the looks, the questions. He'd even managed to smile when Liza Courtland had come by, confirming their date for that evening. It was to have been the start of a wonderful weekend.

Instead, it had turned into a nightmare. Sam realized he was grinding his teeth and forced himself to relax. Funny how returning home had momentarily brought back the old feelings—of fear, of shame, of helplessness. Everywhere in town the word had gone out and the news had been chilling. "Sam Rivers—wanted for questioning in the disappearance of his father, Joe Rivers." Those words had changed Sam's life forever.

By lunchtime, everywhere he went, people stared, whispered. He'd been young and scared and close to desperate, so he'd turned to Mac. But the foreman had already had a visit from Deputy Hayes who'd told him Sam was under suspicion and that he'd better let him go. Surprisingly, Mac had caved in even after Sam had insisted that he hadn't done anything, although God knew he'd often thought about ridding the world of his drunken father.

Sam had panicked then, sneaking out of town before Hayes could haul him in. He knew his sudden departure had been perceived as an admission of guilt by many. Especially since half the town knew about the night some weeks before when he'd hunted down Joe Rivers at his favorite bar and, in front of a dozen witnesses, threatened to kill him if he ever hit Ann or Jim again. After that, Joe had been really careful around his oldest son, so Sam had had no reason to act on his threat. But who would believe him if Mac, his mentor, didn't?

And now, here he was, back home to find some answers and clear his name.

At the top of the curve, he came to the road leading to Courtland Enterprises and paused as he spotted the brass sign in the shape of an arrow pointing the way. A newer three-story brick building, housing the company headquarters, sat at the top of the hill, undoubtedly built by Will Courtland, who would have enjoyed looking down on his vast kingdom. Apparently though, even tycoons had their problems, for Ann had written that old Will had had an incapacitating stroke shortly after Sam had left town, but had waited two years to die. And that had left his daughter Liza in charge of the vast Courtland empire consisting of real estate holdings, a rubber refinery in Akron, a manufacturing plant and several small television stations. Sam had been tracking Courtland stock for years.

He shifted his gaze around the bend to Edgewater Road and, although he couldn't see the Courtland Mansion from where he'd stopped, his memory pictured it perfectly. Big, white and pretentious had been his first impression way back when, and likely still would be. Huge columns out front, antebellum, like a Southern plantation, like Tara. He wondered if Liza still lived there.

Liza. Now we've come to it, Sam thought, running his tongue around his teeth. The real reason he'd been hesitant to return to the city of his birth. Liza Courtland, the girl he'd loved more than the air he breathed. And, incredulously, though she'd definitely been born on the right side of the tracks, she'd said she loved him, too.

But he'd left, sneaking out after dark while he knew she waited for him at the lake cottage, because he'd been certain her wealthy family would never accept a man suspected in the disappearance of his own father. He should have stayed, toughed it out. But by the time he'd realized that, his pride wouldn't let him go back, not until he could do so with head held high and money in his jeans.

He'd spent a year wandering from state to state, working odd jobs, living in dingy places, making no friends, wondering where on earth Joe Rivers had gone. He'd called home and sent money to his mother whenever he could, and he'd asked how things were. Fearfully she'd told him that the sheriff still wanted him for questioning. So he'd moved on, working long hours each day and lying awake nights reliving every moment he'd spent with Liza, dreaming of her, wanting her. To keep his sanity, he'd come to believe that Liza Courtland had been only a fantasy, one he needed to forget.

But that had been then and this was now.

The Explorer started forward as Sam pressed down on the pedal. Maybe, if all worked out well, Liza would one day forgive him and understand his reasons. He couldn't snuff out that small measure of hope. But for now, he wouldn't let himself think about what might have been. He needed to concentrate on getting some answers, on clearing up a mysterious disappearance and erasing the suspicions that had caused him to leave in the first place. His main purpose in returning was to show everyone that the kid from the wrong side of the tracks had made something of himself and was someone to be reckoned with, not to renew old romances. Not that Liza would willingly speak to him after the way he'd left her high and dry.

Sadly for her, she'd have to do much more than speak to him since they'd likely be working together. He was certain she had no idea that Sam was involved when, as head of Courtland Enterprises, she'd approved the sealed bid of McDonald Construction out of Akron to develop the subdivision of upscale homes in Oakview Estates.

It had been a long-overdue stroke of luck, meeting Ray McDonald after Sam had been wandering well over a year. Ray had seen something in Sam that Sam hadn't seen in himself back then. He'd worked his butt off for Ray, because the childless old man had believed in him and regarded him more like a son than his own ever had. Three years later, Ray had decided to retire, and Sam had jumped at the chance to buy his thriving business.

With a bank loan that Ray had guaranteed, Sam had become a sole proprietor, albeit an indebted one. Immediately he'd made Dirk Jones, his only close friend and a man as alone as Sam—after losing his wife and child in a house fire—vice president, and together they'd built McDonald Construction into the going concern it was today. Then just last year Ray's wife had died and Ray had followed within two months. No one was more shocked than Sam to learn that Ray had left everything he had to him, enabling him to pay off his sizable mortgage.

Sam had left Ray's name on the company to honor the man who'd been so good to him, which was why when Dirk had recently submitted their proposal to Courtland, Sam knew Liza wouldn't turn it down because of him. They'd won the sealed bid and Sam had experienced mixed emotions. At first he'd thought it best that Dirk do the on-site overseeing of the project while he stayed in their Akron offices. But later, after thinking things over, especially after receiving yet another concerned letter from his mother, he'd decided that it was time.

Everyone said that you couldn't go home again. Sam wanted to discover if that was really so.

Still, he had to admit to a small case of nerves at facing Liza Courtland again. Checking his watch, he saw that he was early for his appointment with the CEO. Perhaps if he circled the bay and looked around, he'd be finally ready to face his past.

"Ninety-eight…ninety-nine…one hundred. Whew!" Liza Courtland released the weights on the arm pulley and leaned forward, bracing her hands on her knees, catching her breath. "That's enough for today."

"I should think so," Sue Stewart commented as she struggled up from the mat where she'd been doing leg stretches. "You've hit every machine in the place this morning. You got some sort of death wish?"

Liza straightened, rolling her shoulders. "No, just trying to keep from putting on the pounds. You know that sinfully delicious chocolate cake Mom made for Beth's birthday party last weekend? A thousand calories a bite, and I had a huge piece."

"I had two, but who's counting?" Sue's envious gaze took in Liza's slender frame and her long, long legs. "I'll trade you problems." She patted the slight bulge of her tummy. "Andy's six weeks old and I *still* haven't trimmed down this fat belly."

Liza grabbed the towel she'd draped over a nearby Exercycle and mopped at her damp face. "Ah, but he's worth it. What an adorable baby."

Her friend beamed. "He is, isn't he?" Sue fell in step as they headed to the showers, walking around a small group setting up for aerobic exercises. Frannie's Fitness Center, just off Port Henry's Main Street, was a popular spot for young mothers and working singles as well as middle-aged residents who came regularly to fight the never-ending battle of the bulge. "I don't remember having this much trouble losing weight after Sherry was born."

"What a difference a few years can make, eh?" Liza and Sue had attended the same high school, but hadn't really become friends until the summer they'd met again at Palmer Park when both their daughters had been toddlers. Now their girls were classmates and Sue had a newborn. Liza envied Sue's easy-going life and sincerely liked her husband, Lyle, an uncomplicated attorney who adored his wife and kids.

"You had to remind me. The big three-oh looms around the corner." Sue opened her locker. "Have you got time to stop at the Roundhouse for a salad before going back to the salt mines?" Despite envying her friend's great figure and big bucks, Sue had no desire to change places with Liza, who was a single parent with a hugely responsible job.

Liza glanced up at the clock on the wall of the locker room and saw she really couldn't take time for lunch. "Actually, I don't. I've got a meeting in about forty minutes. How about grabbing a health drink at the fruit bar instead?"

Sue made a face. "Lord, why does everything good for a person have to taste so...so tasteless?"

Laughing, Liza entered the first shower stall. "Meet you there in ten minutes."

She made it in eight even with blow-drying her long, blond hair. Setting her canvas bag on the floor, she climbed onto a stool and ordered an orange crimson delight from Frannie who was tending the fruit bar this morning.

"My favorite," Frannie said, reaching for the shaker. A tall, slender woman who admitted to being thirty-five because she knew she could pass for ten years younger, Frannie was a walking ad for her fitness center. "So, I suppose you've heard the big news," she said as she poured fruit juice into a blender.

Liza searched in her purse for an emery board to repair a nail. "What big news is that?" As if there ever was any news in Port Henry that could be considered big.

"Sam Rivers is back in town."

Liza's hands stilled as she raised her eyes to Frannie. "Who told you that?"

"No one had to. Saw him myself not more than half an hour ago, driving along the bay in a tan Explorer. He's sporting a beard these days, but I'd know that face anywhere." The owner's shrewd gaze stayed on Liza's face. "You and he used to have a thing going, as I recall." Frannie's parents owned a pizza shop out toward Crane Lake where Frannie used to help out on weekends during the summer. She remembered a certain corner booth where Liza and Sam had often rendezvoused. They'd appeared to be more than just friends. The only thing Frannie liked better than working out was gossiping. And she could tell that her news had come as a shock.

Liza swallowed around a tight throat. "I wouldn't say that. We knew each other, but it was a long time ago." But not long enough, she thought as she accepted the tall, frothy drink, not if the mere mention of Sam's name could cause her hands to tremble.

Frannie busied herself wiping down the counter. "I wonder what brought him back after all these years."

Bending to the straw, Liza took several long sips. She couldn't help wondering, either. Maybe Frannie was mistaken. Eight years was a long time, and faces changed, matured. With a beard and all, how could she be sure? She'd hold on to that thought, Liza told herself.

Joining them, Sue hoisted herself onto the stool next to Liza and ordered a banana blaster. "Sorry I kept you waiting, but I got to talking with Sandy Roberts. Guess who she saw stopped at a light on Main Street on her way here today?"

At the refrigerator, Frannie spoke over her shoulder. "Sam Rivers, right?"

Surprised, Sue nodded. "How'd you know?"

"I saw him, too. Funny, isn't it, him coming back so suddenly?"

"It is odd," Sue added. "Lyle's kept in touch with him, but he hasn't said a word to me about Sam's plans to return to Port Henry."

"Ann Rivers has done some sewing for me, but whenever I bring up Sam's name, she changes the subject. Not that I blame her. It can't be easy, having your son suspected of doing away with your husband." Frannie finished adding ingredients and turned on the blender.

Frowning at the way Frannie seemed to enjoy reminding

them about a man's past problems, Sue glanced at Liza, noticing that she was awfully quiet and oddly pale. "Are you all right?"

Liza held her glass in a shaky grip. Two people had seen him. Two couldn't be mistaken. Oh, God, why now? She had to act natural, to get outside before she aroused suspicions. The one man who could turn her carefully structured world upside down was back. The question was, Why?

Squaring her shoulders, Liza pasted on a plastic smile. "I'm fine, but I think I might have overdone the exercises today." She pushed her drink aside and tossed a couple of dollars on the counter as she slid off her stool. "I've got to run. I'll call you, Sue. 'Bye, Frannie."

She forced herself not to run out to the parking lot, even as she felt their curious eyes follow her. Later, she'd think up a better excuse if Sue called. The car keys were slippery in her hand. Finally she got the door of her white BMW open and slipped inside. She turned on the ignition, then the air-conditioning, hoping to cool off her damp face.

How could this be, that the thought of having him back in Port Henry would make her knees weak and cause her heart to pound? He'd once had this incredible power over her, but she'd been nineteen back then. Eight years was a long time. She'd changed, grown up. She'd had to, with all she'd gone through—her father's stroke, taking over for him, his death and the birth of her child. Still, she remembered everything about Sam Rivers down to the finest detail. She'd loved him with the fierce joy of youth, then hated him for the pain he'd caused her. But always she'd thought of him, dreamed of him, wanted him. A personal failing, she decided as she shifted into Drive.

Her office was less than a mile away, yet she wasn't sure she could make it as jittery as she was. Drawing in several deep breaths, Liza tried to empty her mind and concentrate on driving. The problem was that Port Henry was a very small town. If Sam was really here, the chances of *not* running into him were nil. How should she react? What should she say? More importantly, did his return have anything to do with her or, please God, could it be a mere coincidence?

Her mind reeling with unanswered questions, she turned into the rear parking lot of Courtland Enterprises and took the elevator to her third-floor office. She had a meeting scheduled with the representative of McDonald Construction regarding the Oakview Estates project shortly. She had to have her mind free of personal entanglements. She'd managed before and she would again.

Approaching her secretary's desk just outside her private office, she saw that Edith looked disturbed. A widow who was raising a teenage daughter alone, Edith usually rolled with the punches. What had happened in the hour and a half she'd been gone? Liza wondered. "Hi. What's up? You look troubled."

"Oh, probably I'm making a mountain out of a molehill. You know how we mothers obsess." Edith ran a hand through her short dark hair. "You remember I told you that Kristen's dating this young college fellow and I wondered if he might be all wrong for her?"

At seventeen, Kristen was old enough to date, Liza thought, but then, perhaps she'd be equally as protective when Beth got into her teens. "Yes. Is something wrong?"

"I hope not. I had lunch at the Roundhouse and the place was just buzzing. It seems that Kristen's young man's brother just returned after being gone for years. The shocking part is that I heard that the brother was run out of town by the sheriff before we moved to Port Henry. They say he's under suspicion for the murder of his own father who was a hopeless alcoholic. Good heavens, I can't have Kristen mingling with that sort.'' Edith removed stylish black-framed glasses and began polishing them vigorously.

Not in her own office building, too. Liza felt as weary as if she'd run a marathon. "Kristen is dating Jim Rivers?''

"Yes, that's right. Do you know the family?''

You could say that. "I haven't met Jim, but I do know this town. Don't believe everything you hear, Edith. I remember when all that took place, the rumors, the gossip. If Sam Rivers had killed his father, don't you think Sheriff Hayes would have found him and dragged him back here before this?'' It felt odd just speaking Sam's name aloud. The problem between them notwithstanding, Liza knew Sam was not a killer.

"Well, I suppose the whole thing took me by surprise. Jim seems like such a nice boy, but you can never tell these days.'' Replacing her glasses, Edith peered up at Liza. "You know this Sam Rivers, then, and you don't think he did anything wrong?''

That would depend on how you define wrong. "I would never believe that Sam Rivers is capable of murder.'' Liza stepped past, effectively ending the conversation. "When the representative from McDonald Construction arrives, buzz me, please.'' Hopefully he'd be late, giving her time to get herself under control. She walked into her office, closed the door and sat down at her desk.

Leaning back, Liza sighed and closed her eyes. Why couldn't Sam have stayed wherever the hell he'd gone? She'd spent years angry, hurt and resentful that he'd left so suddenly, without a word of explanation to her, of all people. She'd known better than most how he'd felt about his father, but she hadn't believed a word of the nasty, suspicious talk.

Ed Hayes hadn't helped the situation any, fueling the

flames. He'd been a deputy then and had badly wanted to be elected sheriff. And he had been, at the next election, based almost solely on his earnest pursuit and ongoing investigation of Joe Rivers's disappearance. But Joe had never been found, nor had a body surfaced, even after Ed had had the whole town searched and sections of the bay dredged. Liza hadn't the slightest idea where Joe had gone, but she was very certain that Sam had nothing to do with his departure, and she'd told Ed that very thing repeatedly. He'd answered that he was just doing his job, and she supposed that was true.

The thought that had bothered her ever since was why Sam hadn't just gone in and answered Ed's questions. Even if he had to leave for whatever reason, why hadn't he at least called her to explain? And later, why hadn't he answered her letters after she'd gone to all the trouble of finding out his address? Liza rubbed at the beginning of a headache above her left eye.

Finally she'd had to face facts, and she'd come to the conclusion that Sam simply hadn't cared enough to tell her he was leaving or why, and he hadn't cared enough to return when she'd written she was pregnant. Obviously, while he'd been the love she'd longed for, to him she'd been a one-summer fling.

Now that he was back, what did he want? Would he ignore her as he had for all these years, or would he walk in, give her that lazy smile and expect her to take up where they'd left off? That could never be. For a while after he'd gone, she'd tried to prepare herself for this eventuality. But she'd never come up with a viable plan. Nor did she have one now. Still, she'd have to be very careful. Above all, she had to protect her child.

Liza's face softened as she shifted her attention to the framed photo on her desk. Her beautiful Beth, seven years old last week. Fierce pride and a mother's protective instincts rose in her as a vagrant thought surfaced. Surely Sam hadn't returned because of a surge of latent fatherhood? Liza felt her breathing go shallow as she tamped down her runaway thoughts.

There was no point in overreacting. She'd done everything she could to ensure that no one could ever take Beth away from her. And no one would, not while she was breathing. Beth was hers and hers alone.

Liza drew in a long, calming breath. Maybe, if the gods were with her, Sam's return had nothing to do with her or Beth, nor would their paths even cross.

Right, and pigs could fly!

Straightening, Liza opened the top drawer of her desk and reached to the back. She removed an object wrapped in a white handkerchief edged in lace. Unwrapping the folds, she stared at two broken halves of an ivory-and-gold angel.

Funny how she couldn't seem to let go of this eight-year-old gift. Maybe because it represented her broken dreams, her broken heart. Carefully, she rewrapped the angel and tucked it away, safe from prying eyes.

Enough of this. With the self-discipline that had guided her for years now, Liza Courtland put aside her disturbing thoughts and picked up the file on the Oakview Estates project to familiarize herself with the figures before the McDonald representative showed up.

At precisely one o'clock, Sam Rivers arrived at Courtland Enterprises and approached the desk of the receptionist outside the office of the CEO. He smiled at the dark-haired woman. "I'm from McDonald Construction. I have an appointment to see Ms. Courtland." He handed the woman his business card.

Edith returned his smile. "Just a moment, please." She buzzed Liza's phone as she read the man's card. Suddenly her smile slipped and her eyes widened. "Uh, your name is Sam Rivers?"

"That's right." Sam waited, wondering what Liza's reaction would be if this woman who didn't know him looked so startled. Surely the forty minutes or so he'd driven around Port Henry hadn't been long enough for someone to recognize him and warn her that he was back, although he had noticed several measuring glances.

Recovering, Edith indicated a couch against the wall as she replaced the phone and stood. "Won't you have a seat, please? I'll tell Ms. Courtland you're here." She hurried to the office door, gave a quick knock and walked in. "Liza, I think you'll want to see this," she said, carrying the man's card to her boss.

"Is there a problem?" She took the card and read it, then read it again. "What? Sam Rivers, President of McDonald Construction? That can't be." Nerves jangling, Liza looked up at her secretary. "Did I miss that name on the paperwork?"

"No, I'm certain you didn't." Edith spotted the Oakview Estates file on Liza's desk, picked it up and began thumbing through the signed contracts.

Not only was he here in Port Henry but involved in her latest pet project. *Oh, Lord!* Liza felt like weeping.

"Here's the authorizing signature," Edith stated, moving around the desk to show her. "Dirk Jones, vice president. I believe he's the man you were expecting. Of course, we didn't ask the name of the president."

Liza sighed heavily. "No, we didn't." Because until this morning, who'd have dreamed Sam would be here? What could this mean? she asked herself. Perhaps that he was interested only in the project and hadn't come about the child he'd never seen? She'd focus on that thought.

"What do you want me to tell him?" Edith asked.

But Liza's mind lingered in the alcove outside her office as she tried to picture Sam Rivers there. "What does he look like?"

Edith had taken inventory before she'd known his name, and been plenty impressed. "Better looking than his younger brother, but only by a hair. He's tall, broad-shouldered, with this dark beard and a killer smile. His eyes are deep blue and not friendly. My impression is he's not a man to mess with."

Liza swallowed over a rising lump in her throat. Except for the beard, Edith had described the man she remembered most accurately. Perhaps Sam hadn't changed, but she had. She was no longer a trembling nineteen-year-old awed by the handsomest man in town. She was the woman who'd never forgiven that same man for not loving her enough.

But in this office she was, first and foremost, a businesswoman, cool and in control most of the time. And so she would be today, despite this unexpected turn of events. Rising, she walked to the credenza to pour herself a cup of coffee. "Ask Mr. Rivers to step in, please, Edith."

"Certainly." Hiding her curiosity admirably, Edith went to the door. "Ms. Courtland will see you now, Mr. Rivers," she told Sam, then stepped back to allow him to enter before reluctantly closing the door.

Sam walked in a ways and stopped, his hungry eyes devouring her. It was immediately obvious that he'd walked away from a girl and was now facing a woman. She was standing half-turned toward him, the morning sun flowing through the double windows glinting on her hair, richly blond, lushly thick, falling just past her shoulders. His hands, his mouth, his heart remembered every inch of that slender body, hidden now beneath a businesslike navy suit and a tailored white blouse buttoned over full breasts. Her legs seemed endless, and on her feet were demure navy pumps.

Some men might have trouble getting past that marvelous body and would miss a truly lovely face. High cheekbones and flawless skin tanned golden. A mouth full and inviting, yet unsmiling; her nose small and straight. Her chin, bearing the slightest indentation, held a stubborn tilt. But it was her eyes that drew his attention—a frosty green which was no less than he'd been expecting by way of welcome.

"Hello, Liza," he said softly.

Setting down her cup and saucer before her trembling hands would reveal her nerves, Liza faced her opponent. "Sam." The word was rife with meaning, with emotion. Because her knees weren't as steady as she'd have liked, she moved behind her desk and sat down, indicating that he take the single chair facing her.

Taking his time, Sam glanced around her office, approving the view of the bay outside the large, arched windows, the pale gray and deep burgundy decor, the wall of bookcases. There was even a small fireplace at one end and a bar built into the oak-paneled wall. It appeared that the lady CEO had spent a lot of time and money on her home away from home. "Nice place you have here," he commented as he crossed his long legs. "Impressive yet cozy. A tough combination."

There was that lazy smile, the one you could never read, Liza thought, carefully folding her hands atop her desk. Damn him for being even more attractive than she'd been picturing in her restive dreams. The beard suited his craggy face, yet the hint of danger it lent him was unnerving.

How many times had she shoved her hands into his silky

black hair, loving the feel of it? About as often as she'd kissed those hooded blue eyes, or trailed her fingers along his strong, square jaw that even his dark beard couldn't disguise. He was the first man who'd ever touched her and, God help her, the only man who'd ever been able to make her blood heat and her senses swim.

But she'd been young and trusting back then, unlike now. Now, when she needed to remind herself that he hadn't loved her enough to acknowledge the part he'd played in her pregnancy.

Composing herself, making an effort to put on the cool demeanor that she'd learned worked very well in her business dealings, Liza cleared her throat. "So, the prodigal son returns at last."

Sam caught the hurt, the flash of pain in her eyes, and thought she was entitled. "Like a bad penny, I've landed back home." His smile turned sardonic. "I guess I shouldn't have hoped for a warm welcome."

"No, you shouldn't have. You left under a cloud and returned under a deception. Why couldn't you have at least been honest enough to let me know you own McDonald Construction?" It was impossible to keep the anger, the bitterness out of her voice.

He had no idea if she'd believe him, but he had to try. "I didn't intend to work on site when we bid on the Oakview project. Usually Dirk Jones does that. But a family situation my mother needs help with came up, and I changed my mind." Which wasn't all of it, but enough for now.

To give her restless hands something to do, Liza toyed with her pen. "I doubt that in eight long years, this is the first time your mother's needed you." She'd kept track of Ann Rivers and knew she'd had a hard time after Joe's disappearance. "Why now, suddenly, did you turn into a caring son?'' She'd heard that Sam had built a spacious house on Woods Lane for his mother a couple of years ago, but Ann had needed more than financial aid.

Sam shifted in his chair, unused to being on the carpet. He could tell her that his family relationships were none of her business, but his guilt over leaving her so cruelly had him answering. ''Because it's time that I find out what really happened to Joe Rivers, to put my mother's mind at ease, and my own.''

That was one she hadn't figured on. ''You came back to look into that old case?''

''I came for the Oakview project and to give my mother a hand, but yes, I also intend to do some investigating on my own. Despite what you undoubtedly heard, I had nothing to do with my father's disappearance, Liza.''

''I never thought you did.'' The problems between them had had little to do with Joe Rivers.

Her words gave him a small measure of hope. ''Thank you.''

His pleasure would be short-lived. ''It's really a shame you didn't stick around long enough to protest your innocence to the sheriff at the time.''

Sam's posture became defensive. ''I had my reasons.''

''The same reasons that kept you from letting me know you were leaving that night while I waited for you at the lake cottage without so much as a phone call?'' She heard the suppressed rage in her voice, but was helpless to control it. *All these years...*

''I regret that more than you can know, Liza.'' His words were low, heavy and heartfelt, though he doubted she believed him.

''As much as you regret not answering all the letters I sent you?''

Guilt had his lips thinning. ''That was cowardly, I admit.

I read the first few, but I didn't know how to answer you when you asked when I was returning, because I had no idea. I honestly felt you'd be better off forgetting you'd ever met me. I threw the rest away unopened because it hurt too much to be reminded of all I'd lost.''

Liza straightened, unable to believe what she'd just heard. ''You...you threw my letters away, after the first few?'' She hadn't told him about the pregnancy until perhaps the sixth or seventh letter, hoping she could persuade him to return without being reduced to begging him to. Could this mean he still didn't know about the baby? ''How many letters exactly did you read?''

Sam shifted again, running a hand across his bearded chin. He'd suspected that this meeting would be rough, but he hadn't known just how rough. ''Three, maybe four.'' He raised his eyes to her face, wishing she would understand, knowing he hadn't the right to hope. ''I'm truly sorry, Liza. If I had it to do over...''

Liza slumped in her chair. He didn't know she'd had their child, didn't know he had a daughter. All the years she'd been blaming him for abandoning her when she'd really needed him, he hadn't even read her letters. She felt her world tilt as she struggled to accept this new knowledge.

Carefully she studied his face. He certainly looked sincere, or he'd become one hell of an actor. Perhaps it was better this way. He would make no claims on Beth, would pose no threat. Maybe he was sorry he hadn't called or written, but the unadulterated truth was that he hadn't cared enough to inquire how she was doing in all those long eight years. Apparently he'd wanted her for a short time, but he'd never loved her.

Like so many other women before and after her, she'd

mistaken lust for love. Liza felt the heat rise in her face, felt the humiliation stain her cheeks.

"Are you all right?" Sam asked, genuinely concerned. She looked so wounded, so vulnerable. He wished he could march around her desk, take her into his arms and make the past go away. "Was there something in your letters I should know?"

Not anymore. "No, nothing." Shoving back her chair, Liza walked to the credenza and poured herself a glass of ice water. Sipping it, she commanded herself to calm down. Never let them see you sweat, the saying went. Or cry.

Brushing back her hair, she swung back toward him and nearly stumbled. He was holding her daughter's photo and studying it carefully.

"Mom wrote me that you'd adopted a daughter," Sam commented, smiling at the blond little girl grinning into the camera despite two missing front teeth. "She's lovely. What's her name?"

Liza's smile felt frozen. "Thank you. We call her Beth, after my mother, Elizabeth."

If only he hadn't been such a damn fool, Sam thought, perhaps he and Liza would be married now. He could have given her children so she wouldn't have had to adopt. Annoyed with his thoughts, Sam replaced the photo. Suddenly he was anxious to get this session over with. "So, who's going to work with me at Oakview?"

Liza forced her mind back to business. She'd gone over possibilities before she'd known Sam was McDonald's representative. Of the available ones, only Dave Enright could handle the work, but he was in the hospital with a multiple fracture of his right leg. She needed her right-hand man, Arnie West, in too many other places. That left only one choice.

"I will," she said, though she didn't look forward to

working closely with a man whose presence was still so damnably disturbing. However, the Oakview project was too important to lose and postponing was out of the question. "I hope that's all right with you," she added, watching him carefully. He still had that enviable ability to mask his feelings, which made reading his expressions difficult.

"I have no problem working with you, Liza."

"Fine. Let's get started by looking over these preliminary figures." She handed him several sheets. "I think our first priorities are to visit the bank and the water commission. They promised piping along that section and, according to my last conversation with your foreman, who's already over there…uh, Jeff, I think his name is—"

"Jeff Barnes."

"Yes. According to Jeff, they still haven't approved our tapping into the water main."

Sam thumbed through the papers. "I agree that those two things are important. However, the zoning commission is what's really holding things up. Suddenly they're not happy with the area we'd all previously agreed would be set aside for the park. We've platted all our lots around that section. A change now would mean replatting, a considerable expense and an indeterminate delay."

Liza sighed. "This is partially my fault. Initially I'd assigned this project to Andy Brewster, a man who's been with us since before I went away to college. Dad trusted Andy as one of our best. However, a month or so ago, Andy learned he has cancer and he went into denial. His work's suffered because he refuses to admit how ill he is. When I took over the file, I saw that several things had been done incorrectly and more left undone completely. I apologize and I promise you I'll stay on top of things from now on."

"What happened to Andy?"

She frowned. "I insisted he take early retirement. Why? Did you think we tossed him out on his ear?"

"No, I didn't think that. Just as you never believed I was involved in a crime, I always believed in your innate goodness, Liza." Enough to think that perhaps one day she'd forgive him for hurting her.

Her face softened somewhat. "Thank you."

Sam stood. "I've taken up enough of your time today. Do you want to schedule a meeting with the zoning commission, or shall I?"

"I'll try to get one for tomorrow and I'll call you when it's set." Feeling the need to move, she got up and walked toward the door, trailing after him. "Just how do you plan to go about looking into your father's disappearance?"

Sam turned to face her. "I'm not sure yet. Visit his old haunts, for starters. See if I can find someone who knows something. Try to track his movements during that time to see if he might have been in some sort of trouble that caused him to leave." He shrugged. "Grasping at straws, but I have to start somewhere."

"Maybe you should talk with Ed Hayes first. He spent a lot of time and money searching for Joe. He even had sections of the bay dredged looking for a body."

Sam nodded. "That's because he was trying to prove I killed Joe and got rid of the body somewhere."

Liza frowned again. "You really don't believe that. Ed's not so bad. He's like a big teddy bear."

Sam's brows shot up. "What? You can't be serious. A teddy bear? More like a barracuda."

"Hardly that. He brings his niece over to play with Beth quite often. They're the same age. He's always polite and even funny." Liza knew she always took the side of the underdog, which Ed was, despite his family background and his badge.

Sam ignored the quick jolt of jealousy. "Are you seeing Ed Hayes socially?" That couldn't be, could it? The same age as Sam, Ed had been big in high school, earning the nickname "Beefy," which had irritated the hell out of him. On the football field Ed had been awkward and clumsy whereas Sam had been strong with quick hands, a natural athlete. Girls had also been a problem for Ed, the same ones who were drawn to Sam despite his indifference. Those two reasons had fueled Ed's dislike for Sam, which had carried over into his law enforcement. He'd particularly enjoyed dragging home a drunk Joe Rivers and dumping him on the front porch, sneering at Sam as he drove off. Joe's suspicious disappearance had been tailor-made for Ed to exercise his prejudices, and he had.

"I don't date him, if that's what you mean," Liza said, noticing the barely concealed anger in Sam's dark blue eyes. "What if I did, though? I'm a big girl now and I choose the men in my life without checking with anyone." If he only knew how few there'd been.

Sam cursed himself for overreacting because of his distrust of his old nemesis. "Sorry I asked." She was standing close enough that he noticed her scent, the one he'd tried unsuccessfully to dislodge from his memory bank over the years. His blood started to churn as she stared up into his eyes.

He wanted nothing more than to reach for her, to kiss her until they were both weak and breathless. But he knew what a mistake that would be right now. "I'll expect your call." He left, closing the door behind him.

Back at her desk, Liza sank into her chair. She'd get through this somehow. She had to. But it was going to be a long, long summer.

Chapter Two

The meeting with Liza left Sam unnerved and far more shaken than he cared to admit. The years spent trying to convince himself that she was out of his reach had been terrible. Even harder to accept was seeing her face-to-face and realizing that she would probably never forgive him.

The bayside road angled to the left, but Sam took the right fork into the town square and pulled to a stop at the light at Main Street's six-lane intersection, heavily trafficked in early afternoon. He looked up at the statue of the late Ohio senator, Robert A. Taft, standing as it had for years, a constant in a sea of new buildings and renovated older ones. Nothing stayed the same.

Suddenly Sam felt an odd prickling at the back of his neck and glanced toward the far lane. There he was, Ed Hayes, sitting in a black car with the sheriff's insignia on the door, his eyes hidden behind huge mirrored sunglasses yet obviously studying him. He hadn't seen Ed since before he'd left Port Henry, yet he'd have recognized him without his official car and uniform. He'd been an annoying deputy, and since he'd been elected sheriff, he undoubtedly was worse.

The look held for several more seconds, both men expressionless, until an impatient honk behind Sam let him know the light had changed. Returning his attention to the front, Sam shot the Explorer forward, pleased to notice in his rearview mirror that Ed had been held up by a slow vehicle turning right, in front of him.

The new house he'd had built for his mother was on Woods Lane coming up fast on the right. But he decided to take a circuitous route and avoid the big, bad sheriff for now, in case Ed had nothing better to do than follow him. Zigzagging through streets once as familiar as the back of his hand, Sam realized he was clutching the wheel in an iron grip and forced his fingers to relax.

It wasn't that he was afraid of a confrontation with Ed Hayes, but he'd rather put it off until after he had a chance to talk with his mother. In retrospect Sam realized that he'd let himself be intimidated by the burly deputy eight years ago because he'd felt no one would believe the word of someone named Rivers over a lawman's. So he'd run.

But this was a different day and he was a different man.

Twenty minutes and several miles later, Sam saw that the road was clear behind him, so he headed toward Woods Lane. Gliding around the curve, he spotted the two-story colonial in the cul-de-sac, and pulled into the drive of his mother's house.

It was nothing like the home he'd grown up in. Thank God, he thought. If it had been up to him, that shack would have burned to the ground long before he'd been able to move his mother out of it.

Sam climbed out, stretching the kinks from his shoulder

muscles caused by the tension of his homecoming and his chat with Liza. He stood for a moment gazing at the tiny crocus shoots and tender hyacinth buds that would soon be in bloom in front of the house he'd designed. Four bedrooms and two baths, a fieldstone fireplace, a large, airy kitchen and a fenced backyard with trees, a rolling lawn and more flower beds. Ann Rivers had fought him all the way, but she'd finally agreed to resettle. For Jim's sake.

But she'd adamantly refused to stop taking in sewing, because she didn't feel right letting her son support her totally. Sam understood pride and hadn't argued further, though he'd kept on sending her a supplemental check for whatever else she needed, including Jim's tuition. He'd have sent the money even if she'd thrown it all away. His penance, Sam thought, for leaving her and his little brother, for running away like a coward.

Finally he stepped up on the porch and pushed in the doorbell.

Ann Rivers took the steaming raspberry pie, Sam's favorite, out of the oven and placed it on the cooling rack, her nerves jumping at the sound of the doorbell. Tossing aside the pot holders, she removed her apron and walked to the front, patting her hair with shaky fingers. That would be Sam, here at last. She'd both longed for and dreaded this day.

Taking a deep breath, she swung open the door, then stood still, her pale blue eyes scarcely able to take him in all at once. When had he gotten so tall, his shoulders so wide? And the beard, changing his angular face, giving it a dangerous quality. The eyes were the same, a striking blue that darkened and changed with his moods. Her first-born, home at last.

"Sam." Ann's voice trembled as she pulled him close

for a hug, tears forming behind her closed lids. Not a day had gone by in eight years that she hadn't thought of Sam, worried about Sam, prayed for Sam. She wasn't an affectionate woman by nature, but this reunion broke down her natural reserve. "I can't believe you're here."

There was hardly anything to her, Sam thought as he took a step back to study his mother. Ann Rivers had always been small, but she was even thinner now, the rose-colored blouse and slacks just hanging on her slim frame. Although he knew she had yet to see fifty, her short, dark hair was already liberally sprinkled with gray.

A muscle in his jaw tightened as he realized her appearance was a direct result of years of Joe Rivers's abuse, both verbal and physical. Her husband had been gone eight years, but Ann still had that haunted, defenseless, skittish look about her, as if he might walk in any second and start swinging. For all the damage that man had done to his mother, Sam wished he could even the score. Guiltily, he had to admit his being gone had undoubtedly contributed to her decline as well.

He watched her brush aside a tear as she stepped close for another hug. This generous affection was new. He remembered his mother as one who hid her feelings even from her sons. Apparently the years had changed her, too. "I'm here now, Mom. Everything's going to be okay."

"I know it will, son," Ann said, then cleared her throat. "You were always stronger than any of us." Moving back, she glanced out on the porch. "Where's your bag?"

"In the car. I'll get it later." His eyes traveled the length of the living room, through the arch into the dining area. Wet plaster walls and hardwood floors, coved ceilings and leaded windows. They'd followed his instructions and built her a quality house. "Do you like the place?"

Her eyes were shiny with unshed tears. "I love it, Sam. I never dreamed I'd live in such a fine house."

He wondered if she'd ever lose that ingrained humility, that servantlike approach that had her feeling overwhelming gratitude for the smallest thing anyone did for her. He wondered if she'd forgotten how to smile.

"Shall I give you a tour and show you the rest of the house?" Nerves had her jumpy, habit had her anxious to please.

"Maybe later." He cocked his head and sniffed the fragrant air. "Is that raspberry pie I smell?"

Finally Ann gave a hint of a smile. She'd worked extra hours to buy the off-season berries, but the look on Sam's face was worth it. "Yes. Let's go into the kitchen and I'll cut you a big piece." She slipped a hesitant arm around his waist as they walked, marveling that this strong, solid man was her son. "And I'm making your favorite chicken and dumplings for dinner. Jim will probably be home by then and—"

"Jim?" Sam sat down at the butcher-block table while his mother hustled to cut the pie. "Are classes out already?"

There was no easy way to tell him. "No, not for another month or so. Jim left college early, said he needed some time off." Worry emphasized the lines on her brow as she served his pie along with a tall glass of cold milk. She sat down, one fidgety hand plucking at the sleeve of her blouse. "But there's more."

She hadn't told him in the letter just what was wrong, but Sam could see that whatever it was troubled her. More than just ditching school early, bad as that was. "Lay it on me, Mom. And by the way, the pie's wonderful. I haven't had anything this good since…well, in a long time."

"There's plenty more." Ann hurried to get him a napkin,

buying a little time. She hated having to upset Sam his first hour home, but she didn't know what to do. Jim was so distant lately and she feared he was veering out of control. "He doesn't seem to want to do much, just lay around the house. He sleeps late, then drives off with his friends. Stays out all hours, and I don't know where he goes. When I ask, he just tells me he's a big boy now." She shook her head. "And then last week, he was arrested. DUI. His court appearance is in ten days."

Sam drained half the glass of milk before responding. "I can see that Jim and I are going to have to have a talk. Did you tell him I was coming?"

"Sort of. I told him what you'd said, that your company had won the bid to build the Oakview Estates homes and that you'd decided to oversee the operation. He just said, 'That's nice.'" She caught Sam's frown as he finished the last bite. "He's not a bad boy, Sammy. It's just that, without a father and all…"

"Don't!" Sam set down his fork, his eyes darkening. "Don't think for even a minute that Joe Rivers could have kept Jim—or me for that matter—on the straight and narrow. If anything, he'd have made things much worse." He hated the fact that she blamed herself for Joe leaving, instead of rejoicing that he was gone. Her letters had been full of self-recrimination. She knew she was better off, yet felt guilty about it. He'd have to try to change her thinking.

In a subconscious habit, Ann rubbed hands that ached from years of sewing. "You're not going to be bringing all that up again around here, are you, Sammy? I mean, I'd hate to be going into town and have people not looking me in the eye again, whispering behind my back. That's mostly over now, except for a few, and I—"

"Mom." He took her small hands into his. "Don't worry, please. I'll do everything I can to shield you. But

I've got to find out what happened. Don't you see, there are people here who still think I had something to do with that bastard disappearing? I can't have that, not anymore."

Ann's face crumbled as she struggled not to cry. "I don't know if I can go through all that again. Why don't we let sleeping dogs lie, Sammy? Talk dies down and—"

"I can't. I love you, Mom, but I can't. Not this time. I ran away once, and I shouldn't have. Things are different this time around and—"

The harsh ringing of the doorbell interrupted, startling both of them. Immediately fearful, Ann jumped up and went to the dining room window, carefully peering out between the drapery folds. "Oh, Lord, no. The sheriff's car's out front."

Word travels fast in small towns, Sam thought as he looked into the unfriendly face of Sheriff Ed Hayes. He'd been expecting him. Even if he hadn't run into Ed at the light, he knew several residents would have called Hayes by now, only too happy to report on his return. He hadn't exactly been trying to keep his homecoming a secret.

"Well, if it isn't the law," Sam said slowly as he stood squarely in the middle of the doorway, checking out how the years had treated Hayes. He was still a solid man with massive shoulders, but he'd slimmed down some. He wore his brown hair in a crew cut, a style Sam had noticed most lawman preferred. Liza had called him a teddy bear which Sam thought was truly a stretch.

"Get out of the way, Rivers," Ed said, shifting the toothpick he was chewing on to the corner of his mouth. "I'm coming in."

Sam reached up, his big hands settling on both sides of the door frame. "That so? I don't believe you are, not without asking. That is unless you have an invitation or some kind of warrant that would allow you to force your way into my mother's home.''

Color climbed up from Ed's thick neck as he removed his mirrored sunglasses. His dark eyes narrowed and locked with Sam's cool gaze.

Standing his ground, his stance casual but firm, Sam knew he'd better win this round or old Beefy would think he could still intimidate him. Behind him, he could sense Ann all but wringing her hands. Calmly, he waited.

Ed shifted his gaze to Ann and decided to use her. He knew how to be charming if it suited his purpose. Putting on his best smile, he spoke directly to her. "Good day, Mrs. Rivers. I wonder if I could step in and ask you all a few questions?"

Sam wasn't fooled by Ed's good-old-boys ploy, but he stepped aside, knowing how agitated his mother was as she hurriedly invited him in.

Brushing past Sam, Ed walked over to Ann's side, aligning himself with her. "Kind of springlike out there, isn't it?" he asked as affably as he knew how.

Ann swallowed around a dry throat, her nerves causing one eye to twitch. The sheriff hadn't stepped foot in her house since that hideous weekend Joe had disappeared. She didn't like him, didn't trust him, but he did represent the law. And she'd had plenty of reason to fear the law all the times they'd brought Joe home drunk, the times she'd had to swallow her pride and bail him out of jail for disorderly conduct, the pity she'd see in the eyes of every lawman as she'd lied about the beatings and tried to hide the bruises on her arms and face.

She had no idea why Ed Hayes was here now, unless Jim was in trouble again. Nerves jumping, she indicated the couch or chair. "Sit down, won't you?"

"Thank you, ma'am, but I believe I'll stand." Finished

with the niceties now that he'd gained entrance, Hayes zeroed in on Sam. "So, you're back, eh?"

At six-three, Sam stood half a foot taller than Ed, and knew that he looked formidable as he crossed his arms over his chest. "That's right." Never say too much, he'd learned the hard way. Just answer the questions.

"Why?"

"Why?" Sam feigned innocence. "Why, to see my family, that's why. Any law against that, *Sheriff?*" The emphasis on his title fell just short of disrespectful.

Ed's semi-amiable attitude completely disappeared as his eyes bore into Sam's. "Listen, I want no trouble in my town. Folks here respect the law and, like it or not, *I'm* the law around here." He gave them a condescending smile. "This family's had some trouble in the past." He watched Sam's eyes turn cold and hard, but he knew even he couldn't deny old Joe's drunken rages. Pointedly he glanced at Jim's picture on the mantel, then back at Sam. "And it looks like the apple didn't fall far from the tree."

Sam's open hand slammed against the front door, causing his mother to gasp and a flash of fear to leap into Ed's dark gaze. "That's it. You're out of here." He yanked open the door and stood waiting.

"I'm not finished yet..."

"Yes, you are." Furious and trying valiantly to keep his temper in check, Sam stepped closer, so close he could smell the onions Ed had recently eaten on his breath. "Get out of this house and don't come back unless you have official business here." None too gently, he ushered the sheriff through the open doorway.

Shocked at finding himself on the porch, Ed's face flamed with a mixture of humiliation and anger. "You haven't heard the last of me, Rivers." He turned somewhat clumsily and clomped down the steps as Sam slammed the door shut.

"Oh, my. Did you have to do that?" Ann flinched, listening to the squeal of the sheriff's tires as he zoomed away. "He's not a good man to have for an enemy, Sammy."

"Yeah, well, neither am I, Mom. Hayes has pushed us around for the last time." Awkwardly, because he knew he'd upset her without intending to, he bent to kiss her cheek. "Please, don't worry so much. I'll handle the sheriff. Now, why don't you finish making dinner while I get my bag from the car?"

Sam parked the Explorer alongside the McDonald Construction site trailer, just beyond the gate that opened into Oakview Estates, and got out. A late-afternoon sun was playing hide-and-seek with some big, puffy clouds, and the scent of the water from the bay teased his nostrils. He'd missed this town, Sam realized. Port Henry, with its rolling hills, the boats coming in off Lake Erie, the dairy farms just outside the city limits, the feeling of wide-open spaces, still drew him. He'd missed the town, but not too many of the people.

On the drive over, he'd been surprised at the number of folks who'd gawked at him from their cars and from sidewalks where he'd paused at lights. He'd thought the beard would offer some anonymity, at least for a while, but it seemed the older residents, especially, recognized him anyhow. He'd grown the beard as a lark five years ago and rather liked the subtle protection it offered. Apparently it hadn't shielded him from his former neighbors.

The door to the trailer was ajar. Sam had told his foreman that he'd be arriving today, but not exactly when. He gave a quick knock, then stepped up and inside. "Hey, Jeff. How's it going?"

Jeff Barnes looked up from where he sat at the built-in desk and grinned. "Better, now that you're here. Man, I hate this paperwork." A short man with dark hair and a full mustache, Jeff was energetic and honest, both a requisite in a good foreman. He'd worked on half a dozen projects with Sam and felt they made a good team.

"Yeah, me, too." On a laugh, they shook hands. Sam leaned against the file cabinet. "Everything going according to plan?"

Jeff grunted. "Does it ever? Remember that job we had down Canton way where they shipped the wrong beams, incorrect cement mixture *and* the lumber was all warped?"

"Not again, not that bad." No job went smoothly, but to have things go wrong this early wasn't a good sign.

"Bad enough. It just quit raining two days ago after a week-long downpour. I've been interviewing for two weeks and managed to hire only six guys. There's a real shortage of available bricklayers, electricians and finish carpenters around here."

"Swell." Sam grabbed a folding chair and sat down backward, leaning his arms on the backrest. "We can't do much about the weather, but let's get some ads in right away. Local papers and nearby cities. Offer bonuses. We've got to get moving here. I'll call Dirk and see if he can spare anyone who might want to come over for the duration."

"That's a start." Jeff ran a hand through his already ruffled hair. "The zoning commission's giving us a real hassle about details that we'd been assured had already been taken care of. Stuff that should have been approved weeks ago hasn't even gone to committee. Mostly minor, but we still need it in writing. You're going to have to meet with the Courtland rep and iron things out."

"I met with Liza Courtland earlier, and she's setting up an appointment with the zoning board."

Jeff's brows rose. "The lady herself. I heard that old man Courtland used to handle all building projects on his land parcels himself, but somehow I didn't think his daughter would. I mean, can you picture her strolling around out there in a hard hat?"

Actually, he could. "She's an enterprising lady, no doubt about it. Where you staying?"

"Courtland Inn. Is there anything in this town they don't own?"

"Not much." He hadn't asked, but he wondered if maybe Liza's wild younger sister had straightened out and was now also working in the company. Or perhaps Liza's mother, Elizabeth Courtland, had gotten more involved after Will's death. Sam had slipped in a question now and then about the Courtlands to his mother during his infrequent calls, but he hadn't wanted to appear overly interested. He'd also subscribed to the *Port Henry Gazette*, but the small weekly paper had revealed very little, and nothing personal. But then, Liza had always been a very private person.

"You want to meet the guys? It's almost quitting time."

"Sure." Sam followed Jeff out to where a handful of men at the far end of the complex were working on putting up the first home that would serve as the model. As they walked, he glanced at his watch. He needed to get back by dinnertime. He wasn't much looking forward to it, but he had to talk with his brother.

It was almost like looking in an old mirror, Sam thought as he stared at his younger brother. Jim had to be six feet tall with the same lean, rangy build as his and hair just as black as his own, though his eyes were a lighter shade of blue. There was a hint of wariness in Jim's expression, but you had to look past a defiance Sam hadn't expected.

"Guess I've changed a little in eight years, eh?" Jim asked, looking up at Sam. He'd always been a little afraid of his big brother. Hell, even their father had been afraid of Sam. But he wasn't about to let him see.

"You sure have." Uncertain whether the boy would welcome a brotherly hug, Sam held out his hand instead.

A bit awkwardly, Jim shook hands. "Welcome back."

"Thanks." Sam winked at his mother, nervously watching the reunion from the kitchen doorway, then sat down in one of two comfortable chairs flanking the fireplace. "So, how're things going?" He'd decided to let Jim tell his story his own way.

Jim slouched on the couch, his face guarded. "Okay, I guess."

Maybe he'd have to prod a bit. "You're home a little early, aren't you?"

Jim shrugged, his eyes downcast. "Couple weeks is all. Lots of guys drop a semester now and then. I've been going to school forever. Thought I'd take a little time off."

"Uh-huh. What are your plans for the summer?"

Another shrug as Jim crossed an ankle onto his knee, his fingers tracing the sole of his sneakers. "Hang out. You know."

Sam leaned forward slowly, bracing his elbows on his knees. "No, I don't know. I never had the option of hanging out. I had to work since..."

"Since you were twelve. Yeah, I know." Jim rose, walked to the window, then turned, facing his brother. "You worked, you held the family together, you pay my tuition and put food on the table. *I know.* Mom tells me constantly. And me, I'm just a screwup. I dropped two classes so I wouldn't get a failing final. And I got arrested.

Drunk driving. Now, you know it all, big brother.'' Embarrassed, ashamed and angry at being called on the carpet by the one person he admired most yet resented deeply, Jim swung back and glared out the window.

Silently, Sam regarded him, wondering what would be the right thing to say. Long moments passed. He waited.

Finally Jim turned around, more out of curiosity than fear. Why wasn't Sam giving him hell like he'd expected, like their old man would have? ''Aren't you going to say anything?''

''I have only one question, Jim. Do you want to stay in college, or do you want to quit, get a job now and start supporting yourself?''

Jim didn't much like the question. How could he support himself at nineteen when even part-time jobs were hard to find? The fight drained out of him as he sat down and rubbed along the back of his neck. ''Look, I don't know what happened.'' When Sam didn't say anything, he went on. ''Yeah, I guess I do. They put me in the honors program because last semester I made the dean's list, and suddenly, everything was so damn hard. I started getting behind, so I skipped a few classes. Only made things worse. I couldn't catch up so I dropped out.''

It wasn't as bad as Sam had feared. ''It happens. So what do you want to do?''

''Finish school. But I'll have to take some classes over. It'll take longer to graduate.'' He met Sam's eyes. ''That'll mean more money.''

''Yes, it will. You'll have to get a job and make up the extra money that ditching classes cost.'' He stared into Jim's eyes and saw the quick flash of annoyance, but he didn't back down. ''If you do that, then I'll know you're serious and I'll continue tuition payments in the fall. Maybe I can help you get a job.''

Jim thought that over and realized it was the best offer he was likely to get. "All right, but I'll find my own job." He was tired of being beholden to Sam for every damn thing.

"Fair enough. What about this drunk driving?"

Jim's face got defensive again. "It only happened once."

"Once is enough if you get caught." Sam took a deep breath, feeling his way. "Look, Jim, I don't want to lecture you, but it seems to me you've got some problems to work through. Are you in with a crowd that drinks quite a bit? You're under age, you know, and..."

"Yeah, yeah. I know. All right, I get the picture." Scowling, he glanced toward the kitchen doorway, saw that his mother wasn't there. "She's been on my back since I walked in the door—morning, noon and night. I made a mistake. I admit it. One damn time and I'm nailed to the cross. She's comparing me to the old man, telling me I'll never measure up to you. I'm sick of hearing it." But he wasn't as brave as his words indicated, especially not about the summons to appear in court. Swallowing hard, he looked at Sam. "What do you think that clown of a sheriff's going to do to me?" He'd spent one night in jail after the arrest. The thought of going back had given him nightmares.

Beneath the complaints and the bravado, Sam spotted a very real fear. Perhaps that fear would keep Jim from making a second mistake. "I've kept in touch with a guy I went to school with. Lyle Stewart's a lawyer here in town. I'll go see him tomorrow and feel him out."

Jim didn't bother to hide his relief. "Thanks. I... thanks."

"Dinner's ready, boys," Ann said from the doorway, hoping Sam had been able to accomplish what she hadn't.

Sam rose. "One thing, though. I want the drinking stopped, *now*."

"Yeah, okay." Jim got to his feet, but he needed to say something. "Sam? I didn't mean to screw up. I just…"

"I've screwed up a time or two myself. Nobody's perfect, Jim. I'm not going to dismiss a failed semester or a DUI as insignificant. But the thing to remember is to not make the same mistakes twice. You know what caused the situation. Fix it."

"I will. Honest, I will."

Sam threw an arm across his brother's shoulders. "I believe you. No matter what Mom's told you, I'm no saint. Let's go eat."

Liza Courtland stood at the railing of her back porch sipping a glass of chilled white wine and watching the sun drip bloodred colors into the bay as it inched its way down. It was a sight she never tired of, yet tonight she saw something more in the evening sky. Dark, tousled hair and a pirate's beard, piercing blue eyes wary and watchful.

Had someone told her as she'd left home this morning that she'd be standing here tonight picturing Sam Rivers, she'd have denied it. Yet here she was.

She took another cool sip, savored the tart taste on her tongue, then let the liquid slide down her throat. She rarely drank evenings, since she often brought home work to do and because she needed a clear head to deal with her daughter. Tonight was a rare exception.

What would Sam have said if she'd blurted out that Beth was his daughter as he'd sat in her office studying the child's picture? Would he deny her, since Beth's coloring so matched Liza's own? Or would she recognize his daughter's blue eyes as a gift he'd given her? A moot point since she wasn't about to reveal anything to anyone. All these years she'd guarded her secret and she would continue to do so at any cost. Beth must not be hurt.

The sun was slipping lower into the bay, slowly, slowly, with paintbrush colors drifting across a cloudless sky. A freighter horn could be heard way in the distance. The water was peaceful and calm.

As her life had been until today. Liza drew in a shaky breath and went inside to check on Beth.

Dark blue eyes several miles away also gazed out on the bay waters as Sam stood at an upstairs bedroom window in his mother's house. He'd loved living near water during his growing-up years, had missed the scent and sounds ever since moving away. He remembered renting a sailboat once and taking Liza out to Put-in-Bay. They'd anchored on a small sliver of land and picnicked there, getting sunburned and slightly drowsy after lunching on tuna sandwiches and warm beer. They'd napped in each other's arms. It had been wonderful.

Sam thrust his hands in his pockets as the scene before his eyes disappeared, replaced by the face he'd been remembering for eight long years. She'd been angry today, thinking he'd deceived her again by not putting his name on the McDonald papers. He hadn't meant to mislead her, hadn't intended to come to Port Henry. But his plans had changed and he couldn't help wondering how Liza would handle working with him on their mutual project.

Whatever happened, it would be interesting, he thought as a smile formed.

Chapter Three

Lyle Stewart's smile revealed a chipped eye tooth he'd acquired in a football game in his senior year at Port Henry High, courtesy of Sam Rivers's elbow. But there was warmth in the smile as he greeted his old friend, shaking hands across a huge desk piled high with files, folders and books. "Long time, no see, my friend."

"Yeah, you could say that," Sam answered as he sat down in the chair Lyle indicated. They'd lost track of each other when Lyle had gone away to college, then law school. Oddly enough, they'd run into each other in Akron when Lyle had been in town on business. He was one of a select few that Sam trusted. "And Port Henry's just as friendly as I remember."

Lyle, too, had been something of an outcast, because his father had left his mother with two small boys to raise. She'd gone to work in a bar which hadn't sat well with some folks in Port Henry. Lyle leaned back in his swivel chair. "Are they getting to you already?"

Sam ran a hand over his bearded chin. "I can't drive down the street without people stopping and staring. I guess folks around here have long memories."

"Boredom is what it is. Their lives are pretty ordinary, then you reappear and they start wondering all over again about Joe's disappearance and your involvement and all that. Drama is back in their dull little lives." He brushed a lock of sandy hair back from his forehead. "You should have expected as much. People don't change a whole lot."

"You're right. Actually, I want them to remember because I want to talk to each and every soul who might know something about what happened that night. I'm going to get to the bottom of this thing once and for all."

Lyle had rather thought, when Sam called to say he was back, that the building project wasn't all he'd be working on. "Can't say I blame you. Time to put it to rest. If you need my help, just say the word."

"Thanks, I appreciate that. First, though, I have something else to clear up." Sam removed the folded sheet from his pocket and handed it to the attorney. "You might have heard already. My brother, Jim, was cited for a DUI."

Lyle put on his gold-rimmed glasses and read the summons. "Arrested last week by our eminent sheriff. Zigzagging on a two-lane road at one fifty-eight in the morning. Failed the breathalizer test. Arrested, jailed overnight, released to his mother's custody. Court date in—" he glanced at his desk calendar "—nine days. Judge Alan R. Larson." Lyle looked up. "Is this his first offense?"

"So he tells me. I don't know how many points that will get him, though. Sheriff's already been to the house making references to Joe Rivers and his well-known drinking habits." Sam never called his father anything but his given name. He'd never felt the man acted enough like a father to be called one.

Lyle steepled his fingers thoughtfully. "Hayes has no love for your family, that's for sure. However, *if* we've got an otherwise clean-cut kid, good grades in school, no other arrests even in juvenile, *and* since there was no accident and no one injured, nor even property damage, there's a good chance for probation and/or community service on a first offense. Can Jim measure up to all that?"

"I think so. I'd have heard if he'd been in any serious scrapes, but I'll check all the same. He blew a couple of courses this last semester, but I've been getting copies of his grades up to then and he's done well."

"Do you want me to handle it for you?"

"I do, if you have the time." His gaze skimmed the overflowing desk.

"Neatness isn't one of my habits," Lyle said with a grin. "But I've got the time. And I know Judge Larson pretty well. Tell Jim I'll call him a day or two before the court date."

"Thanks, Lyle. I owe you."

Lyle waved a dismissive hand. "Have you been out at Oakview yet? Nice area. I wouldn't mind getting one of those big spreads."

"I stopped in yesterday. First model's just going up. I'll be working with Liza Courtland on the project. Do you know her very well?"

Lyle smiled. "Everyone in town knows Liza Courtland but I doubt many know her well. My wife sees her now and then. So Liza's going to oversee Oakview directly. I'm not surprised. Since she took over, the word is that no decision is made without her okay."

Sam decided asking Lyle a few questions wouldn't hurt since he'd lived all his life in Port Henry, as had his wife,

Sue. "Her sister's not involved in the company? Or the mother?"

Lyle shook his head. "Cindy lives in Boston. I heard she finally straightened out after being pretty wild all those years. Mrs. Courtland has always kept a low profile, even more so after old Will died. She spends most of her time with Liza's daughter."

"I saw a picture of the daughter yesterday on Liza's desk. Pretty child. Looks enough like Liza to be her own."

"Maybe she is." At Sam's surprised look, Lyle went on. "I've always suspected that was the case. See, Liza transferred from Ohio State to the University of Michigan shortly after you left, and went to live with some aunt in Ann Arbor. Scuttlebutt was that she and old Will had a big falling out, so much so that she never came home for holidays or summers. Next thing you know, we heard she adopted a baby girl, Beth. I've got a feeling Liza met some guy in Michigan, got pregnant and that Beth is her real daughter, that she made up the story to avoid talk. But what do I know?"

Sam took a moment to digest that. "So she's never married?" He saw Lyle shake his head. "I didn't know they'd allow a single woman to adopt a child."

"Oh, sure. Money talks, don't you know? If the story's true, she probably did a private adoption through an attorney, not an agency. Maybe the mother was a friend who had to give up her baby. Lots of possibilities."

"When did she return to Port Henry?"

"After Will's first stroke. She came home and took over the running of Courtland Enterprises, no easy task, I can tell you. She got engaged a couple of years later, some guy named Matt Hemmings. They were engaged for over a year when Will died. Next thing you know, Liza broke it off.

Doesn't even date, the way I hear it. Married to her work, they say.''

That wasn't at all what Liza had said she'd wanted, back in the days when they'd dreamed of a future together, Sam remembered. "Don't tell me she still lives in that big old house, the one that looks like an old Southern plantation?" The one he'd never been invited into.

"Sure does. Three generations of women and no men around." Lyle removed his glasses once more and leaned forward. "Do I detect more than a business interest in the lady?"

Sam wasn't sure his attempt at a disinterested shrug fooled his old friend, but he tried it, anyway. "Got to scope out the opposition, you know. We're supposed to be on the same side on this project, but who knows whether or not I'm persona non grata with Liza Courtland. Hayes may have dropped by already and warned her that I eat female CEOs for lunch."

Lyle chuckled. "Now, that wouldn't surprise me. Never did know why that man dislikes you so much."

"We must have been enemies in another life." Sam got to his feet. "I won't hold you up any longer. Thanks for taking care of Jim's little problem."

Lyle rose and walked around to see his friend out, shaking his hand once more. "Good to see you again. I like the beard. I'd grow one myself if Sue would let me." He shook his head affectionately. "That woman rules my life."

"And you love every minute of it. See you later."

Sam was irritated. The old fuddy-duddies who'd been members of the zoning commission for decades were giving them a hard time. Was it because the name Rivers had suddenly appeared on the paperwork, and now they were hesitant? It was three days after his initial meeting with

Liza, and finally she'd called this morning to say the commission had agreed to meet with them at two. Big of them, Sam thought with no small annoyance.

He glanced down at his clothes—denim shirt and jeans. He really didn't want to drive to his mother's to change. He'd spent the early morning with Jeff walking the site, making notes, then a couple of hours interviewing another group of men. At least they'd been able to hire three new ones.

Rising from the chair at the desk in the trailer, he went to check and saw that he'd left his tan corduroy sport coat hanging in the closet where he kept a change of clothes in case he wound up spending the night. A jacket was as far as he was prepared to go toward business attire for this meeting, and if the old geezers didn't like it, too bad.

The ringing phone had him returning to the desk. "Rivers," he said, none too friendly.

"And a good morning to you, boss," Dirk Jones greeted him. "You sound like you've been chewing nails for breakfast."

Sam sat down. "Sorry, but you know that patience isn't my long suit. Everything here is dragging. How do you stand it?" Most of their out-of-town jobs were handled by Dirk, who was patience personified.

"Stay calm. It gets better once all the approvals are in, the men hired and the material shipped and received." He gave a short laugh. "Unless, of course, there's a snag in committee or some of the guys quit on you or there's a shipping strike. You get the picture."

"Thanks a lot. You've really cheered me up."

They talked every day, and it seemed to Dirk that Sam was crankier with each call. "Hey, maybe this wasn't such a good idea. You want me to drive on over and we switch places?"

Sam took a deep breath. It wasn't really the project or its delays that were annoying him. It was more personal than that. "No, but thanks. I'll ride it out. You remember that quote about you can't go home again? You can, but it's probably never anything like you hope it will be."

Dirk stretched out his long legs as he tried to read between the lines. "No ticker tape parades in the old hometown, eh?" Up to today, Sam hadn't said much, just groused in generalities.

"Not exactly, not that I'd expected a rousing welcome. But it's like I'm an oddity. People staring everywhere I go, then turning away. Damn, but I hate it." He'd left after a small taste of notoriety and now he knew why. But he wasn't going to run away, not this time. "However, I intend to change things."

"Have you started searching for Joe?" During their years of friendship, Sam had told his friend all about his father's disappearance.

"Yeah, but it's slow going. Lyle, the attorney I told you about, has been a big help. It seems the best way to look for someone is to try to follow a paper trail. We all have one. I've started by writing to the Department of Vital Statistics to see if there's ever been a death certificate on Joe filed anywhere in the country."

"You think he's dead?"

"At the rate he was drinking eight years ago, he very well could be. But just in case, I'm checking with Social Security, thinking they could have a record of where he might be working, but that may net me nothing. Joe liked to work for shoestring construction outfits that paid under the table. Hell, I don't even know if he had a social security card."

"How about his car? Did you try auto registration?"

"I've written them, too. Naturally, his wallet disappeared

with him so I don't have any old numbers of his past
driver's license to give them. He left a ten-year-old clunker
that only ran half the time. Mom sold it for junk a while
back. As I said, slow going, but Lyle's patient and he's
given me a long list of places I can check. Most will probably be dead ends, but all we need is one good lead.''

"You're still convinced he left town, then?''

"He had to have. I found out that the good old sheriff
had his men digging all over looking for a fresh grave after
I left. He even dragged the bay. He had high hopes of
finding Joe's body so he could pin his death on me. I have
a feeling if Hayes couldn't find Joe, he's simply not anywhere in Port Henry.'' Sam leaned back, stretching. "I
haven't questioned his drinking pals yet, but I plan to.
Wherever he is, I'll find him, sooner or later.''

"I believe you will.'' Dirk hesitated, then decided to ask,
since Sam seemed to have lost his feisty edge while they'd
talked. "How are you and Liza Courtland working out?''

Depends on who you ask, Sam thought. "I haven't seen
all that much of her. One meeting in her office and another
the day after at the bank for a short conference. At least
the financial end seems to be going well.''

"That's a relief. But she's not being hostile?''

Leave it to Dirk to zero in. "I wouldn't say that.'' She'd
sat some distance away from him at the bank and had insisted on driving herself. However, today she'd agreed to
let him pick her up, since her office was on the way to the
zoning meeting. "She wasn't happy that I didn't tell her
ahead that I was part of McDonald Construction. But I
think we're both adult enough to put aside our personal
feelings and get the job here done.''

"Great. Nothing new going on around here. The Wilson
development is almost finished, but you already knew
that.''

"Okay, then. I'll catch you tomorrow." Sam hung up and checked his watch. Nearly noon. He'd have just enough time to grab a bite to eat before it was time to pick up Liza. Why hadn't he heard from Jim? He'd told his brother yesterday afternoon when he'd been leaving for a job interview to call him at the trailer with the results this morning, since Sam had left the house very early. He dialed his mother's number.

She answered on the first ring, but when Sam asked for Jim, Ann stammered and stuttered, sounding vague.

Sam felt his temper rising. "Mom, is he home?"

"Yes, but, well, you know, boys his age like to sleep in."

Everyone liked to sleep in now and then. Jim was making a career of it. "Had he been drinking when he came home last night?" Sam had gone to bed early, but he knew that his mother had waited up for Jim, as was her habit.

"No, really, he was sober."

"Good. Wake him up and put him on."

"Oh, Sammy, I hate to—"

"Mom. Stop. Just go get him." Fear ruled the woman's life, and he probably wasn't making things any easier for her, Sam thought as he waited for his brother. Some things you couldn't do for someone else, like give back a lost sense of pride. Ann Rivers had suffered for years for the sins of her husband. It was time she stopped and held her head up high. However, after the small taste of the suspicious, judgmental nature of most everyone in Port Henry that he'd had over the past few days, he couldn't blame her entirely for how she felt.

"Hello." Jim's voice was blurry with sleep and laced with resentment.

"Did you get the job yesterday?"

"No. They're full up, not even taking part-time."

"All right, time's up. I want you to come out here to Oakview Estates and report to Jeff Barnes, the job boss. We need every able-bodied man we can get."

"Wait a minute. I don't know a damn thing about construction. I'm a math major, remember?" Jim's voice had turned surly and petulant.

"I remember. I also remember that I gave you three days to get a job and this is the fourth. This is a summer job, not a lifetime commitment."

Jim had all he could do not to swear into the phone. "Look, I don't *want* to work for you. I'll find something else and..."

"Not by sleeping till noon you won't. This is no longer a request, Jim. It's an order. Get your butt over here within the hour or the money tree gets chopped down." None too delicately he hung up the phone.

Spoiled rotten was what his brother was. He didn't exactly blame his mother. After the old man took off and Sam had left, she'd lavished all her affection on her remaining son. Jim had grown up learning to take advantage of her. No more. The kid would shape up or Sam would know the reason why. Tonight he'd have a talk with his mother, let her know that the days of pampering a kid who was nearly twenty were over.

Again Sam checked his watch, then on an impulse, dialed Liza's number. Her secretary finally put his call through. He was still frowning when Liza came on the line.

"Why doesn't your secretary like me?" he asked, knowing it was a foolish question.

"I can't imagine," Liza answered. "Edith likes everyone."

"No kidding. Back to charm school, I guess. Listen, have you had lunch?" He didn't pause long enough for her to think up an excuse. "Neither have I. How about we grab a quick bite before this meeting? I think we might need a little fortification. I can be there in fifteen minutes.''

He was like a runaway freight train, just as he had been years ago. But she wasn't that naive, young girl any longer. ''I usually skip lunch and have a yogurt at my desk. But thanks any…''

''That's terrible. Nobody can think on an empty stomach, and I need you to be strong and alert at this meeting. Be downstairs in fifteen. I'll swing by for you. No more excuses.'' He hung up and let out a whoosh of air.

You're plenty nervy, Rivers, he told himself as he left the trailer to look for Jeff so he could tell him about Jim. Liza would either be fuming and decide to keep him waiting again, or too stunned to refuse.

No one was more shocked than Liza to find herself stepping up into Sam's tan Explorer in front of the Courtland Building at twelve-twenty. She settled herself, closed the door and turned to find her escort studying her with his lazy, hooded gaze. ''Did anyone ever tell you that the caveman approach is apt to get you a smack upside the head in this, the nineties?'' she asked.

Smiling, he shifted into gear and cruised out of the circular drive. ''It worked, didn't it?''

''Only because the last yogurt in my fridge has expired and I skipped breakfast this morning.'' At least that's what she'd told herself. If there was a deeper reason, Liza didn't want to think about it just now with the sun shining overhead, the breezes from the bay drifting in through the open windows and the delicious sensation of playing hooky even for a short time, something she so rarely did.

''That's a great dress. Green's your color.'' Linen was his best guess, the material fitted around her full breasts, the skirt short enough to show off those spectacular long legs. He felt an ache begin that he knew would probably remain uncomfortably with him for hours. "I didn't think Port Henry had shops that sold anything with style."

"Thanks. I made it myself."

Turning the corner, he raised a surprised brow. "You sew? I can't imagine where you'd find the time."

"I make the time. I find sewing relaxing. I make most of my clothes and Beth's, too. As you said, there's not much selection close by." Why were they babbling about clothes, of all things? Still, it was a safe subject.

Sam remembered how Liza had always talked about wanting to be nothing more than a homemaker, to sew, to bake, to fill the house with children. Yet he certainly hadn't thought, with her money and her demanding job, that she'd be sewing these days. "Do you do much cooking or baking?" She'd usually fixed their picnic lunches, her special fried chicken and biscuits that melted in his mouth along with chocolate chip cookies. He had yet to taste any better.

"Occasionally I bake cookies on weekends." With Beth, but she didn't want to bring her daughter into the conversation.

"With your daughter, I imagine." Sam downshifted as he swung onto Hillside Road.

Staring straight ahead, Liza swallowed hard. The man seemed to read her mind. Perhaps this lunch wasn't such a good idea after all. Impulses usually weren't. When would she learn?

"Why'd you adopt a baby, Liza?" He'd been wanting to ask since finding out.

Frowning, Liza looked out the side window. "Where are we going?"

"To the Hilltop. I remember that their food's good and the view's great." As he spoke, the old stone building came into sight. He rounded the bend and pulled into a parking space just vacated. It was lunchtime, and the place looked crowded. He switched off the engine and turned to her, draping his arm casually over the back of the seat. "Are you going to answer my question?"

She'd been asked that question before and had several standard answers. Looking him straight in the eyes, she dug out her best. "Because I needed someone of my own to love after you left." Quickly, she opened her door and stepped out.

The panoramic view along with the tantalizing scent of seafood at the Hilltop apparently appealed to a lot of diners. How Sam managed to get a corner table by a back window, Liza couldn't guess, unless the hand the beaming head waiter slipped into his pocket contained a generous bribe. Was Sam trying to impress her, she wondered, or was this usual for him these days? It occurred to her that she knew very little about the man Sam Rivers had become.

Oddly enough, although he was perhaps the most casually dressed man at the Hilltop, he looked terrific. Simple denim and corduroy, like something out of a *GQ* ad. Liza hid behind the menu.

Sam noticed that the woman at the side table was all but falling off her chair trying to figure out where she'd seen him before. Several other heads had turned, their owners looking him over on their way in. He'd seen the dawn of recognition on a few faces and decided to ignore them all. "Would you like a glass of champagne?" Sam asked, picking up the wine list.

He hadn't lost his knack for surprising her. "It's a little early for me, but you go ahead. I'll have iced tea, please," she told the waiter.

"Make that two." Sam smiled as he sat back to look at her. She was undoubtedly the most attractive woman in the room. "You introduced me to my first taste of champagne. Do you remember?"

A vintage bottle she'd confiscated from her father's wine cellar, then hidden in the picnic basket she'd taken to the cottage at Crane Lake. In front of a blazing fire, they'd spent the night sharing far more than the wine. Did she remember? If only she could forget.

Liza leaned forward, crossing her arms. "I don't want to stroll down memory lane with you, Sam. This is a business luncheon. Period."

"I think it might help us both to discuss our past."

Perhaps it would, she thought, but not today and certainly not in public. "There's nothing to discuss. The past is just that, past. Let's leave it alone."

There was plenty to discuss, but he'd leave it alone—for now. "All right. How do you like running a huge conglomerate?"

The waiter appeared with their drinks and took their order before hurrying off. Liza took a sip of tea, carefully considering her answer. "It's not all that huge anymore. After Dad died, Mom and I decided to sell off many of the family's holdings. My executive vice president, Arnie West, does more than I these days. The company was too large for me to manage without involving a great deal of traveling, and I'm unwilling to do that. I want Beth to have a stable home life. Besides, I don't have the killer instinct for acquiring companies just for the thrill of puffing up the Courtland portfolio as Dad did."

Sam regarded her over the rim of his glass. He'd known about the Courtland downsizing since most of it was a matter of public record and he always read the financial news. "Down to your last half-dozen investments?"

"You could say that. You, on the other hand, have been busily doubling and tripling your little kingdom."

So she'd been interested enough to look into his background since their first visit. "Sort of gets in your blood."

"For some, I guess." But her expression was doubtful. "You always said you'd be a big success in time."

"Yeah, but it took a little longer than I'd planned."

"God has a way of changing our plans. I read that on a sampler once."

"Well, needlepoint never lies." Their lunch arrived then, a seafood salad for Liza and broiled halibut for Sam. His noisy stomach reminded him that all he'd had today were several cups of strong coffee. "Mmm," he said, savoring his first bite. "As good as I remember."

"What made you settle in Akron?" Perhaps they could talk a little about the past, as long as it wasn't their shared past.

"Luck and circumstances. I'd been wandering from town to town for way too long, doing odd jobs, always on the move. My old truck finally gave up the ghost on a street corner in Akron. Across the alley was McDonald Construction. I walked in and asked for a job. Ray McDonald gave me one." He broke a steaming roll in half. "But then, you probably already know all that, if you had me investigated."

He wasn't going to make her feel guilty. "I had your *company* looked into, a sound business practice. Not you, personally."

"And how do we rate?"

"A-1 from the day McDonald opened the doors. But you were responsible for its expansion. Or so everyone I spoke with lately has told me. Even Ray McDonald before he died gave you the credit."

"Ray was like the father I always wished I'd had."

Liza suspected that Ray McDonald had considered Sam

the son he'd never had or he wouldn't have made him his only heir. "And you like living in Akron?"

Sam shrugged. "It's all right." He'd built himself a big house like he'd always dreamed of owning, yet spent very little time in it. Amazing how colorless dreams were without someone to share them with. "How about you? Do you intend to stay in Port Henry forever?"

His question took her by surprise yet again. "It's never occurred to me to leave. My family's here, my roots. I can't imagine leaving them, no matter the reason."

He couldn't help thinking that her remark was a deliberate jab at his own sudden departure, the way he'd walked out on his family. "I think it best if we get something said once and for all so you can stop giving me digs. Yes, I left town suddenly, without a word to anyone, and drove away from my mother and younger brother. I had what I considered to be a very good reason. When I realized that Joe probably wasn't returning, I supported Mom and Jim the best I could from whatever job I had in whatever town I was in. I sent money every week, enough so that my mother could have stopped taking in sewing, but she refused to do so. In retrospect, I might do things differently, but what's done is done. Are you going to make me pay forever for that one youthful error in judgment, Liza?"

Carefully she set down her fork and met his eyes. "Now let me tell you how I feel, and then we won't talk about this again. 'Forever' isn't nearly long enough." Pushing back her chair, she stood. "Please excuse me. I'm going to the ladies' room."

Rising, Sam watched her wend her way through the crowded restaurant toward the rest rooms at the front. She'd pretty well let him know she not only wasn't interested in a reunion, but that it would be a cold day in hell before she'd forgive him.

So be it, Sam thought, letting his own anger surface. A business lunch was how he'd view this, too. They'd go to their damn zoning commission meeting and they'd work together as two reluctant colleagues. Until the job was done. Then, after he cleared up his father's disappearance, he'd head home and stay there.

To hell with Port Henry and to hell with Liza Courtland.

Ed Hayes happened to be driving past the Courtland Building just before five in the afternoon and recognized Sam Rivers's Explorer as it turned into the circular drive. He noticed that there were two people in the front seat. Stopping his black sedan just out of sight alongside a cluster of trees, he shifted the toothpick in his mouth and leaned out the window, squinting.

Sure enough, Liza Courtland hopped out on the passenger's side and hurried into the building. He could see Sam's dark beard clearly as he circled the drive and turned left.

Damn! Back only a couple of days and already Rivers was rooting around Liza Courtland. She was the most beautiful, the kindest, sweetest person he knew. Liza never judged someone by their looks nor cared if they weren't as educated or as successful as the next guy. She was nice to everyone, even a low-life like Sam Rivers. She'd never been particularly impressed that Ed's father had once been district attorney in Cleveland.

She deserved better than a man who'd lived on the run for eight years.

Why in hell hadn't Rivers stayed put? But no, he was back, all but physically throwing a man of the law out of his mother's house when Ed had only been doing his job. No one else in his town would have dared do that. No one else would have gotten away with it, either.

He should have slapped the cuffs on him then and there,

locked him up on some charge, like resisting arrest. If he could have come up with something that would have held water, he would have.

Not to worry. Ed's dark eyes narrowed. He'd watch the maverick builder carefully, night and day. Sooner or later Sam would make a mistake. And it would be Ed's supreme pleasure to throw Rivers behind bars where he should have been years ago. Mr. High-and-Mighty would learn that Ed Hayes was the law around here and Sam Rivers wasn't welcome, wasn't fit to mingle with the good people of Port Henry.

That decided, he felt better. Shifting into Drive, he crept forward. He'd just mosey on over to Oakview Estates and set up a watch. It shouldn't take long. Cocky men like Sam thought they were above the law. He'd soon learn differently.

Smiling, Ed cruised off.

Chapter Four

The Watering Hole was located in a seedy section of the docks on the waterfront near where smaller freighters anchored occasionally. It had been Joe Rivers's favorite bar, Sam remembered as he pulled the Explorer into the gravel parking lot. And it was the same hangout where he'd found his father the night he'd threatened to kill him if he ever touched Ann or Jim again.

Walking toward the weathered building with the winking red neon sign, he hoped that Zac hadn't sold the bar and that he had a good memory. The swinging doors squeaked as he entered and paused just inside the doorway to look around. The decor fell a bit short of achieving the nautical look its owner probably intended, mostly because the fisherman's net draped just under the ceiling was dingy and dusty, the wide-eyed fish phony and faded and the imitation seaweed a garish green.

Two older men, probably regulars like Joe had been,

nursed drinks at the bar that ran the length of the left side of the rectangular room. Only one of half a dozen tables was occupied by a tired-looking couple slouched in their cane-back chairs sipping bottled beer. Sam spotted the rotund barkeep with the bald pate and the thick, black mustache polishing glasses. He slipped onto a bar stool at the end nearest the door and waited for Zac to saunter over, his eyes curious.

"What'll it be?" Zac asked, swiping at the wooden bar with a damp rag that had seen better days.

Sam decided it was safest to order a bottle of beer.

Zac set the bottle and a cloudy glass on the bar. "I was wondering if you'd stop in. Heard you was in town."

Bartenders heard everything sooner or later, Sam thought. He hadn't frequented the Watering Hole when he'd lived in Port Henry, but he'd been in several times looking for Joe. "How've you been, Zac?"

Zac patted his ample stomach. "Haven't missed many meals. How about you, Sam?"

"Can't complain." He took a swig of his beer.

"So, what brings you back to our fair city after all this time?"

Sam glanced down the bar and saw that no one seemed to be paying them any attention. "I thought it was time I looked into Joe's disappearance. Do you remember the last night he was in here, Zac?"

"Pretty much. What do you want to know?"

Sam hadn't been sure Zac would open up, thinking that the sheriff might have brainwashed the bartender in his intense campaign to pin something on Joe's son. "Can you tell me the names of the guys who were in here that Thursday night before the Labor Day weekend, men who were friendly with Joe?"

Zac tossed his rag into a sink full of soapy water and

leaned back against the refrigerator directly behind him. "The usuals. Mike Ruggero, for sure, and Tom Novak. And, of course, Waldo Franks. Waldo and Joe were usually together."

Sam wrote down the names in a small notebook he always carried to jot reminders in when he was working on site. "What exactly happened that evening?"

"There was this scuffle. Can't rightly say who started it. Might've been Joe 'cause he was really in his cups. Maybe Tom threw the first punch. I didn't see. Pretty soon, they was all over the place, swearin' and hittin'. After they fell into one of my tables and broke a chair, I tried to pull 'em apart. Joe shoved me hard up against the bar. So I called the sheriff."

"You mean Sheriff Leo Bates?" Sam knew that Bates had been sheriff back then.

"Yeah, him. But he was off sick. You remember, he'd had that first heart attack about then? So Hayes showed up. He separated 'em, all right. They was still snarlin' at one another, but they stopped punchin'."

Sam swallowed more beer. "Then what happened?"

Zac shrugged. "Nothin'. There was only maybe six, seven customers in the place. I offered a round on the house to cool everyone down. Even Hayes had a beer. But not Joe. He cursed Hayes for interfering, mumbling under his breath, and then he left."

"So Joe drove off and—"

"Nah, he wasn't drivin'. He left on foot." Zac gave a short grunt. "Joe was a drinker all right, but he wasn't a fool. I never remember him drivin' here. Always walked. He knew better than to drive drunk, knew the sheriff would put him in jail and throw away the key. Especially that deputy. Mean son of a gun."

"You mean Hayes?" Ed had been one of two deputies back then. "You don't much care for him?"

Another laugh, louder this time. "You got that right. No love lost between me and *Sheriff* Hayes. You ask me, there's a man should never wear a badge. Too damn mean."

While Zac went down to the far end to serve another round to the two men there, Sam sat thoughtfully considering what he'd learned so far. Joe getting in a fight was not news. A couple of drinks and he'd wanted to take on the world. Funny, since he wasn't a big man, not nearly as tall as Sam or Jim. A bantamweight who thought booze made him powerful.

But where had he walked to after leaving the Watering Hole and who, if anyone, had he encountered?

Sam waited for Zac to mosey on back, aware that the bartender felt important being asked his opinion. "Tell me honestly, Zac, what do you think happened to Joe after he left here that night?"

"Truth? I think he's long gone from Port Henry." Zac leaned forward, bracing thick hands on the bar. "Your dad was an unhappy man, Sam. I don't have to tell you that, most probably. He must've told me the story a hundred times. He was training to be a fighter up Cleveland way, a lightweight. Pretty good, too, or so Joe said. But he was seeing your Ma and next thing you know, you were on the way. Joe's father was a mean cuss. Held a rifle to his head and made him marry Ann. Joe had to find a job and give up his dream of becoming a fighter. Might have been a champion, he used to say." Zac shook his head sadly. "Ain't the first man had his life go sour on account of a roll in the hay. No offense, Sam."

"None taken." He'd heard various versions of the same story all his life, and each time, Sam had wanted to plant his fist in Joe's face. As if the man had had the discipline to become a champion fighter, much less the talent. In his dreams. Never once had Joe stopped to consider that Ann had been sixteen and he'd been twenty, the one old enough to know better. Nor had Joe cared what hearing that sort of talk had done to Ann. "You mean you think he hitch-hiked out of town that night, or grabbed a bus or train, what? Because he never came home, never got his clothes or picked up his car."

The bartender leaned closer, looking as if he were about to reveal the secret of the ages. "I think he grabbed a freighter and he's miles from here. Those ship owners are always looking for hands and they're none too particular about papers. Yes sir, mark my words, old Joe's sailing the ocean blue and he's finally free of all his responsibilities. 'Course, by now he could've drunk hisself to death, I s'pose."

A freighter was a possibility Sam hadn't considered. It was something to look into. Shouldn't be too hard to get a list of freighters that stopped regularly at Port Henry eight years ago. Worth a try. "I'll look into that. Thanks. Mean-time, you know where I can find these guys, these friends of Joe's?"

"Let's see. Mike moved to Sandusky near his daughter. And Tom's in a vet's hospital in Toledo. Diabetes. Had to cut off his leg, poor guy. Waldo still comes in now and again, works odd jobs on the docks."

"Do you remember who Joe was working for back then?" Sam knew he could ask his mother and she might recall, but he also knew the conversation would upset her.

"Yeah, Reynolds Construction. I remember 'cause the job boss was Red McGinness, used to come in now and then. He's working on the west side somewhere, I hear."

Taking notes, Sam nodded. "Thanks." Pocketing his

book, he found his money clip and tossed a bill on the bar as he slipped off the stool. "I appreciate your help, Zac. One last question—did anyone else leave shortly after Joe that night?"

Zac scrunched his face up, thinking. "Don't believe so. Most everyone stayed to drink the round I bought. Things quieted down after Joe left." He began polishing the bar again. "Not much to go on. But then, I doubt you'll ever find your daddy. Man that don't want to be found, ain't gonna be."

Words of wisdom from a bartender. "You're probably right, but I've got to try. If you remember anything else, call me at this number." Sam handed him his business card with the number of the trailer phone written on the back. "Thanks again."

Outside, Sam gazed up at a three-quarter moon and wondered if Liza was home looking at the same moon. She'd rocked him a bit at lunch earlier, telling him she'd adopted a baby because she needed someone to love after he'd left her. Although it was an admission that she had loved him once, it also told him she still blamed him for leaving.

Maybe if he told her all the reasons why he'd felt it necessary to go, she'd understand. Then again, maybe not. He'd always hated defending himself. He opened the Explorer's door and got in. She'd been subdued in their meeting after lunch and quiet on the drive back to the Courtland Building. He'd thought it best to leave her alone for a while.

They'd gotten only minor concessions from the zoning commission, and Sam knew there was more work to be done before they had final approval, an approval they needed badly. They'd parted with Liza agreeing to get some figures together, which she would then fax to him for discussion. Best not to contact her until she got in touch with him.

Sam left the parking lot and drove along the waterfront. Only one freighter in tonight anchored in the bay, looking large and looming and slightly rusty with only one string of lights on. He tried to picture his father that night, drunk and belligerent and angry as usual, convincing someone on the boats to hire on. The picture wouldn't compute, but he'd check it out, anyway. Stranger things had happened, he supposed.

Slowly he drove toward Woods Lane and his mother's house where Jim undoubtedly would be sullenly staring at the TV, angry that Sam had insisted he go to work at Oakview. He hadn't seen his brother when he'd returned, but Jeff said he'd put him to work at the far end grading. A job that no doubt Jim thought was beneath him. The kid had quite a lot to learn. Sam wondered if they'd be speaking to each other by the time Jim learned his lesson.

Easing up the hill, he stared out at the moon seemingly following him. A lovely night after a beautiful day. He wished he had someone to share it with, then cursed himself for being a dreamer and a fool as he stepped on the gas.

Sam leaned back in the trailer desk chair and scrubbed a hand over his face, then spoke into the phone. "Thanks for calling me back, Keith." He'd been trying to reach the young man who was Ed Hayes's only deputy all day. Keith Nickles had been a sophomore second-stringer on the football team when Sam had played varsity, someone he'd given some pointers to, cementing their friendship.

"Glad you're back in town, Sam." At his desk in the sheriff's office, Keith glanced at a team picture on the wall of the Port Henry Chargers taken the year he'd been the quarterback who'd led them to the state championship.

He'd never forgotten the upper classman who'd helped him learn to throw. "Staying long?"

"I don't know yet. Listen, I was wondering if you could do me a favor?"

"I'll sure try."

Sam knew that Keith had to be alone in the office because if he were to step out of the trailer, he'd be able to see the sheriff's car parked up the dirt road just the other side of the fence, partially hidden by a cluster of trees. He'd spotted Hayes sitting there watching for hours on and off for several days now. Crime in Port Henry must be at an all-time low for the sheriff to be able to while away half a day keeping a building site under observation, he thought. "I don't know how far back the sheriff keeps records on file, but what I'd like to see are any reports you can find regarding the missing-person investigation of Joe Rivers over the Labor Day weekend eight years ago."

"To tell you the truth, I'm not sure how far back our records go, either. But I'll check it out and fax you any I find. That be okay?"

"That would be great." Sam gave Keith the fax number at the trailer. "I don't want to get you into any trouble with Hayes."

"Don't worry about that. I've been meaning to stop over at Oakview. I hear you've grown a beard. I've been thinking of doing the same."

"Come on over and check it out. I'll buy you a cup of coffee." They said their goodbyes and Sam disconnected just as he heard the low hum of a powerful engine approaching. It was past seven and all the men including Jeff had gone home. He rose, stretching, hoping that Hayes hadn't decided to leave his hidey-hole for a one-on-one chat.

As usual, the door of the trailer was open. Sam stepped

out into the twilight of a spring evening just as Liza climbed out of her white BMW. He hadn't heard from her in two days and wondered what brought her here, especially this late.

"I've been trying to fax you for hours and I can't get through," she said, walking toward him holding a file folder. "*And* your phone line's been busy, too."

Puzzled, Sam frowned. "I've been on the phone, but the fax should be working." Moving out of the doorway so she could step in, he walked over to check the machine and saw the problem right away. "Jeff must have unplugged the fax so he could connect the copying machine. I need to get a couple more outlets in here." He switched the plugs, then turned to face her. "Sorry about that." Sitting down at the small table, he gestured to the other chair. "Come show me what you have."

Reluctantly, Liza joined him. She hadn't wanted to come over, but she was well aware how crucial the zoning approval was to their project, and she had to bring him in on a small problem. Besides, she thought it was time she visited the site and looked around after hours, when the men weren't working.

Pulling out the chair, she glanced around, noting the couch along one wall, a built-in desk and counter holding their office machines, a four-drawer filing cabinet and even a small refrigerator. A door at the back undoubtedly led to a bathroom. The trailer looked new and was far cozier than she'd been expecting with its tweed carpeting, walls paneled in a light pecan and miniblinds on the windows. "This isn't half-bad," she told him.

"I had a couple of these customized last year. You should have seen our old ones. Like metal ovens in the summer and we froze in the winter. Dirk and I spend so much time in them during a project that I thought we might as well be comfortable.''

Sam wondered how she managed to look so fresh at the end of what was probably a long day for her. She was wearing pale gray slacks with a matching silk blouse and a heavy gold chain at her throat. Classic beauty, but then she'd always been that.

He nodded toward her folder. "So what've you got?"

Liza sighed. "I probably should have told you this before. The reason the commission's been so slow is that Courtland owns that building at the far corner of the property."

"Uh-huh." He recalled that it was a square brick structure, one story, about two thousand square feet, that used to house a hardware store. "And you want to exclude it from the zoning requirements?"

"No, I want to *include* it as part of the parcel, which the commission's been reluctant to do." She held out the folder. "I've put together yet another proposal, but they're stubborn."

He took the folder, but didn't open it. "I don't get it. What do you want to use that building for?"

"A teen center." She leaned forward, eager for him to understand, to agree with her. "There's a real need for that kind of thing in Port Henry. The location's perfect, with easy access from half a dozen neighborhoods. You have no idea how restless and bored kids around here are evenings, weekends and all summer long. And there's no place they can go where there're organized activities, counseling for those who need it by adults who're used to working with that age group, even vocational guidance. The schools can't do it all, and the parents don't.''

Sam was thoughtful for a long moment. "How's Cindy doing?"

She almost smiled. Uncanny the way he could see through even her roundabout explanations and guess that she wanted to create something that might have helped her sister a while back. "She's okay now. At least, I think so. You never know with Cindy when the other shoe will drop."

"I heard she moved to Boston."

She nodded. "About six months ago. She was home for Christmas and seems to be clean and sober. Miraculously, she didn't have some guy with her this time after the string of losers she's dragged in. She works at a boutique, of all places. If you could have seen how she used to dress." Liza shook her head in wonder. Two years younger, Cindy had been wild for ten years and a huge disappointment to her parents. Liza had lost track of the number of times she'd had to bail out her sister. "Ah, but we hope for the best." She met Sam's eyes. "And yes, she's the reason I want to open the center."

"I think it's a great idea. My brother could probably use something like that right now."

Liza frowned sympathetically. "I heard he'd been arrested on a DUI."

No secrets in small towns. "Yeah. I've got Lyle Stewart working on it. Do you remember him?"

"I know Lyle. His wife Sue works out at the fitness center where I go a couple of mornings a week. I didn't know you and he were still friends."

"We kept in touch." Keeping in touch was not a topic Sam wanted to pursue. "Getting back to your building—the commission doesn't want to let you include it and that's our holdup?"

"More or less. You saw how many old geezers are on that commission. They haven't had a new thought in the last millennium. They think that the center will attract all sorts of riffraff. Their word, not mine. And that the property owners who're spending a bundle on the new houses in this neighborhood will object. What do you think?'' In a flash of déjà vu, Liza remembered the many times they'd talked together about issues just like this, sometimes agreeing, often not. But their conversations had always been interesting, stimulating. She'd missed that, missed his quick mind, the fair and honest way it worked.

Stop! she reminded herself. No sweet, sad memories. That way lay madness.

''I think it's a terrific idea. Let me ask you, how are you planning to work this—the renovation, the maintenance, the operation, hiring, etcetera? Donations, private funding, bonds?''

''Strictly a Courtland enterprise. We'll finance the whole thing. I want to personally interview and hire the staff, oversee the decorating, all of it.'' Liza watched those incredible blue eyes study her, assessing what she'd told him. She'd never before or since met anyone with eyes that same cobalt, that rich blue tinged with green. They seemed to change with his moods, turning almost gray when he was angry, darkening to deep blue when he was aroused, when he touched her just so and... Clearing her throat, she shifted on the hard chair. ''Why do you want to know?''

''Because that basically makes it a charitable operation, in which case you can apply for a new zoning ruling, tax exempt. You don't need the commission's approval to donate your building, especially for such a worthy cause.''

Her eyes lit up. ''That's possible?''

''Sure. Let's exclude the building from the Oakview project and tomorrow, you fill out the paperwork on the new request. We had something similar on a development Dirk handled outside Akron in Canton last year. Worked out much better financially for the owners, I can tell you.''

Liza frowned. "I wonder why our attorney never thought of that."

Sam shrugged. "Don't know. It's not that unusual. But, to be on the safe side, have him check it out before you make your move." He rose, walked to the refrigerator. "Want something cold to drink?"

Liza followed, bending to peer inside the compact fridge. "What've you got?"

"Beer, soft drinks, juice." He grabbed a small orange juice for himself."

"That cranberry looks good." She straightened as Sam, holding both bottles, shoved the fridge door shut with his hip and turned toward her. He was much closer than she'd realized. Suddenly, their eyes locked together as awareness surged through her system.

Sam set the bottles on the counter before pulling her to him, watching her eyes shift to an emerald green.

"Sam, don't. I..."

But his hand was already reaching up to tuck a lock of thick blond hair behind her ear. "Don't what? Don't look at you, don't touch you, don't want you? If only I could stop." There might be hell to pay, she might slap him and walk out, but the reward was worth the risk. He lowered his head and took her mouth.

He caught her off guard. Of all things Liza hadn't expected during this meeting, a kiss was at the top of the list. But she was in his arms, her mouth locked to his, before she could dodge him. And in another heartbeat, she didn't want to.

There it was, the heat, the incredible heat he alone released in her. Like a match set to very dry tinder, he had but to touch his lips to hers and she was hot and needy and filled with renewed longing. She'd dreamed of this, consciously and unconsciously, week after solitary week. And now it was here and eight lonely years fell away.

Fire. There was such fire in her. Her response was instantaneous, like a fallow field springing to life, like a dead man suddenly awakening. Yet he could sense her inner struggle as her hands moved restlessly up and down his arms, then finally bunched in the denim of his shirt as she tightened, shifting closer.

Her mouth was the stuff dreams were made of. Where had she learned to kiss like this, her lips greedy on his, her tongue slipping inside without hesitancy? Then he felt her hands inch up his back and curl around his shoulders as she pressed her slender frame against his. And he was lost in the wonder of her.

Familiar. How could that be after such a length of time? Liza asked herself. Yet he felt and tasted familiar. Still, there were subtle changes. His hold on her was more self-assured, for the seeking boy had been replaced by a confident man. He'd always been clever, his hands roaming her body with a thoroughness that had stolen her breath away. Now, there was no hesitancy, but rather a certainty to his touch that was even more thrilling.

She had no willpower when Sam touched her, never had had. She was like a puppet who danced to his tune, like a piece of clay he molded to his liking. Never had anyone ruled her so completely or stolen her breath along with her firm resolve.

So she stepped closer to the flame and let the fire take her.

Sam had wondered how she'd react, if she'd struggle out of his grasp and curse him for daring to touch her. From the moment he'd walked into her office that first afternoon, he'd wondered if she would taste the same, respond the same. His heart leaped to realize that she'd opened to him as if they'd been apart a mere eight days rather than eight years.

A homecoming. It was like a homecoming, the feel of her in his arms once more, her generous mouth moving under his, the soft sounds she made that he remembered from long ago. Pressing her closer, he thrust his hands into her hair and deepened the kiss.

Later, Liza was to wonder what would have happened if the phone hadn't rung just then, startling them apart. She opened her eyes and saw the jolt of irritation in his at the interruption. Breathing hard, she stepped back as he turned to answer the call.

"Rivers," he all but snarled into the phone. He listened to the hesitant, worried woman's voice as his heart rate settled. "What did you say again?" She wasn't quite hysterical, but plenty upset. Finally her words penetrated his muddled mind. "Oh, yes, Mrs. Courtland. Liza's right here. Just a moment." He held out the phone. "For you. Your mother."

Always, Liza's first thought was Beth, knowing her mother never tracked her down unless there was a serious problem. "Mom, is Beth all right?" She listened for several seconds, her concern growing. "No, no, it's not your fault. I'm on my way, Mom. Please calm down."

Anything but calm herself, she hung up rather clumsily. "I've got to go. Beth's had an accident. Mom's taken her to Port Henry General, to Emergency."

Sam dug his keys from his pocket. "I'll drive you. What kind of accident?" He handed her her shoulder bag, then hustled her outside, quickly locking the trailer door.

Liza brushed back her hair with a nervous hand. "I bought her this videotape of *The Little Mermaid*. Apparently she was pretending to be the mermaid, leaped down over several steps on our back stairway and landed all wrong. Mom thinks she broke her left leg.'' She stopped, realizing he'd opened the door to his Explorer. ''No, I have my car right here and…''

''You're in no condition to drive. I'll take you and get your car back to you by morning. Get in.''

Rarely did Liza take orders well. However, this was one of those times. She got in, too upset to argue. Her baby in Emergency. ''Please hurry.''

Liza rushed into Port Henry General and saw Dr. Gerald Tracy tending her daughter. ''There's Mommy,'' he said, looking up as Liza approached. ''Let's tell her what a brave young lady you are.''

''Beth, honey, does it hurt a lot?'' Liza bent over the table where her daughter lay stretched out, leaning close to brush back strands of blond hair the exact shade of her own.

Beth's small face was a little pinched, and there were tear tracks on her cheeks. ''Uh-huh.'' But she tried a brave smile. ''They're gonna put on a cast, Mom. My friends can sign it.''

Elizabeth Courtland rose from the bedside chair. ''They've taken X rays, Liza. It's a simple fracture. Dr. Tracy says it should heal beautifully.'' Her voice was anxious, guilty. ''I'm so sorry, darling. It all happened so fast. I had no idea she'd jump down *five* steps.''

Liza squeezed her mother's hand. ''Of course you didn't.''

''We need you to sign this permission slip, Ms. Courtland,'' the doctor said. ''Then we'll give her something for the pain and put the cast on.''

''Certainly.'' Liza scanned the paper, then signed her name.

''Thank you. I'll be right back.'' Tracy left.

"Mommy, who's that man?" Beth asked, peering at Sam standing in the doorway.

Liza took hold of her daughter's hand. "That's Mr. Rivers. He and I are working together on building those houses I told you about." She stroked the dear little freckled face. "Whatever made you try to jump so far, Beth?"

"I was the little mermaid, Mommy," Beth insisted, as if that explained everything. Looking around her mother, she smiled at the tall man. "Hi. My name's Beth."

Charmed, Sam stepped closer, noticing the flash of annoyance on Liza's face and the keen look of interest on her mother's. "Hi, Beth. I'm Sam. Can I sign your cast, too?"

She gave him a gap-toothed smile. "Sure." But a wave of pain swept her and she flinched. "Mommy, it hurts."

"I know, honey. Just a minute or so more." Even in pain, Beth was drawn to an adult male, always had been, Liza recalled. That longing for a father that no amount of mothering could satisfy.

A short nurse wearing a name tag marked Rhoda and carrying a syringe on a small tray bustled in. "We're going to take care of that pain right now, sweetie." She smiled at the little girl, then looked at the adults. "I'm going to have to ask you all to step out into the waiting room for a little bit. The cubicle's small and we need moving-around room to put on her cast."

"You're going to put the cast on right here?" Liza asked.

A second nurse wearing rubber gloves walked in and heard the question. "Yes, indeed. We do it all the time. Rhoda's worked in orthopedics for years. You can wait right over there." She pointed toward a small room with plastic chairs and a wall-mounted television.

"Why don't you two go ahead?" Liza said to her mother and Sam. "I'm staying right here with my daughter." The look she gave the two nurses brooked no argument. "I'll keep out of your way," she added as a concession. She had no intention of leaving Beth, knowing she was in pain and frightened, as well.

"After you, Mrs. Courtland," Sam said. He winked at Beth. "See you shortly." And he followed the older woman into the waiting room. "I don't believe we've met. I'm Sam Rivers." He held out his hand, wondering if she'd reject him.

Gracious as always, Elizabeth Courtland shook hands. "Thank you for bringing Liza over. I worry about her driving when she's upset."

"I remember she used to have something of a lead foot a while back when she had that red Corvette." They used to leave his unreliable truck parked in an apple orchard just outside town and tool around in her Corvette.

"You knew my daughter years ago?" Elizabeth couldn't recall Liza ever mentioning Ann Rivers's son, although she remembered that he'd left town rather suddenly some time ago.

Mistake! Sam thought, then recovered quickly. "Sort of. I'd see her driving by." Reaching in his pocket, he hauled out a quarter. "I've got to make a couple of calls. Excuse me, please." No way was he staying in that small room with those shrewd eyes on him for the length of time it took to put on Beth's cast. He headed for the bank of public phones.

"Okay, now, Beth, you just slide that arm around my neck and I'll ease you out of there," Sam told the child as he bent toward the Explorer's back seat. He'd driven the three generations of Courtland ladies home with Mrs. Courtland in front alongside him and Beth stretched out in the back, her head in her mother's lap.

''Like this?'' Beth asked, her hand snaking along his shoulder, then curling around his neck. The pain medication was still in effect, making her quite woozy.

''That's right.'' He shifted her into his arms easily, mindful of the bulky cast, and turned to see both women watching him anxiously. ''She's fine. Where would you like me to deposit her?''

''On the couch, probably,'' Elizabeth said, searching in her purse for her keys. ''We can take her upstairs later.''

''No, Mom. We'll never be able to manage Beth with that heavy cast.'' Finding her own keys, Liza moved to the front door. ''Would you mind carrying her up to her room, Sam?''

''Certainly not.'' He smiled down into the child's huge blue eyes. ''It isn't every day I get to hold such a pretty young lady.''

Beth giggled. ''You're nice.''

''You're pretty nice yourself.'' Sam walked through the door Liza held open, thinking that this was the first time he'd ever stepped into the Courtland Mansion, as it was known all over town.

''This way, Sam.'' Liza walked toward the winding stairway leading up from a white marble foyer larger than his mother's living room.

Climbing up on thick gold carpeting, he noticed that the walls were covered with silk wallpaper, and a huge sparkling chandelier hung from the second level. The impression was elegant but too colorless for his taste. He followed Liza along a wide hallway to a heavy walnut door on the far right. She shoved it open and stood aside so he could enter with his drowsy bundle.

Sam had an impression of a good-size sitting room as he followed Liza across a large bedroom containing an enormous four-poster bed and on through an archway into a pink-and-white room that was fit for a princess. "This must be your room," he said as Liza quickly pulled back the covers on a canopied bed.

"How'd you know?" Beth asked, her words slow and slurring.

"A lucky guess." Gently he laid her down and saw her fight sleep as her mother removed her polo shirt and slipped a Garfield nightshirt over her head. "You rest now, sweetheart."

"Will you come see me soon?" Beth asked, her eyes already closing.

"You bet, real soon." He watched Liza kiss her lingeringly on both cheeks, then draw the comforter up before turning away.

"I can't thank you enough," she said, leading him back through her room and on into the sitting room. Although she was used to fending for herself, for being the strong one even in family situations for so long now, she had to admit the ordeal had been easier with Sam to assist her. "It's the very first time Beth's had a broken bone or anything serious. She had me scared."

"Understandable." He glanced around, wanting to see how she lived. Here was the color missing from downstairs, shades of vivid green mingled with rich blues and touches of ivory. Potted plants, hanging ferns and vases of wildflowers, large and small, were everywhere along with assorted hardcover books, needlepoint pillows and colorful framed prints, mostly of horses. "This is nice."

Liza rubbed along the back of her neck. "I had this apartment made up after I came home when Dad had his first stroke. I thought that Beth and I needed our privacy." She nodded toward the French doors leading to a porch. "We even have our own entrance. Too much togetherness can kill family relationships."

"I'm sure you're right." Not that he'd had much togetherness in his family ever. "But I kind of expected a few servants around in such a big house."

"There were, for a long time. Dad had upstairs maids and downstairs maids, a cook, a gardener, even a chauffeur. Then after his stroke, we added round-the-clock nurses, doctors coming and going. Mom got awfully tired of it, so after Dad died, she got rid of all but a cleaning woman who comes twice a week and a yardman. Of course, she's closed off a good many rooms that are rarely used."

Sam saw her knead the muscles of her neck and guessed that she probably was struggling with the aftermath of tension. He wanted to reach over and massage the pain away, have her lean back against him. Instead he checked his watch. "I'd better be going."

Liza walked downstairs with him. Licking her lips, she realized she could still taste the lingering flavor of his kiss. She didn't dare look up at him for fear he would read the longing in her eyes. Instead, she opened the door, gazing out into the darkened sky, at a loss for words.

"I'll get both cars back to you early tomorrow." He'd get Jim and Jeff to help him before work started.

"No rush. I think I'll take tomorrow off and spend it with my daughter."

Sam raised a quizzical brow. "The workaholic takes a day off?"

"There are some things that come before work." All too often, she hadn't been able to be there for Beth, especially when they'd first come to Port Henry and the company had to come first. That guilt still weighed heavily on her. "Thanks, again."

"Don't mention it. Good night."

Liza watched the Explorer until the taillights were out of sight. She was about to close the door when she saw the headlights of a car flash on just beyond the trees at the bend in the road. It was too dark to see the car clearly, but she saw it turn and follow Sam's Explorer down the incline. Odd, she thought as she locked up.

"Liza," Elizabeth Courtland said as her daughter walked toward the stairs, "come have a cup of tea with me."

"Can I have a rain check, Mother? I'm really beat." The last thing she needed right now was to be questioned by her own mother. From the look on Elizabeth's face, she had a feeling that Sam Rivers would be Topic A.

Elizabeth rarely pressed. "All right, dear. Rest well."

Liza's foot was on the bottom step when her mother called her name. Turning, she looked back over her shoulder questioningly.

"Did you know your lipstick's smudged? I just wondered if you were aware of it, since you're always so well groomed. Good night, dear." Slowly, Elizabeth walked into the library.

That, Liza thought as she touched her lips with a fingertip, is what is known as a *gotcha*.

Chapter Five

Judge Alan R. Larson wore thick glasses and a calm expression as he reviewed the papers Lyle Stewart had handed him. The courtroom was quiet, save for the judge's secretary shuffling through files at her desk off to his right. Several public defenders sat somewhat impatiently at the attorneys' table, waiting to plead their clients' cases while the defendants lounged in the sequestered area. Wearing a smug smile, the sheriff leaned against the railing, his shifting glance taking in everything. On a wooden bench in the gallery behind the rail, Sam sat silently watching the scene play itself out as Lyle waited alongside a fidgety Jim Rivers.

Although this was the preliminary hearing, Lyle had prepared Jim long and seriously. The young man was clean shaven with a new haircut, wearing navy slacks, a white shirt and striped tie. His demeanor was sober and repentant. At least, Sam *hoped* his brother was repentant.

Certainly the courthouse building with its high ceilings and hushed hallways, its metal detectors at each entrance and guards wearing guns standing along the corridors should be enough to sober up any clear-thinking individual, Sam thought. But who could see into the mind of a teenager?

Judge Larson finished reading the collection of character letters Lyle had gathered from Jim's professors at Ohio State, his old Port Henry teachers, the minister at the church Ann attended regularly and, of course, Sam, attesting to the boy's integrity. The purpose was to show the judge that Jim was a decent young man who'd made an honest mistake, one he regretted and wouldn't repeat.

"Well, Mr. Rivers, this is an impressive list of people who seem to feel you won't turn into a repeat offender," the judge said, looking directly at Jim. "What do you have to say for yourself?"

Jim cleared his throat. "I've learned my lesson, Your Honor. I've got a good job working for my brother's construction company. I intend to work hard all summer, to save my money and go back to Ohio State in the fall, sir."

Sam listened to the well-rehearsed speech and hoped Jim meant every word he said.

"I see." Larson shifted his attention to Lyle. "Mr. Stewart, let's hear what you think."

Lyle stepped forward. "I think Jim Rivers regrets his mistake, Your Honor. As you read, he's on the dean's list at college, he's never been in trouble before, and there was no accident or injury, nor even property damage involved in this incident. I believe he poses no further risk to the community."

Larson looked toward the arresting officer who'd moved closer to the bench. Sam could swear he saw a flicker of dislike cross the judge's bland features, but it was gone before he spoke. "Sheriff Hayes, have you anything to add?"

"Your Honor, I respectfully disagree with Mr. Stewart. This young man quit college and has been out drinking and running around every night since. I've got witnesses who've seen him. He also has a questionable family background. His father's a known alcoholic, his brother up and left town under suspicious circumstances and..."

"*Sheriff!*" The judge's tone was loud and impatient. "We're here to discuss a simple DUI, a first offense. The young man's family is not on trial, nor is any of their background relevant. I've been assured Jim Rivers is returning to Ohio State for the fall term and that he's gainfully employed for the summer. If you have anything *new* to tell the court about this arrest, please do so now. If not, you may step back."

"Nothing else at this time, Your Honor." His face flushed, Hayes stepped back.

"Thank you, all of you." Larson folded his hands and looked at Lyle. "I'm inclined to be lenient this morning since this is your client's first offense. I'd like to see him begin attending AA classes a minimum of three times a week, and I'm going to assign him fifty hours of community service. I'm also going to restrict his driver's license so he may operate a car only to and from his job, AA and the service I mentioned for a period of sixty days. If after that time there's been no violation and Mr. Rivers here has completed everything, we'll purge his record and erase his debt to society. Can you and he live with that, Lyle?"

"Yes, we can, Your Honor. And thank you."

Jim joined in. "Yes, thank you, Your Honor." Over his shoulder, he smiled nervously at Sam.

"See you in sixty days," the judge said. "Next case."

Sam watched Hayes shove his sunglasses into place, but

not before he'd caught the glimmer of rage in his dark eyes.
A public reprimand when he'd been expecting a jail term
for Jim, the young man's greatest sin not the DUI but the
fact that he was related to Joe and Sam. Some officer of
the law Hayes was.

Rising, Sam reached to shake Lyle's hand and embrace
Jim. "You've got a second chance here," he told his
brother. "Don't blow it."

"I won't, honest. Thanks, both of you." The three men
left while the sheriff stood glaring after them.

Sam had just finished a call to the last shipping line on
his list of five and hung up when the phone in the trailer
rang again. "Rivers," he answered absently, his thoughts
on the last call.

"It's Keith, Sam." The deputy's voice sounded puzzled.
"I've run across a problem here."

Just what he needed, another problem. Sam leaned back
in his squeaky chair. "What's that?"

"Well, you know that file on your father's disappearance
that you asked me to look into for you?"

"Right. Did you find it?"

"There is none."

Sam straightened. "No file at all?"

"That's right. I wasn't working here back eight years
ago, but I remember what went on around town. Hayes
questioned anyone and everyone. He had whole fields dug
up, the bay dredged, Joe's work site and several bars gone
over with a police hound in tow. He logged a lot of hours.
And yet there's no file, no interview sheets, no expense
vouchers, no record of anything."

Sam was thoughtful, considering possibilities. "Maybe
it's misfiled or perhaps Hayes took it home."

"It's not misfiled. I went through every drawer. Naturally, I don't know if he took it home. I'm at a loss to explain this."

Why would Hayes deliberately destroy or hide a file on the biggest case of his career, one still unsolved, open and pending? He had to have it in his possession. But why? "Well, I appreciate the search. Maybe it'll turn up yet."

"Yeah, right." Disbelief was clear in Keith's voice. "Doubtful, but if it does, I'll let you know. Sorry."

"Not your fault. Talk with you later." Sam got up and walked outside. Midafternoon and the crew were hard at it. Things were moving along now that the zoning problem had been taken care of and the new men were on payroll. The weather had been near perfect with sunny skies and temperatures not too hot yet, even though tomorrow was the first of May. If the spring rains would hold off awhile, they'd get most of the cement in and dried, at least.

Hands jammed in his back pockets, he gazed to the far perimeter where the building Liza was renovating stood. She'd gotten the okay and was in the process of hiring people to revamp the place. He had to admire her for wanting to help the community. The soft side of Liza Courtland.

He'd also seen the tough side of her the night in the Emergency ward when she hadn't caved in to the nurse's request that she leave while they put on Beth's cast. The mother bear protecting her cub. And a pretty little cub she was.

Sam hadn't spent much time around kids. One of his foremen in Akron had a son about nine, and he used to bring him around occasionally. The boy had seemed drawn to Sam, always wanting to talk. At their last company picnic, he'd found an old mitt and they'd played catch awhile. Cute kid. Not as cute as Beth.

He wondered if Beth was Liza's natural daughter and, if so, who the Michigan college kid who'd fathered her was.

Had she loved him? Or used him to get the baby she'd apparently wanted, someone of her own to love, as she'd told him? An unkind thought, but a possibility. Or was she telling the truth and she'd really adopted Beth? He hadn't ever known her to lie when the two of them had dated years ago. Still, people changed. With her family so prominent, she might have told the lie to save her folks from the embarrassment of an illegitimate child. Her parents had had enough to deal with after the drowning death of their only son and the youngest daughter who'd been so out of control.

Yes, he could picture Liza lying to prevent someone she cared about from getting hurt. Yet Lyle had said she'd been estranged from her folks, not even returning for holidays until after Will's first stroke. What had that been about? Sighing, he decided there was a great deal about Liza Courtland he didn't know.

Turning, he checked the spot where Hayes always parked the sheriff's car and saw that it was there, all right. What kick did that creep get out of watching Oakview's operation? Sam knew Hayes was even more furious since he hadn't been able to throw Jim in jail. If you can't get the man, get the brother. Hayes was a sick SOB. How had he gotten elected sheriff?

And what had he done with the file on Joe Rivers? Surely there had to be one. As deputy back then, he'd have had to obtain permission and expense approval for all the digging and dredging and searching. With all that, Hayes hadn't been able to locate Joe. Sam doubted if he would, either, since not a one of the five shipping lines he'd contacted had ever hired a man by that name or social security number. Damn discouraging.

Enough of this fruitless brooding. Sam glanced at his watch. He had an errand to run, one that he looked forward to for a change. He had in mind something he wanted to buy, if only he could find it. Closing up the trailer, knowing Jeff had keys, he climbed into the Explorer. As he whizzed past Ed hunched down behind the wheel of his cruiser, Sam honked and waved at the sheriff simply because he knew it would irritate the hell out of him.

"That's great, Edith," Liza said into the phone. "Thanks for taking care of that for me. Please remind Arnie to cover the meeting in Toledo for me. I'll be in early tomorrow morning." Hanging up, she glanced across the room at her daughter who was studying her collection of movies spread out on the coffee table, wondering which to choose for their matinee. "Find one yet?" Liza asked, moving over to join her on the couch.

Beth sighed dramatically. "It's between *The Little Mermaid* and *Beauty and the Beast.* I can't decide."

In the three days since the broken leg, Liza had rearranged her schedule at the office, going in late mornings or returning home by midafternoon so she could spend more time with her restless daughter. Beth hated the confinement of the cast, not being able to ride her bike around the property and the worst, hardly ever leaving their small apartment since Liza refused to allow her to manipulate her crutches on the stairs unless she was present to help. "I think we can rule out the mermaid before she gives you any more ideas."

"Okay." Beth scooted back on the couch and handed her mother the other videotape. "Did you make some popcorn?"

Liza shoved the tape into the VCR in its niche below the television. "I did better than that." She picked up the large can decorated with playful kittens. "I bought caramel corn, but we can't overdo or we'll rot our teeth." It was Beth's favorite and something Liza let her indulge in very infrequently.

"Oh, wow, thanks, Mom." Nestled in the corner of the couch, she stretched out her leg with the cast and accepted the small bowl from her mother.

Liza settled in the opposite corner, watching her daughter watching the introductory credits roll and munching in time to the music. She never tired of looking at the beautiful child who was hers alone. She suspected that there was some speculation about Beth's parentage around Port Henry and even in her own family despite her carefully worded adoption story, still no one knew the whole truth. Not even Aunt Margaret who'd taken her in when she'd moved to Ann Arbor had known everything.

And Liza intended the truth to stay hidden, for to bring it all out, especially now, would be disastrous. Occasionally she felt twinges of guilt about denying the father of such a lovely girl the right to know his own daughter. But basically she felt that men who walked away from their responsibilities didn't have the same rights as those who stayed and became loving and committed fathers. If she was wrong in her assessment, so be it. Saving Beth from getting hurt should that man choose to walk away again was worth most anything.

The first song had barely begun when Liza heard a knock at the door of their sitting room. Since her mother was the only other person in the house, she called out to her. "Come in, Mother."

Elizabeth pushed open the door, entering a bit hesitantly, then stepping aside to allow her guest to step in. "You have company, Beth." She sent an apologetic smile to Liza before going on. "Mr. Rivers has brought you a get-well present."

Looking none too pleased, Liza clicked off the movie while Beth gushed an enthusiastic welcome.

"I was hoping you'd come visit me," the girl said with the forthright honesty of youth. "You said you would."

"And here I am," Sam said. "I try to keep my promises." His gaze shifted to Liza, as he wondered if she was remembering a promise he'd broken on a long-ago rainy night, a promise to meet her at the Crane Lake cottage. He saw her green eyes turn cool as the Caribbean Sea on a choppy day, and he knew she was.

"You brought me a present?" Beth asked, staring at the wrapped gift.

"You bet I did." He handed her the pink-and-white box with the big bow as Elizabeth sat down in the rocker.

Liza stood. "So nice of you to think of Beth. Why don't you come sit here?" She walked around to settle on the arm of the couch alongside her daughter, feeling suddenly protective.

She was saying all the right things, Sam thought, but Liza's voice lacked warmth. Her unwelcome attitude had him wondering if it was because she was reluctant to share her daughter or if she was cool because of their unresolved past. Today, wearing jeans and an oversize green shirt, her hair caught up in a ponytail tied with a piece of yarn, she looked enough as she had back then to cause his breath to hitch. His hands itched to yank off that yarn, to sink his fingers into the blond thickness and slowly massage her scalp so he could watch her eyes grow hazy with arousal. Then he would...

Swallowing hard, Sam tugged his attention back to Beth who'd made quick work of removing paper and ribbon, then the lid from the box.

Separating the folds of tissue paper, Beth drew in a quick

breath as she saw what was inside. "Oh, look, it's an angel and she's got stars all over her gown."

Elizabeth leaned forward. "I believe it's also a music box. Isn't that right, Mr. Rivers?"

"Yes, and the name's Sam."

Beth held the music box up for Liza to see. "Look, Mom, isn't she beautiful?"

"She's lovely." Liza kept her eyes lowered, trying to push back a rush of emotion. Had he forgotten the angel he'd given her that long-ago night or was he trying to taunt her?

Studying Liza's face, Sam wondered why she had that pinched look around her mouth. Years ago she'd told him she loved angels, so he'd given her one. Naturally, he'd thought her daughter might like them, too, so he'd gone looking. Apparently he'd inadvertently done something wrong, though he hadn't a clue what.

Feeling her mother's eyes on her, Liza shook off the mood and smiled at Beth. No matter the cost, she wouldn't let Sam know how she felt. "Let's wind it up and see what tune it plays."

Beth listened, then smiled as she recognized "When You Wish Upon A Star." "That's Jiminy Cricket's song." She turned to Sam, reaching out her hand to him across her cast. "I love it. Thank you."

"You're very welcome." Sam stretched for a hug. "Now open the lid. There's something else inside."

"More? This is my lucky day. Uncle Ed brought over a teddy bear earlier." She pointed to a blue bear wearing a plaid ribbon around its neck, propped on the end table. "Isn't it cute?"

Sam frowned. "Uncle Ed?"

"You know, the sheriff." Oblivious to Sam's scowl

deepening or the look he sent her mother, Beth took off the lid and pulled out a small angel pin.

Swallowing his annoyance, Sam leaned closer. "They tell me you're supposed to wear that on your shoulder so your guardian angel is always with you." He felt a little awkward with the sentiment, but that's what the clerk had told him.

He leaned back, willing Liza to look at him, but she had her eyes averted. Why would she allow Hayes into her home, yet respond so coolly to Sam's visit? She'd defended Ed the last time his name had come up, too. Surely she wasn't romantically interested in that fool, was she?

"An angel watching over you is a lovely thought, isn't it, Beth?" Elizabeth asked, aware of the increased tension in the room. Only Beth seemed happy. Something going on here, Liza's mother decided.

"Yes, it is. Mom, pin it on for me, please."

Liza fastened the pin to her red sweatshirt at Beth's shoulder. "There. Now she'll watch over you always." And she wished she still believed in such childhood magic, wished she could accept Sam's gift to Beth at face value. And why should it matter to Sam that Ed Hayes is kind to her daughter? It was none of his business. She wished he would leave.

Wanting to give Sam something in return, Beth offered her bowl of caramel corn. "Would you like some?"

Obligingly Sam thanked her and grabbed a few pieces.

"Mom and I were just going to watch *Beauty and the Beast.* Why don't you stay and watch it with us?" He was so nice. She didn't want him to leave. "It'll be fun. You can sit with me," she added hopefully.

"Beth, I'm sure Sam has a lot of things he has to do," Liza said, gathering up the wrapping paper and ribbon. Maybe, just maybe, he'd get the hint. Two hours in his company watching a sentimental love story, albeit in cartoon form, was not her idea of fun by a long shot. Torture maybe, but not fun.

Why'd he come bearing gifts, being nice, winning over Beth's vulnerable little heart? Like mother, like daughter, Liza thought grimly. For she wasn't immune to his presence, not by a long shot. Why'd he have to look so damn appealing? Usually, she disliked beards, and he certainly hadn't dressed to impress with his khaki slacks and black cotton shirt. Was it because she still remembered that hard, exciting body close up against hers or that she'd felt that soft beard graze her face as he'd kissed her breathless just days ago? Remembered and wished she could forget.

Liza was sending him a message loud and clear, Sam decided. She wanted him gone. Apparently, obnoxious as he was, Hayes had something he didn't have: the past several years to establish a relationship with Liza and her daughter.

Rising, Sam shook his head. "Thanks, Beth, but I have to get to an appointment. I just wanted to give you a little something for being so brave in the hospital the other night."

Beth wasn't one to give up easily. "Maybe you could come back after your appointment. We're having fried chicken for dinner, right, Grandma? He can have dinner with us." She looked from one adult to the other and no one would meet her eyes. Confused, she turned back to Sam. "Are you sure you have to go?"

He gave her a smile. "Yes, but I'll see you again real soon."

"All right." Beth sounded dejected. "'Bye and thanks again."

"I'll see you out," Elizabeth said, opening the door.

He should have known better than to come, Sam thought.

He'd been a welcome guest the other evening when they'd needed his help, but today Liza was treating him as if she wished he'd disappear. To hell with it. He'd go back to the site and lose himself in work. And not waste time thinking about someone who obviously wanted him gone.

With a curt nod, he followed Elizabeth out and closed the door.

Slowly, feeling suddenly tired, Liza walked back to sit on the couch. "Shall we put the movie on again?" she asked Beth.

"I don't want to anymore." Disappointment clouded her small face as she wound up the music box and leaned back, listening to the tune again.

If only it were as easy as wishing on a star, Liza thought sadly.

It was nearly nine in the evening when Sam locked up for the night and got into his Explorer. He'd spent time checking out the progress of the model home, made a bunch of calls and finished a pile of paperwork. And he'd conferred with Dirk for nearly an hour about their various jobs. Suddenly he was bone tired.

He'd been tempted to skip dinner altogether, to tell his mother that he was going to sleep in the trailer tonight. But when he'd phoned her, she'd sounded kind of sad and said she'd made her special chili. He owed her the dubious honor of a few hours of his company after his long absence. So he started the engine and swung out of the complex.

The evening was balmy. He rolled down the windows for air he badly needed to stay awake. There was very little traffic out. Like most small towns, Port Henry pulled in the sidewalks after sundown. He'd just cleared the hill outside of downtown and was rounding the curve toward Woods

Lane when he heard the siren behind him, rapidly coming closer.

A glance into his rearview mirror told Sam all he needed to know. The good sheriff was out hunting bad guys. With red light flashing, Hayes brought his cruiser up close behind the Explorer, motioning him over. With a weary sigh, Sam pulled to a stop along the shoulder and waited.

His footsteps heavy, Ed sauntered over to Sam and stared in at him. "Let's have your license."

There seemed no reason to cause a ruckus. Sam handed over his driver's license and waited.

"Registration," Hayes demanded.

Sam handed that out next and waited again while Hayes looked over the papers in the beam of his big flashlight. "What seems to be the problem, *Sheriff?*"

At his tone, Ed spat his toothpick onto the ground. "Speeding. You were speeding."

Sam gave in to a rush of anger. "The hell you say. I was doing forty in a fifty zone."

Hayes smiled. "Prove it. I say sixty." Not another car on the road either way since he'd stopped Sam's vehicle. "My word against yours, and I'm the law."

"Fine." Sam's voice was calm and hard. "Write me up, but you better have a radar readout to prove sixty because I'll be in that courtroom calling you a liar to your face. Seems to me the judges around here aren't exactly in your pocket, Beefy."

At the old nickname, Hayes turned crimson, his eyes narrowing. "I don't like you, Rivers, and I don't want you nosing around my town. If you were smart, you'd go back to where you've been and stay put. Decent folks don't want to have anything to do with scum like you and yours." He tossed Sam's license and registration at him through the window. "Go on, get out of here. But you watch yourself, you here? 'Cause anything else happens and I'll be all over you like a cheap suit.''

"You're the one who'd better be careful, Hayes. I know you're hanging around the building site watching us. Ever hear of harassment, of stalking laws? My men and I are making note of every minute you're sitting there wasting taxpayer's money. Push me too far and I'll slap a lawsuit on you that you'll never get out of.'' He flipped into gear. "So long, *Sheriff.*''

Sam took off with a childish squeal of rubber tires, pleased that he'd stirred up enough dust to coat Beefy's smartly pressed uniform.

Cursing, brushing himself off, Ed walked back to his cruiser and got behind the wheel. Damn Rivers. Life had been moving toward perfect until that renegade had returned. He'd spent years trying to trash the man's reputation and still nearly everyone in town remained oddly unconvinced. Folks were looking him over curiously, but many were welcoming him back into the fold as if he hadn't walked out on his family, as if he hadn't left under very suspicious circumstances. Ed had worked so damn hard to put doubts in everyone's mind about Sam's character, yet suddenly, all was forgotten. And forgiven.

Angrily, he dug a new toothpick from his shirt pocket and stuck it into his mouth, clamping down on it hard. Even Judge Larson, who was a hard nose if ever there was one, had gone easy on Jim Rivers. What was it with these Rivers brothers? Well, Sam could threaten him with a lawsuit all he wanted, Ed wasn't about to stop watching him. It was the duty of a lawman to keep his eye on a suspicious man. Sam's lawsuit, if he was stupid enough to file one, would be thrown out of court.

But it was Liza Courtland that bothered Ed the most. Ed felt that with his family background, he was more suitable for her than Rivers ever could hope to be. Over the years, as a respected lawman, he'd carefully insinuated himself into her life by bits and pieces, gaining her trust. He'd volunteered on his own time to train the security personnel for Courtland Enterprises. After an attempted break-in at the Courtland Mansion, he'd spent hours securing the place with a new burglar alarm system and dead-bolt locks so the three Courtland ladies would feel safe.

And he'd made sure that Beth and his niece were good friends. It was all part of his patient plan to win Liza over. One day he felt certain she'd realize how loyal and devoted he was to her and her family. Perhaps then she'd begin to look at him as a man, to care for him. It was a dream Hayes had harbored for a long, long time, patiently waiting until she'd returned from Michigan and settled back into life in Port Henry. Finally he'd felt she was warming up to him and would soon make his dream a reality.

Until Sam Rivers had come back.

Hadn't he told Liza repeatedly that Sam was a loser? Hadn't he warned her to stay away from everyone named Rivers? The two of them working together was bad enough, but why had Sam been at the Courtland Mansion earlier today? Twice now, he'd noticed Sam's car parked in their circular drive. What in the world would a lovely woman like Liza want with a man whose father was a drunken bum and whose younger brother was following in the old man's footsteps? Maybe Sam was a boozer, too. Or worse, a coward who'd run away.

Ed perked up. That was the answer. He'd do some careful checking as to Sam's whereabouts all those years. Maybe the guy had a record, say in another state. He'd dig up all the dirt he could, then make sure Liza found out. She was a very protective mother. Hayes was certain she wouldn't have anything to do with Sam much less allow him near Beth if she had proof he was an unsavory character. Sam would surely leave if that happened.

If that plan didn't work, he'd think of another, Hayes decided. He simply wouldn't rest until Sam Rivers was out of Port Henry.

And life would return to normal once more. With renewed purpose, Hayes took off down the road.

"You can't sleep, either?" Elizabeth asked as she stepped out onto Liza's large upstairs veranda.

Liza glanced up, then shook her head. "Too much on my mind, I guess." She'd been watching night birds scurry through the trees as busy as her scattered thoughts.

Uninvited, Elizabeth sat down in the wrought iron chair across from Liza's lounge, then turned to study her daughter's face in the splash of light coming through the open French doors. Liza had that melancholy look she so often wore. It was nearly ten, a peaceful evening, with the tall pines along the back property line standing guard in the moonlight and the heavy-limbed maple trees swaying in a light breeze. Only, Elizabeth didn't feel peaceful and doubted that Liza did. "I love these spring evenings. I think we're going to have a hot summer since May's already so warm."

Small talk. Liza had a feeling her mother hadn't sought her out tonight to discuss the weather. Hoping she might be wrong, she didn't answer, but kept on gazing out over the waist-high railing.

"Are you going to tell me or are you going to make me grill you?" Elizabeth finally asked.

Despite a flash of annoyance at the question, Liza almost smiled at her mother's uncharacteristic phrasing. "Grill me? You've been watching too much TV, Mom."

"Don't pretend you don't know what I'm talking about

and insult us both, Liza.'' Her voice was low so as not to awaken Beth asleep inside, but firm with resolve.

Liza let out a ragged sigh. Hadn't she known that the day would come when she could no longer avoid this subject? ''What exactly do you want to know?''

''You and Sam Rivers knew each other rather well before he moved away, although you hid your relationship. Am I right?''

Something inside Liza struggled against revealing what she'd concealed for so long. Yet every secret, she supposed, came out sooner or later. Perhaps it was best if she told her mother in her own words rather than have her making wild assumptions.

''We were friends, yes.'' There was reluctance in her voice and a fair amount of resignation.

''I'd say you were more than friends.'' Elizabeth had been stewing ever since Sam had left this afternoon. She'd never been a confrontational woman when Will had been alive, trusting him to take care of things right or wrong— to take care of all the family matters. However, after his stroke, she'd had to come out of her comfort zone, to call Liza and all but beg her to return, despite the fact that their oldest daughter had refused to even visit their home after her hasty departure.

Elizabeth hadn't wanted Liza to leave, but she'd been put in the dreadful position of having to choose between the wishes of her husband of twenty-five years and her daughter's stubbornness. If she had it to do over, Elizabeth thought, she might do things differently. But the past couldn't be changed.

She'd been so grateful to have Liza back, with Will speechless and confined to a wheelchair, that she hadn't questioned her. She'd accepted Liza's brief explanation, and they'd resumed their lives with much left unspoken between them. But the fact that she and her daughter had never really cleared the air had bothered Elizabeth more as she grew older. After this afternoon, she felt that this was as good a time as any to put the past to rest.

"I've not questioned you before, but perhaps it's time. I had the feeling some weeks before I learned you were pregnant that you'd been seeing someone secretly that summer, though you never mentioned a name, never brought a boy home. It was Sam Rivers, wasn't it?" Her hazel eyes watched Liza through fashionable bifocals, hoping her daughter would be honest.

Liza met her mother's clear-eyed gaze. "How did you guess?"

Relieved that Liza wasn't going to fence with her nor did she seem angry, Elizabeth shrugged. "Something Sam said at the hospital and the tension between the two of you when you're together. I've always thought Beth looked just like you, except for the eyes. They're a very unusual shade of blue. I'd never met Sam until the night Beth broke her leg, so I hadn't realized that her eyes are identical to his. I'm surprised he hasn't noticed."

"Fortunately she has my coloring, and eyes, well, how often do we actually stare in the mirror at our own eyes and think they're unusual? I doubt Sam ever thinks much about his looks."

"Why didn't you tell me back then?"

The sound Liza made was more sob than the ironic laugh she'd intended. "Oh, Mother, how can you ask that? Look what happened when Daddy found out I was pregnant? He threw me out, told me I was a tramp like Cindy." Her expression became imploring. "But I want you to know that Sam is the *only* man I've ever been with, back then and since. If making love with the only man I've ever loved makes me a tramp, then I guess I am. However, if you ask me, Daddy wasn't angry that I'd gone to bed with someone, only that I got caught, as he so charmingly put it. He measured Cindy and me by a very harsh yardstick.''

Loyalty ran deep in Elizabeth. ''Perhaps, but he loved you both.''

''Did he? Not nearly as much as Drake.'' The entire family had been devastated when her brother had drowned at fourteen, but none quite so thoroughly as Will.

''Perhaps if your brother hadn't died, your father might have concentrated more on him and been more forgiving of his daughters. Don't judge him too harshly, Liza. Every parent tries their best.''

''No, Mother, they don't. Not *every* parent. Look at Sam's father. Selfish, irresponsible, pathetic. And look what havoc that caused in Sam's life, then and now. As for Daddy, he demanded perfection, from all of us. Drake drowned trying to prove to his father that he was a champion, the best. He wore himself out practicing dives that day, then overly tired, he miscalculated and hit his head. I know because I was there.''

Elizabeth stiffened. ''I don't believe that. It was an accident.''

''Yes, an accident caused by Drake trying to be perfect, to please Daddy. Cindy tried, too, but she couldn't get her grades up high enough to satisfy him, nor was she pretty enough to win his praise. So she gave up altogether and got his attention by doing every rotten thing she could think of.''

''Now who's using a harsh yardstick?'' Elizabeth had reason to regret ever beginning this conversation, but she couldn't back down now. ''You shouldn't have left like that, Liza. All Will wanted to know was the name of your baby's father.''

''Is that what he told you?'' Liza let out a bitter laugh.

"Not quite, Mother. When I refused to name the father, Dad wrote out a check, handed it to me and told me to go have an abortion and we'd never speak of my little fall from grace again."

"Oh, no." Elizabeth's shock was real. "I had no idea. Why didn't you tell me?"

Because Liza was certain her mother would have taken her father's side, as she always had. She thrust both hands into her hair, brushing it back. "It was easier to just leave."

"But you came back." That, to Elizabeth, was the bottom line.

"Yes, I came back. For you, Mom. Not for him. Never for him."

Elizabeth's eyes grew damp and she reached over to squeeze Liza's hand. "Thank you. I—I'm grateful that you did."

"I don't want your gratitude, but I could use your understanding. Nothing would have been gained by revealing the father. Besides, by the time I discovered I was pregnant, Sam was gone already." And she'd been left on her own. Thank God for Aunt Margaret who'd taken her in and taken Liza's secret to her grave like the caring, honorable woman she'd been.

"But why didn't you tell me later, when you came back?" Guilt was making Elizabeth's voice shaky, guilt over not standing up to her husband when she'd felt he was wrong.

"Oh, Mom, let's not do this." Liza got up and went to stand at the porch railing. The moon was nearly full, but there was a nip to the air. She shoved her hands into her jeans pockets. "You had a full plate with Daddy's illness, and Lord knows I did, what with trying to learn all I could about the company and worrying about Beth adjusting. It didn't seem like a good time to play true confessions."

Elizabeth had to agree. "I don't suppose you'd have told me even now if I hadn't guessed, would you?"

"Probably not. What purpose would it serve?"

It was Elizabeth's turn to sigh. "It took your father's illness to give me the strength of my convictions. I might have at least empathized with you, especially if I'd realized that you were in love with Beth's father. And you still are."

Slowly, Liza turned, unaware that her face was infinitely sad. There was no point in denying the obvious. "Unfortunately, ending a relationship doesn't end your feelings. All these years, I've tried to hate Sam and only wound up wanting him more. But I'm an adult woman with a child now, not a teenager carried away by first love. Sooner or later we all have to learn that we can't have everything we want."

"Maybe not everything, but perhaps Sam, too, has matured. I watched him this afternoon, Liza, the way he looks at you. He cares for you, I'm sure of it."

"That's no longer enough. I have to think of Beth. Maybe Sam does care, or thinks he does, but does he care *enough?* What if he gets bored or restless or whatever, and decides to leave again? I might be able to handle it, but would Beth? Did you see her today? She hardly spoke to me after Sam left because she blamed me for not encouraging him to stay for dinner. She's totally smitten. It's the very thing I've feared, that one day he'd come strolling back into our lives and make us *both* care about him again." Liza blinked, struggling with tears that threatened to fall. "And he doesn't even know she's his. What if he finds out and wants to take her away from me?"

"Oh, Liza, he could never do that."

"Read the papers, Mom. Fathers have rights, too, and Sam's not a poor boy any longer. He's got resources and connections. He could take me to court and fight for shared custody and win. That push-pull thing between quarreling parents can be devastating to a child. I don't want Beth hurt.'' Her face tortured, she looked into her mother's eyes, letting her real fear surface. ''I can't lose Beth, Mom. I can't.''

Chapter Six

Red McGinness came by his nickname honestly, Sam thought as he approached the job boss for Reynolds Construction. He was a short, wiry man with thinning red hair and a pale, freckled complexion. He was also the man in charge of the last known job his father had worked.

Stopping several feet from where the foreman stood, Sam waited until he looked up from his clipboard. "Red, my name's Sam Rivers. I believe Joe Rivers worked for you some years ago."

"I know who you are," Red said, his brown eyes revealing nothing. "Heard you were back in town."

"I was wondering if you could tell me anything about the last day you saw Joe. How he seemed to you, if anything was bothering him, that sort of thing."

"Why do you want to know, after all these years?"

"I think it's time we learn the truth about Joe's disappearance."

"Makes sense. I'd want to know, if it was my old man."
Red scratched his head with a hand that had a missing ring
finger. "There isn't much to tell. Joe was Joe. A hard
worker when he wasn't drinking heavy. He'd go weeks
fairly sober and I'd begin to think he was through. Then
he'd show up staggering drunk, mean and ugly, aching for
a fight. He usually found one, too. That last week wasn't
any different from many others."

Sam remembered that Joe hadn't come home at all that
Thursday night, and the next morning he'd begun hearing
stories about the sheriff being called in to break up a fight
at the Watering Hole. By midday, the gossip had shifted to
rumors that Joe's son had something to do with his disappearance and was wanted for questioning by Hayes. "Did
he show up for work on Friday?" Maybe his father had
slept it off somewhere, then gone straight to work.

"Nah. I threw him off the site Thursday around four
because I'd caught him swiggin' from a bottle. He wandered off cussing at me. I never saw him again."

The afternoon sun hot on his face, Sam shifted so a slice
of shade fell on him as he thought over Red's words.
There'd been a lot of nights when Joe had gotten stinking
drunk, but he'd always turned up sooner or later. Countless
times they'd found him curled up asleep on the porch swing
or in his car. The man had had an amazing capacity to
recover, usually making it to work the next day even when
he'd passed out the night before. "Nobody seems to remember seeing him after that ruckus Thursday night at the
bar."

"So I heard. I remember thinking it was pretty odd because Friday was payday. Not too many guys missed coming in on payday, even if they were hung over. The following week, when Joe still hadn't come around, I decided he
was probably on a bender somewhere. He hadn't ever done

that, but he'd been drinking more and more, it seemed. Then the sheriff showed up asking all kinds of questions. Hayes, you know. He was a deputy then, I guess.''

"What happened to his paycheck?"

"I mailed it to his house about two weeks later. Figured your mom could use it. At least that way Joe couldn't drink it up. Didn't she tell you?"

"I didn't ask, but I'm sure she received it. Tell me, how'd Joe get along with the other guys? He couldn't have had too many friends if he got mean and ugly, as you said.'' Certainly Sam couldn't recall a single incident where one of Joe's friends had come to the house.

Red shrugged. "You know construction guys. Lots of 'em drink and get into fights. 'Course some never do. Union's in now and things are different. Back then, some guys who worked hard all day felt they were entitled to play hard, too. Joe wasn't a bad guy. He was kind of funny when he was sober. Used to tell jokes, kid around. Waldo Franks was a friend of his, both of them carpenters and all. Waldo's quit construction and quit the boozing, too, I hear. He runs some bait and tackle shop these days.''

"Did you ever hear Joe say he was thinking of taking off, maybe that he'd *like* to take off, go somewhere else and start over?'' He hadn't gotten a positive response from the boats, but Joe could have slept off the booze, then hitch-hiked out of town or hopped a freight train. His father had always hated responsibility. The only reason he'd shown up for work was so he'd have drinking money. Maybe it wasn't a stretch to imagine him leaving without another thought to the family he'd leave behind.

Red's lined face broke into a smile. "Hell, son, all of us dream about taking off and starting over. Even you, am I right?''

There it was, the censure he'd hoped wouldn't come, but

knew probably would. Everyone in Port Henry knew the Rivers family history. "Yeah, Red, even me. Thanks for your help."

Slowly Sam walked back toward the road where he'd parked the Explorer. He hadn't learned much, not that he'd expected to. But one thing did stand out. Joe would have picked up his check if he'd been around, if he'd been able. His father had never walked away from money. If he'd planned to leave, he'd have needed some traveling dollars.

At the road, he turned to look back at the west-side development of small starter homes going up. All his adult life, Joe Rivers had worked on sites like this. He'd been a scrapper who'd often provoked fights, perhaps to prove to himself that he was still contender material after he'd had to abandon that dream. Yet basically, he'd been gutless, a coward who'd taken out his frustrations on his hapless wife and innocent boys until a grown-up Sam had threatened him.

Still, the facts didn't support a planned departure, or even an impulsive leave-taking. Sam seriously doubted if Joe had ever been able to save a dime, which meant that without his paycheck, he'd been penniless. Even in an alcoholic fog, he wouldn't have suddenly left with only the clothes on his back and no money. So what had happened to Joe Rivers after he left the Watering Hole late that Thursday night?

Could someone have followed Joe and ambushed him, someone new in town, unaware that he had very little money on him? It wouldn't have been difficult if he'd been as drunk as the bartender had said. The road back to the shack where they'd lived at the time would take Joe past a wooded section, dark and deserted at night. Then, after discovering that Joe was broke, after all, had the would-be robber become enraged and beaten up on him? If so, where did he leave Joe's body? Sam had seen his father stagger home after some of the fights he'd been in and had wondered how he'd found the way much less been able to walk. But he'd always made it.

What had been different that night? Even if Joe had died from the beating, his body would have been found since Hayes had searched just about every inch of Port Henry, even the bay. Apparently he was on the wrong track, Sam told himself.

Getting behind the wheel, he started the Explorer as another possibility occurred to him. Suppose Joe had acted out of character and hitchhiked home that night. What if someone had picked him up, driven out of town and then decided to rob him? Finding him penniless, the driver could have shoved him out of the car anywhere along the highway. But then again, the body, alive or dead, would have been found sooner or later.

Letting out a frustrated whoosh of air, Sam shifted into Drive and headed back to the trailer. One dead end after another, each theory not holding up under scrutiny. He had a whole file folder filled with negative responses from Social Security, the Department of Motor Vehicles and the Department of Vital Statistics. He still had a few other old friends of Joe's to interview, but he had to admit to a fair amount of discouragement.

Two things kept him going: the need to clear his name and his reputation along with the belief that *no one* can vanish without a trace. Somewhere there was someone who knew where Joe Rivers was, and Sam was absolutely determined to find that person.

Checking the time, he saw that it was three o'clock. He had half a thought to go home and visit with his mother for a while, maybe take her out for an early dinner. But he decided instead to go back and get some paperwork done.

When he drove up, he was glad he'd changed his mind, for Liza's BMW was parked just inside the cyclone fence that enclosed the site. She and Beth were standing by the steps talking with Jeff.

He parked and got out. "Well, look who's here," he said to Beth.

The little girl beamed a smile at him. "We thought we missed you. I came by to show you my new walking cast." One hand braced on her mother's car, she held up her leg, encased in a more compact cast. "See, it's not so heavy and now I don't have to use crutches."

He walked over to her, smiling down at her eager grin. "Hey, that's terrific. Next thing you know, you'll be running relay races with it."

"I don't know about that." She shifted closer to him, enormously pleased that he'd shown up. It had taken her a very long time to talk her mother into driving over. Beth couldn't figure out why her mother got that funny look on her face every time she brought up Sam's name. He was by far the neatest man they knew.

"How are you, Liza?" Sam asked, very aware that she was watching the two of them carefully.

"Fine, thanks." She'd almost made it, Liza thought. With Beth insisting they stop by, she'd had to appease her daughter, but had been inwardly relieved when Sam had been out. As luck would have it, he'd returned before she'd been able to take off.

"I've got to go check on a couple of things," Jeff said. "See you all later." And he took off at a run, moving toward the model home under construction.

"Now that Sam's seen your cast, we'd best get going, Beth," Liza said, moving over to help her daughter get into the car.

"But, Mom, you promised." Beth's look was pleading.

"What did I promise?" Liza was hesitant, trying to recall.

"Remember when Sam couldn't stay for dinner the other night? You told me that maybe one day when we go out for pizza, we can ask him along. At the doctor's office, you said that we'd have a late lunch at Spanetti's if I didn't make a fuss. And I didn't." Triumphantly, she turned to Sam. "Can you come with us, *please?*"

Sam almost laughed out loud at the trapped look on Liza's face. "Well..."

"Beth, Sam's a very busy man. You can't expect him to drop everything and..."

"I'm free, it just so happens." His smile was wide, the corners of his mouth twitching just a little. "Lucky you came by. I was just craving some pizza."

"Yes, lucky," Liza murmured. However, she knew when she was licked. "Why don't I drive? It might be a little tricky getting Beth up into the Explorer."

"Great." Beth was thrilled. "I'll get in back. You sit with Mom, Sam." A bit awkwardly she stepped aside so Sam could help her in. "Have you ever been to Spanetti's?"

"Can't say I have." Located close by, the Italian eatery was one of several that had cropped up in his absence. He closed the door after Beth as Liza got behind the wheel.

"They put on lots of gooey cheese and big chunks of ham. Do you like green peppers? I don't. But anything else is okay." Tickled to be out of the house for the first time in ages and to be with Sam, Beth gazed at the two adults in the front seat. They looked good together. Really good. Maybe...

The pizza turned out to be as scrumptious as Beth had said. Sam watched the little girl take a big bite and stretch the stringy cheese several inches from her face, then giggle as she chewed her way back to the source. The way she did it reminded him of another girl and another time. He shifted his gaze to the mother.

"I wonder, is that pizza place near Crane Lake still there?" he asked. "Their food was the best for miles around, remember?"

Of course she remembered, Liza thought, trying hard not to let her annoyance show. The Pizza Palace owned by Frannie's parents, the Frannie who owned the fitness center. Why did Sam do this every chance he got, toss in little reminiscences of shared memories? Was he trying to mellow her or get a rise out of her? In either case, she wasn't going to play his game.

Setting down her frosty mug of root beer, she tried for nonchalance. "There are so many good Italian restaurants around. It's hard to say which is best. Beth, use your napkin, sweetie." Why, Liza wondered, had Sam chosen to come along when she'd given him a perfect out? Surely he had better things to do than eat pizza with a child. Or had he joined them because she'd made no bones about not wanting him around the other evening? He'd never been perverse when she'd known him before, but that had been a very long time ago. They'd both changed.

Beth swiped at her mouth. "Mom said you used to live here a long time ago. Did you and Mom know each other then?"

Sam saw no reason to lie. "Yes, we did."

"How come Grandma never met you before?" Beth wanted to know.

"Beth," Liza interrupted, "it's not polite to ask so many personal questions. Remember you told me that your teacher talked about that in class a couple of weeks ago?"

"I'm sorry." Not looking in the least bit sorry, she took another big bite.

Liza found herself wondering what Sam was thinking as he contentedly ate his pizza, his eyes moving between Beth and her. Did he have a suspicion about the little girl who appeared to openly adore him? She shouldn't have allowed Beth to talk her into coming here, Liza decided as she chewed without tasting a thing.

Sam supposed it was natural for a child who'd never known her father to take to any man who was nice to her. Hell, Beth even liked Ed Hayes, or so she'd indicated. He hadn't stopped to consider why he was drawn to Beth Courtland, although it was probably because she belonged to Liza. If things had worked out differently so long ago, maybe he and Liza would have married and had children, a beautiful daughter like Beth.

Growing up as he had, his mother downtrodden, his father a drunken disgrace, Sam had always longed for a real family, a loving wife and kids, a reason to get up in the morning and come home at night. Was it too late for them? Could Liza get over their hurtful past, forgive him and allow him back into her life? Would she share her child with him, as protective as she was? Maybe he could make it happen.

They ate in silence for several minutes before Sam decided he would ask a few questions of his own. "Do you like school, Beth?"

"Mmm-hmm." She swallowed before going on. "I like vacation time, too, 'cause I like to go swimming. School's out in just two more weeks."

Sam leaned back, watching her animated little face. She really was a pretty child. "I like swimming, too, but school's important. Next year you'll be, what, a first-grader?" She looked to be about six years old, which would fit the story Lyle had told him about when Liza had adopted a child.

"Oh, my!" Liza exclaimed. "Look at the time. Beth, honey, we've got to get going. I promised Grandma I'd pick her up at Hazel's by four." A discussion of Beth's age would bring him perilously close to the truth. She was small for seven, so Liza had prayed he wouldn't ask. Nervously she glanced at Sam. "Mother plays cards on Wednesday afternoons. We dropped her off at noon." She signaled for the waiter.

"But Mom, I've only had one piece," Beth complained.

"You can finish at home." The waiter stopped at their table as Liza reached into her purse for her wallet. "Can you box the rest for us, please? And I need the check. I'm late for an appointment." Turning back, she sent Sam an apologetic look. "I'm sorry to have to leave like this, but I completely forgot about Mom. She gets nervous if she's kept waiting."

"No problem." But he did think it odd that the super-organized Liza Courtland had forgotten that she had to pick up her mother. He touched her hand, preventing her from pulling out money. "This one's mine, I insist."

None too happy to have things end so abruptly, Beth nevertheless noisily slurped the rest of her root beer through the straw, finishing as the waiter reappeared with box and check.

"Here you go." Sam handed him a folded bill and helped Beth out of the booth while Liza took the boxed pizza. Walking outside, he couldn't help thinking that Liza seemed oddly nervous. Then again, she always was when he was anywhere near her daughter.

At the trailer, Sam got out of her car, then leaned a hand on the open window ledge. "Thanks for inviting me." His eyes were on Beth but his words included Liza, although he could sense she was chafing to be on her way.

"Will we see you again, Sam?" Beth asked, her voice anxious.

"Count on it, sweetheart." He stepped back and waved as Liza gunned it and left, whipping up a cloud of dust. A difficult woman to figure, Sam thought as he unlocked the trailer.

He'd been in Port Henry several weeks now and things were moving along. The exterior of the model home was nearing completion. The floors were in as well as the tubs and sinks. The cabinets had arrived, and then there'd be finish work, final roofing, plastering, painting etc. The preliminary ads they'd run were garnering a fair amount of interest. Liza was looking into selecting a Realtor to sit in the model and take orders.

Liza, Sam thought as he gazed up into a sky streaked with wispy clouds. What was there about this one woman that had him churning and craving as he had for no other? He'd done everything he could from a distance of several hundred miles to forget her over eight long years. And nothing had worked.

Now that he was back, seeing her frequently and spending time with her casually as well as for business, dormant feelings had reawakened in him stronger than ever. Would it always be like this? Would it always be Liza Courtland, the one woman for him? If so, he might well be setting himself up for a big fall, since she obviously didn't trust him nor had she forgiven him for walking away from her. He could understand that. What he couldn't understand was her reluctance to discuss their past, to clear the air and allow them to start over, to go on from here.

So the question was, did he want her badly enough to insist she listen to his explanation, weak though it was? In his mind's eye, he saw her lovely face, that fantastic body and remembered how it had felt to hold her, to love her. He saw her with Beth, protective and loving. He pictured her at the meetings they'd attended—quietly assertive, calm and confident. And he recalled the powerful kiss they'd shared, her quick, passionate response that had held nothing back.

And his heart that she always had owned yearned for her.

She was still the woman he wanted, the only one he'd ever loved. He knew he and he alone was responsible for killing the love she once had for him, for destroying the trust. He'd been young and afraid back then, but he was neither now. He'd learned a few of life's harsher lessons and was a better man for it. He knew what he wanted out of life and who he wanted to spend his life with. Unquestionably, Liza Courtland.

It wouldn't be easy, convincing her to listen, making her realize that she also cared, that she'd never really gotten over him, either. Liza never did things in half measure, not her work nor her feelings. When she loved, she loved for all time, Sam believed, much as he did. Which was why he felt confident that she'd adopted Beth. She couldn't have turned off her feelings for him so soon after he'd left and taken up with someone else.

He'd have to pin her down, make her listen. And soon, because each time he was with her, he wanted her more. He hadn't had to work hard to win her the first time, but Sam had a feeling the second time around wasn't going to be a walk on the beach.

Stepping inside the trailer, he decided he'd begin his campaign the next time they were alone together. For now, he needed to call Dirk and get updated on what was happening back in Akron.

* * *

Electrical storms were not uncommon in Ohio in the spring, some bordering on hurricane intensity. The one that hit on Tuesday night was a humdinger, knocking out power for miles around, the wind gusting up to forty miles an hour and causing considerable property damage. Pleasure boats anchored in the bay slammed into docks, some overturning and others even sank. Roofs, freestanding garages and sheds were especially in jeopardy, particularly in older neighborhoods. A number of trees were uprooted and the statue of the late Ohio senator, Robert A. Taft, in the town square toppled off its pedestal, breaking his left arm.

By late afternoon the worst was over, the rain a mere drizzle and the winds were quiet once more. Sam and Jeff had phoned the men, instructing them to stay home, but by four, Sam could no longer stand the suspense. Relieved that his mother's house had escaped any damage, he'd driven to Oakview Estates to check things out for himself. On the way, he passed both sheriff's vehicles out assessing storm damage. For once, Hayes wouldn't be parked in his usual spot spying on them.

All things considered, they were pretty lucky, he decided after gingerly walking the grounds. Roofing shingles just recently added to the model house lay scattered all over the area. Pieces of sawed-off wood apparently had been lifted by the wind and sent flying into several windows, breaking them. The tarp covering stacked lumber was in a wet heap some yards away, but the boards were intact, though thoroughly soaked. The entire terrain was a mud bath with brown puddles everywhere. It would take several hot days to dry things up.

Even so, the damage was comparatively minimal and, if the sun broke through the cloud cover tomorrow, they'd lose only a few days. Not bad considering the intensity of the freak storm. The drizzling rain had dampened his hair, and he brushed it back off his face. Shifting a section of furnace duct that had landed in his path, Sam tossed it off to the side, then yelped out loud as he let go. Examining his hand, he saw that he'd cut a good-size gash in the fleshy heel. Swearing under his breath, he dug out his handkerchief and wrapped it around the cut, stepped carefully around an overturned sawhorse and headed back to the trailer.

It was darker than usual at dusk due to the aftermath of the storm, and Sam wished he'd brought his flashlight as he picked his way through more rubble. He'd just made it down a muddy incline when he saw headlights turn into the complex and come through the cyclone fence gate he'd left standing open. Slogging nearer, he recognized Liza's BMW as it pulled to a stop. He watched her climb out wearing a pair of very unfashionable ankle-high rubber boots.

"Look at you," he said, reaching the steps. "I wouldn't have guessed you owned anything as practical as those boots."

"This isn't my first visit to a site in bad weather," she commented as he unlocked the trailer door. "I take it you've already checked everything over. Any major damage?" Restless in storms as always, she'd waited until the rain had died down before deciding to visit Oakview. Courtland Enterprises had a lot of money tied up here and she needed to know firsthand just how they'd fared.

"Not bad, considering." Sam quickly snapped on the desk lamp, removed his work boots, then moved to the counter. He found a hand towel and wiped off his face, then ran it over his hair. One-handed, he opened the cupboard and took out the first aid kit.

Liza stepped out of the oversize footwear and walked

over to see what he was doing. Noticing his bound hand, she took the kit from him. "What did you do?"

"I cut my hand, Mommy. Can you kiss it and make it better?" Because it was easier than arguing, he let her take over. He could smell the spring rain in her hair mingled with her special scent, and felt his stomach muscles tighten.

Ignoring his words, she unwrapped the cut and saw that it was fairly deep but wouldn't require stitches. "Nice job. I can see we can't let you play with the big boys anymore." She found cotton and alcohol, then bent to clean the wound. When he flinched, she looked up at him. "If you're really brave and hold still, you can have a lollipop when I'm finished." If she kept it light, the flush of awareness she felt in the close confines of the shadowy trailer might go away.

"Gee, thanks." He watched her work efficiently, as he'd guessed she would, her blond head bent over his hand. She was dressed casually in yellow cotton slacks and matching sweater buttoned to her throat. It never mattered what she wore, for his memory removed every stitch and his mind's eye roamed over every delicious curve. In minutes, she'd put antibiotic cream on the cut and had it bandaged.

He was too quiet, too watchful, those deep-set eyes never leaving her face, Liza thought as she put away the first aid things. She needed to fill the silence and to add some distance. Stepping back and across the small area, she sat down in his desk chair. "You're sure there's no damage to speak of? On the way over, I ran across a big maple that had been split by lightning blocking the road, and a wooden fence broken apart like so many matchsticks."

Sam leaned against the counter, crossing his arms over his chest and described all he'd seen on his walk-through. "The repairs won't take our men more than a day or two, providing the rain stops soon and the sun comes out."

"That's good." His eyes had that dark, hooded look. It was time to leave. She stood. "I'd better get back home, then. Beth's not real good in storms." And neither was she.

"How's she doing?"

"Fine. Healing nicely. She's beginning to itch beneath the cast and that bothers her, but otherwise she's fine." She bent to pick up a boot.

Now or never, Sam thought as he stepped closer, taking her arm and turning her toward him. "Don't go." He let his eyes say the rest, the look between them holding for long, sizzling moments.

Her breath backed up in her throat as anticipation set her heart to pounding. But a frisson of fear raced up her spine, fear that if she let him touch her again, she wouldn't be able to turn away. "I...this isn't a good idea, Sam."

"It's the very *best* idea." Before she could react, he tugged her up hard against his chest and pressed his mouth to hers.

He was not a man who'd ever force a woman. He'd never had to. If she had protested, by word or deed, he would have backed off in a New York minute. Surprisingly, she didn't.

Liza wanted to protest, had thought she should, but every nerve cell in her body celebrated his touch and reached out for more. And still more. He held her close, but she could easily have broken free and they both knew it. They also both knew that deep inside she had no desire to be free of him.

He was a hard man who'd worked hard jobs all his adult life, but his mouth was surprisingly soft, Liza thought. There was raw heat in the way he kissed, causing pleasure to whirl throughout her entire system. Who could resist such temptation?

Long, wakeful nights Sam had imagined this, dreamed

this, yet even those vivid pictures couldn't match the real thing, he thought. The special flavors his tongue sampled on her lips were the ones he'd been seeking all his life. As if in generous welcome, she opened to him and, like a drowning man, he drank deeply from her.

He'd forgotten how small she was, how delicate her bone structure. Yet the breasts that heaved with each breath against his chest reminded him that she was every inch a woman. Despite her slender frame, there was strength here in the arms that wound about his neck and the hands that thrust wildly into his damp hair. Outside, he heard a deep rumble of thunder that lent a primitive feel to their embrace. Like jungle drums, the sound came again and then the rains took up the beat, slamming against the windows of the trailer, isolating them in their small world.

Liza heard him murmur her name as he backed her up against the door, his hard body shoving closer while his greedy hands raced over her aroused flesh. His rough hands grazed her soft skin, and she welcomed the touch. Her heated blood churned as a moan she couldn't prevent came from her throat. Needs clamored inside her, needs she always kept so carefully chained, now bursting free. The one man who could satisfy them was raining kisses on her face and her upraised throat while outside, the torrent picked up momentum.

She was scarcely aware when his fingers began pulling at the buttons of her sweater, pushing aside fabric in a feverish rush to press his mouth to the swollen tips of her straining breasts. Eyes closed to hold in the feeling, she buried her hands in his hair as he took possession.

He wanted her more than he wanted his next breath, more than a desert walker wants water. It was more than wanting, more like an elemental need that no one else could fulfill, that no other woman could assuage. He had to have her, to make her his once more, to never let her go again. Moving his lips up, he took her mouth in a kiss that stole her breath away.

Unable to hold still, Liza arched her back, feeling the solid door behind her as he deepened the kiss. If he let go of her now, she'd surely sink to her knees, for they were already trembling. It had been so long since she'd let her senses rule and the devil take the hind road.

And then she felt his hands slip her sweater from her shoulders and move to unclasp her bra.

The sudden realization that she was about to drop to the floor in a bout of mindless sex like a randy teenager hit her like a cold splash of water. Hadn't she done just that once before and look where it had gotten her? "No!" she cried out.

It took but two seconds for the word to penetrate Sam's foggy brain. He dropped his hands and took a step back, breathing hard. It was a full half minute before he could speak. "What's wrong?" he asked in a voice still thick with desire.

"I can't walk down this bumpy road again, Sam." Her shaky fingers could scarcely rebutton her sweater, but she finally managed. She needed to leave, but knew she had to take a few minutes to steady herself first or she'd never be able to drive in this downpour. As Sam turned aside, she made her way hesitantly to the table and sat down, gingerly touching her face still tingling from contact with his beard.

What was wrong with her? Liza asked herself. Hadn't she learned her lesson the first time? Didn't she remember the high cost of loving Sam Rivers? Leaning her head into her open hand, she closed her eyes, waiting for her heart to stop pounding.

The undeniable truth was she'd never gotten over him. That much was painfully clear. She had loved in secret; a love she would have denied had it been discovered. Love was a dance, music she moved to without conscious thought, with unconscious desire. How could she put herself through all that again?

Sam was honestly confused. There was no mistaking her response, her desire, every bit as strong as his. He knew she wasn't involved with anyone else, nor was he. They were both adults, more mature than before. Why, then, did she go just so far, then slam on the brakes?

Wearily he walked over and pulled out the other chair, making sure he didn't sit too close to her. "Liza," he began, praying for patience, "I don't understand. I know that wasn't a faked reaction just now. I think you want me and I sure as hell want you. What's the problem?"

Her hand shook as she raised her head to look him right in the eyes. For a long moment, she just stared. He honestly hadn't a clue. Amazing. She searched her mind where to begin.

"I need to know, in your own words, why you left that Friday night before Labor Day eight years ago without getting word to me, when you knew I was at the Crane Lake cottage waiting for you. Even later, you never called, never tried to contact me. All this time, I've wondered. I think I deserve an honest answer." She kept watching him, trying to read his expression, to judge the veracity of his explanation.

Sam ran his fingers through his hair. Finally she wanted to talk about the past, yet suddenly he felt queasy and reluctant. It wasn't a pretty story, and he had no idea how she'd respond. He crossed his legs and nervously began tracing the seam of his jeans, his eyes downcast. "You're right. You deserve the truth. I left because I was a coward."

"Oh, bull! Sam, that's not true and you know it."

He shook his head. "You're wrong. My father had disappeared and Hayes was spreading the word that I'd killed him and hidden the body. I heard it whispered everywhere I went. I'd worked for Mac for three years, yet when I showed up that morning, he fired me on the spot. Never even asked for an explanation. He told me the sheriff's deputy had been to see him and said I was guilty and there was probably a warrant out for my arrest already. Hayes told everyone that he had half a dozen witnesses who'd overheard me threaten to kill Joe.''

"That's ridiculous."

Finally Sam raised his eyes. "No, it isn't. I did threaten to kill him, weeks before he disappeared. I'd gone home one night and found he'd been using my mother and brother as punching bags. I tracked him down and told him if he ever laid a hand on either of them again, I'd kill him. I meant it, too.''

"You never told me that."

He gave a grunt. "Why would I have? I was in love with you. I didn't want you to think of me as a violent man."

"I wouldn't have. You should have trusted me more. You didn't kill your father. I *know* you didn't."

It was the second time he'd heard her profess her faith in his innocence, and her words warmed him. "No, I didn't. But I might have, if he'd hurt my mother again. The intention was there. I guess that's what Hayes picked up on.''

"But you were innocent. You could have stayed and fought back instead of staying away for eight years.'' There was so much he didn't know about what she'd gone through during most of those years he'd been gone.

"You think I could have fought and won? I was young, penniless, without an alibi. And there was a lawman who had it in for me, one I believed wouldn't have hesitated to frame me if he could have. I was the son of a drunk, and we lived in a broken-down shack. Who in their right mind would have believed me, Liza?'' Instead of pleading or angry, his voice sounded defeated even to his own ears as all the frustration of those running years engulfed him.

"I would've believed you, and I'd have helped you, too.''

Again, Sam shook his head. "You were nineteen. Are you going to sit there and tell me that Will Courtland—the same father you'd been afraid to introduce me to all summer—would have let his daughter get mixed up with a guy suspected of causing the disappearance of his own father after threatening to kill him? Be realistic. I cut out before I could be handcuffed and publicly humiliated in front of you or quite possibly shot in the back by our good deputy sheriff while I was supposedly trying to escape.''

"Oh, come now. Ed's a bit overzealous, but he wouldn't have killed you. And you're wrong about Daddy. He was a great defender of the underdog.''

Sam shoved a hand through his hair. "You're living in a dreamworld. That would never have happened.''

Liza sighed sadly. "We'll never know now, will we?'' So much pain that she'd had to endure all alone. For eight long years, she'd been angry and hurt that he hadn't cared enough to come to her in person, to confide in her. It was hard to let go.

There were some things two people might never see eye to eye on, Sam knew. That didn't mean they couldn't get along. Reaching over, he took her slender hand in both of his. "Look, Liza, if I had it to do over again, I'd do things differently. I didn't run away from you, but from what I thought was a hopeless situation. You can't know how much I regret not calling you and at least letting you know *why* I left. I should have, but I was ashamed. Plain and simple. No one who runs away is very proud of themselves. I thought if I made a clean break from you, you'd forget me and get on with your life. You were young. I felt you'd find someone else, someone who made better choices than I. What could I have offered you on the run for years, always looking over my shoulder. I decided you should forget all about me.''

That sure worked, Liza thought. "I tried finding you. You have no idea how difficult it was for me to ask your mother for your address. And then, when you never answered any of my letters…''

Something else to hang his head low about. "I told you I was a coward.''

Perhaps she, too, carried some of the blame, Liza thought somewhat reluctantly. She had to admit that her father hadn't been very understanding, so what made her think he'd have willingly helped Sam?

She sighed tiredly. "You're no more of a coward than I. I shouldn't have insisted we sneak around like we were doing something wrong that summer. I should've stood up to my father and introduced you from the beginning. I should've taken a tougher stand.'' Thinking of all that might have been and could never be recaptured, Liza felt her eyes fill.

He noticed and couldn't stand to know he was the cause of her tears. "Don't cry, please. We both made some mistakes, me far more than you. But it's not too late, Liza. I've never forgotten you. I've never loved anyone but you, and I still do.''

Tears trailed down her cheeks like the raindrops sliding down the windows outside. Her emotions were in a jumble, sadness and regret weighing down her heart. Brushing a hand across her cheeks, she got up. "I've got to go. I can't talk anymore right now.''

He stood, touching her arm. "Please don't go like this. I need you to know I mean what I say. All these years, I kept seeing your face. I pictured you the last time we were together. You were wearing a green shirt and white shorts, and your hair was tied in a ponytail with a piece of green yarn. You were so beautiful.'' It was his turn to sigh. ''I know you've led a busy life and that you weren't sitting around pining away for me, but I want you to know you were never out of my thoughts. Never.''

Silently she walked over and tugged on her boots, the small act taking her quite a while. Her back to him, she dabbed at her eyes, then turned around. ''Blue,'' she said quietly.

''What?''

''You were wearing a blue plaid shirt and jeans with brown work boots. You came by and gave me an ivory-and-gold angel that last morning.''

She did remember. He wanted to rush to her, to swing her up into his arms and never let her go. But he stayed where he was. ''Do you still have it?''

''It fell and broke in two the night I waited for you. I still have the pieces.'' She turned, put her hand on the doorknob. ''I think we both have some thinking to do, Sam.''

''You're probably right.''

Without turning around, Liza nodded, then stepped out into the rain.

He walked to the door and watched her bolt to her car and get in. The BMW's lights flashed on, the wipers did their thing, and in seconds she'd circled around and was gone. He stood there gazing out for a long while, but it wasn't muddy ground he saw or a rainy sky. It was beautiful emerald green eyes awash in tears. Tears that he'd put there.

After a while he closed the door and lay down on the couch, hands behind his head, staring at the ceiling. Afterward, he couldn't say how long he lay there, his jumbled thoughts chasing each other around in his head. Finally he rose, turned off the lights, put on his boots and locked up.

Nine o'clock and it was pitch-dark outside. Apparently the floodlight above the trailer door had somehow gotten disconnected in the storm. He'd fix it tomorrow. Feeling bone tired, Sam got into the Explorer and slowly left the compound, stopping to lock the chain-link gate.

The road leading away from Oakview was two-lane and rain slick. He crested the top of the hill, then started downward. The big engine picked up momentum too quickly for the weather. Sam tapped his brakes to slow down. Nothing happened. Coming alert, he sat up taller and shoved down harder on the brakes. They weren't holding. He was traveling fifty, then sixty down a wet road, gaining speed every second.

It was then that he spotted a truck coming toward him, its bright lights on. Quickly, he flashed his lights, but the truck kept coming, unable to move over because of a deep ditch alongside the road. Sam was zigzagging, skidding all over the slippery pavement. Fear was a metallic taste in his mouth as he leaned on the horn. The truck driver didn't seem to hear him, didn't even slow down.

Almost to the bottom of the hill, Sam swerved off the road to avoid a collision, heading into a field filled with pine trees. He whipped past the first few, but his luck ran out just as the muddy marshland grabbed at his tires. With a roaring crash, he careered into a full-grown pine, creasing the passenger side mightily. Sam's tight grip on the wheel loosened as his head fell forward and he lost consciousness.

Then there was only silence save for the gentle rain falling in the dark of evening.

Chapter Seven

Liza leaned against the padded back of the machine, curled her arms around the weighted side arms and began her series of shoulder exercises. It was seven in the morning and Frannie's Fitness Center was crowded with early birds who chose to work out before heading for their various jobs. Stifling a yawn, she concentrated on counting mentally.

She hadn't slept well after the unnerving encounter with Sam in his work trailer during yesterday's downpour. The storm had contributed to her unease, but it was Sam's kisses that had kept her awake half the night. Even now, she could almost taste his unique flavors on her lips.

Puffing out shallow breaths, she let her mind wander. So far, she'd learned why Sam had felt it necessary to leave town and what had happened to her steady stream of increasingly desperate letters. A part of her couldn't blame him for reacting the way he had to the near witch hunt that

Ed Hayes had engineered against him back then. The other part of her still had trouble understanding why he hadn't cared enough to trust her, to confide in her.

Liza felt certain he was telling the truth as he saw it. He hadn't guessed, even after seeing Beth, that she was his daughter or that Liza might have gotten pregnant that summer. That afternoon at the pizza place, she'd panicked when Sam mentioned Beth's age and rushed them out of there, yet he hadn't caught on. She'd put together a very believable story about the adoption, and apparently people didn't question her as much as she'd suspected. Now she was caught in a trap of her own making.

Stopping, Liza sagged against the machine to catch her breath. Her dilemma was many faceted. If she told Sam about her pregnancy and the resulting child, how would he react? Would he even believe that Beth was his and not another man's? Would he leave, as he had before?

What did *she* want? What would be the best scenario? Liza asked herself, trying to be painfully honest. Did she love Sam still, did she want him in her life, as a husband, as Beth's father? Loving Sam was almost a given, something she'd been doing for so long it was like second nature. Through all the hurt, the anger, the loneliness, she'd never truly stopped loving him. But loving someone and being able to make a life with him were often two separate things.

What would be best for Beth? Any fool could see her daughter longed for a father, an adult man in her life, and that she was very taken with Sam. She'd been too young to relate to the grandfather who couldn't speak or interact with her. In an effort to protect her daughter, Liza had allowed no other man to become important to Beth. Beth was also the reason Liza hadn't dated much, hadn't permitted herself to get genuinely close to another man all these years. Now if she gave in and let Sam into their lives even more, provided he wanted to, would he wind up hurting them both?

So many questions without answers. And one of the worst: even if she did nothing, what if he found out and confronted her, furious and accusing? As a young man, Sam had had strong convictions. Eight years later, he was even more formidable with a dangerous slant that only a foolish few would dare challenge. But with her, in her arms, he was tender and thoughtful, the wondrous lover she'd spent countless hours dreaming of, longing for.

She was only twenty-seven, Liza reminded herself. Was it her intention to live the rest of her days without a love of her own in order to protect her daughter from harm? Or could she have it all, Sam's love and his commitment to Beth and her? In the nineties, or so the magazine articles said, women could have the whole enchilada. Liza wished she believed that.

With a weary sigh, she resumed her arm exercises as Sue Stewart came out of the changing room and walked toward her. Deliberately Liza set aside her mind meanderings and smiled a welcome to her friend. "You're late this morning. Oversleep?"

"Gosh, no, I didn't sleep very well. I never do when Lyle's gone. He got a call last night around midnight and had to go to the hospital." Sue finished adjusting her sweat bands before continuing. "You probably heard about the accident."

"I didn't catch the news this morning. What accident?"

"Sam Rivers lost control of his vehicle and crashed into a tree. What a mess."

Liza went still, as her heart leaped into her throat. "Lost control? Is he hurt?"

"Hardly at all, the lucky son of a gun." Sue began her

warmup and stretching exercises. "Apparently, he swerved into this wooded field and the empty passenger side of his Explorer took the brunt of the hit. Lyle and the sheriff's deputy are over talking to the mechanic at the station where they towed it."

Letting go of the machine, Liza drew in a deep breath. "Then Sam's all right?" She knew she was arousing Sue's interest, but she had to know.

"Far as I know. Lyle said he had a mild concussion and a badly bruised left arm. The hospital's running more tests." Sue straightened, noticing her friend's sudden pallor. "Are you okay?"

Liza ignored the inquiry. "When did the accident happen?" She'd been with Sam until past eight, but she had no idea when he'd left the trailer.

"Sometime last evening. I guess the hospital insisted they notify someone, and Sam didn't want to upset his mother, so he gave them our number." Squinting, she studied her friend, her expression curious.

Liza took the towel from around her neck and dabbed at her face. "I've got to make a call, Sue. I'll see you later." Moving quickly, she headed for the locker room.

Her back to the few women in the changing room, Liza huddled in the telephone cubicle and waited impatiently to be connected to the information desk at Port Henry General. Finally, someone came on the line. "I'm inquiring about the condition of a patient, Sam Rivers."

"Yes, ma'am," the impersonal voice said, "are you a relative?"

She wasn't about to give her name, so she opted for the first lie that popped into her head. "Yes, his sister." And she hoped they hadn't taken a history on Sam and left it with the operator.

"Just a moment and I'll check."

Pulling at the towel around her neck, Liza waited for what seemed a very long time. Finally, the woman came back.

"I'm sorry, ma'am, but Mr. Rivers has checked himself out."

"He has? But I was told he'd been in a fairly bad automobile accident and—"

"That's true, but we can't hold a patient against his will if he signs off. It was against doctor's orders, I might add."

How like Sam to ignore everyone's wishes but his own. "Thank you." Hanging up, she searched her mind as to where he might be. He had to have gone home, probably to rest. It was almost impossible to rest in hospitals. Quickly, she looked up the phone number for Ann Rivers and dialed again.

"Hello!" The voice was young, male and quite annoyed.

"This is Liza Courtland. I'm looking for Sam Rivers."

Jim rubbed his unshaven face in a gesture very much like his brother's habit. He'd grabbed the phone because he knew his mother had just lain down after being up and worrying for hours after the call from the attorney. Lyle had assured his mother that Sam wasn't hurt badly, but she hadn't believed him until the two men had shown up a short time ago. She'd wanted to tuck Sam into bed, but he would have none of it. He'd taken a quick shower and left again with Lyle. "He's not here," Jim said around a yawn.

Not at the hospital, not at home. Where on earth had he gone? "Do you know where I might find him?"

Naturally, Jim knew who Liza Courtland was. Everyone in Port Henry knew. He also knew she had something to do with the Oakview development. But why she sounded so tense about his brother's condition and why she was hell-bent on finding Sam, he couldn't imagine. "Probably over checking with the mechanic about his Explorer. He said he would be going to the trailer afterward if we needed him."

"The trailer? But it's far too wet to work today."

"Yeah. He had Jeff call all the guys and tell them to stay home until at least tomorrow." Glancing outside, Jim could see that the rain had let up again, but the skies were still gray. He hoped it would start pouring so he could have several days off.

He heard the woman let out a ragged sigh. "Thanks. I appreciate your help."

"Sure." Jim hung up and glanced at the clock. Only seven-thirty. He hoped his mother slept awhile so she wouldn't nag him to get up. He didn't get many chances to sleep late these days since Sam had climbed on his case, so he'd better take advantage of the rainy day. Truth be known, he was kind of enjoying the work at Oakview, though he hadn't said as much to Sam. It was tiring, but he could see results at the end of the day, good results. Chet, one of the older carpenters, said that Jim had a real knack for working in wood.

On that thought, Jim closed his eyes.

The fenced-in work site at Oakview was a muddy mess, Liza thought as she drove through the open gate. A gray Porsche was parked near the steps with no other vehicles in sight. By the time she'd showered and dressed, she figured Sam had finished with the mechanic and had been driven here. She got out and knocked on the door.

The tall, sandy-haired man wearing gold-rimmed glasses who opened the door definitely wasn't Sam. Lyle Stewart's face didn't register even a hint of surprise as he stepped aside to let her in. "Hello, Liza. Haven't seen you in a while."

"How are you, Lyle?" she asked, looking past him to the man her eyes had been seeking. Sam Rivers was seated on the back couch, his left arm in a pouch sling, his face pale against his dark beard.

"I'm a lot better than our friend over there." Lyle shook his head. "Maybe you can convince him to get some rest. I can't seem to get through his thick head."

Nerves had Liza tight-lipped and frowning as she walked over and sat down alongside Sam. She hadn't actually believed he was really all right until this moment, until she could see with her own eyes that, although he wasn't in top form, he seemed relatively unhurt. "Do you want to tell me what happened after I left here last night?"

Lyle raised a questioning brow, but remained silent. The two of them had been here in the trailer last night? Interesting.

Sam caught his friend's quick, curious look. "Listen Lyle, I appreciate all you've done. Let me think about things and I'll get back to you."

"Okay. You're sure I can't talk you into going back home? You haven't slept all night."

"That's all right. Liza can take me later."

So the man wanted to be alone with the lady. His gaze skimming over her, Lyle couldn't blame Sam. "Talk to you soon. Bye, Liza."

She gave him a distracted wave, then waited for the trailer door to shut behind him. "Are you in pain?"

Sam leaned back, then rubbed the bridge of his nose with his free hand. "I'm all right. Just a wrenched shoulder and a slight concussion. They gave me a bottle of pain pills, over there on the counter. But I don't like that fuzzy feeling, so I took a couple of aspirin instead."

She'd dealt with a stubborn man before: her father. She knew better than to argue with him just now. "What happened?"

Sam's full lips moved into a thin line. "Someone tampered with my brakes. All the fluid leaked out. I was on my way home, going downhill. Brakes wouldn't hold. This truck was coming at me. It was slippery and I couldn't keep it steady in the lane. So I turned off into the field. That slowed me down, but I couldn't steer well because of the mud. I saw the tree ahead, but I couldn't stop. That's all I remember." Fortunately the mud had slowed the Explorer enough to save his life, so the mechanic had told him.

Liza's hand reached out to grip his free one. "You passed out? Who found you?"

"Another truck driver. It seems my lights stayed on, and he spotted me from the road. When I woke up, I realized I couldn't get out. The crushed-in dash had my left side pinned. I tried leaning on the horn, hoping the battery wouldn't wear out before someone heard, but not too many cars went by."

"How long were you out there, I wonder."

"I left here about nine. The trucker found me about eleven and radioed for help. I had the hospital call Lyle."

Two hours he was out there alone in the dark, hurting and probably wet. She hoped he didn't have pneumonia. "Your arm isn't broken?"

"No, just bruised." He looked into her eyes for the first time, noting the concern there. It warmed him. No one had worried about him in a very long time. She was wearing one of her power business suits, this one a glen plaid with a pale gold blouse, obviously dressed for the office. He was flattered she'd detoured to see him. "Who told you about me?"

"Lyle's wife, Sue, at the fitness center." She squeezed

his hand, her emotions close to the surface as the shock wore off. "You could have called *me*."

He'd thought fleetingly of doing just that, but he didn't want her to perceive of the accident as playing to her sympathies. "I needed Lyle to look into things for me. The mechanic said no way was this an accident. Someone deliberately gouged a hole in the brake line."

Convinced finally that he wasn't badly hurt, Liza focused on his words. "But who? Who would do such a thing and why? You didn't have trouble with the Explorer before coming here yesterday?"

Sam shook his head. "I'm telling you this was deliberate. Someone had to have come on the premises while I was walking the site checking for storm damage, or later when you and I were in here, or even after you left. I didn't close and lock the fence gate. I should have, but it hardly matters. If someone wanted to disable my car, they'd have found a way to get in. Locks won't stop a person that determined."

Letting out a shaky breath at the implication, Liza sat back, her hand still holding his. "But who wants to harm you? You've only been in Port Henry a few weeks. All you're doing is trying to get some houses built."

Sam had his own theory. "And I've been asking questions all around town about my father's disappearance. Suppose the person responsible thinks I might get too close, might find him out. Maybe disabling the Explorer was a warning for me to get out of town. Or maybe he figured he might as well finish me off and he'd be safe again."

Liza angled her body so she could look at him. "Then you're thinking someone killed Joe Rivers. But why? As you've told me, he had no money to steal."

"I've heard that if you concentrate on motive, it'll lead you to the guilty party. So who could gain from Joe's death? The only thing I can think of is that Joe must have seen something, knew something or witnessed something that would get this person in deep trouble, which is why he did away with him. No witness, no risk. But then I come along, after he's felt fairly safe for eight years, and people start wondering all over again. Not about me this time, but about what might really have happened. This guy gets worried. He's killed before. What's to stop him again?''

His words had her shivering. ''Oh, Lord, I don't know. That sounds so…so sinister. I can't believe this someone is here, living in Port Henry all this time, friends with all of us, most likely, pretending innocence. It's like the plot of a bad movie.''

''Yeah, it is.'' Sam moved to sit up and almost moaned aloud at the sharp pain in his shoulder. ''Only it's real, all right.''

''Are you going to bring this to the attention of the sheriff?'' Not that she had much faith that Ed Hayes would very willingly look into someone trying to harm Sam Rivers. He'd probably be glad if the incident would cause Sam to leave town.

''Keith Nickles met us at the garage and heard what the mechanic said. I asked Lyle to call the deputy because I don't trust Hayes, but Keith's all right. He's going to look into the matter. So far, all we have is a criminal act, but no suspects. The guy's smart. Who'd be out on a stormy night to see him crawl under the Explorer and punch that hole? Hell, everyone stayed home last night.''

''Except you and me. And I wish we had, too. Maybe this wouldn't have happened then.''

''Maybe. But if not this, then something else would have happened. If this guy wants me gone, he'll keep trying.'' Sam stifled a yawn. He was tired and achy, but unwilling to quit. He needed to get to work on finding the person responsible. ''I've tracked down one of Joe's old cronies.

Tom Novak's in Veterans' Hospital near Toledo. He recently had a leg amputated due to diabetes. I need to go talk with him and see if he remembers anything about that weekend.''

Liza noticed his fatigue, the pained yet stubborn expression. ''That's all well and good, but first you need to rest. You've had a bad jolt to the system.''

''I'll be all right. I want to get moving on this and...''

''I'll make a deal with you. You get some sleep, and afterward I'll help you any way I can. I'm sure the Explorer won't be fixed right away. I'll drive you to see Tom Novak, if you're a good boy.'' He could easily rent a car, she knew, but she didn't want to let him out of her sight in this condition for reasons she didn't want to examine too closely at the moment. Rising, she dangled her keys. ''Let me take you home.''

''No. My mother'll drive me crazy fussing.'' In the half hour he'd been there to clean up, she'd all but chained him to the bed and spoon-fed him chicken soup. He glanced at the couch. ''This makes into a bed. I'll just take a short nap and get Jim to bring me his car.''

No way was she leaving him here alone, injured and without wheels, vulnerable to some maniac who could easily return. ''Listen, there's a time to be brave and bullheaded and a time to listen to the voice of reason.'' She moved to his good side and took hold of his arm. ''You're coming with me. We have a whole upstairs wing at the house that no one ever uses. You can have peace and privacy, and no one will know where you are. I promise we won't fuss over you, either. Agreed? Good. Come on, lean on me.''

His eyes were grainy and his limbs heavy. He didn't have the energy to argue any longer. ''All right, but I can walk without help.'' Bracing himself, he stood. The first step was wobbly, but after that he managed to walk on his own, to lock up and get into her car.

As they cruised along toward the Courtland Mansion, however, Sam leaned his head back and closed his eyes. In moments, he was asleep.

He didn't remember climbing the back steps at the Courtland Mansion or letting Liza settle him in the big mahogany bed in the upstairs corner room. Later, he was vaguely aware of shadows moving in the big, pleasant room and a soft voice that insisted he sit up and take a pill with a large glass of orange juice. He dimly recalled sinking back into huge, fluffy pillows as the door clicked shut. The next thing he knew, it was morning and a bright sun was pouring in through snowy white sheers at the tall double windows.

Moving gingerly, Sam sat up and became instantly aware of a dull ache in his left shoulder. But the headache was gone, thank goodness. Testing, he got to his feet and was pleased to note that he was fairly steady. Across the room was a door that probably led to a bathroom. At least he hoped it did.

What a hostess. Clean towels, an electric razor and a fresh toothbrush. After a shave and shower, plus two aspirins he'd found in the medicine chest, Sam felt more human. He got dressed, strolled to the window and gazed out.

It was a beautiful sunny morning, looking quite warm, which meant the mud would be drying at Oakview. He'd left word yesterday for Jeff to put everyone to work on cleanup detail as soon as possible. A glance at his watch told him it was just after six. He hoped Liza was an early riser. He needed a quick ride to the trailer where he kept some clean clothes. Then he'd check in with Jeff before renting a car and driving to Toledo to see Tom Novak.

After what had happened, he needed to step up his investigation of his father's disappearance.

He was just putting on his boots when a light knock sounded at the front door. "Come in."

Liza, dressed in navy slacks and a striped top, walked in, her smile a bit hesitant. It wasn't every day she greeted a man first thing in the morning. She glanced at the big rumpled bed that lent an air of intimacy. "Did you sleep well?"

"I hope to tell you, for about eighteen hours." He finished lacing up the boots and straightened. "Did you drug me?"

"No, but I did manage to get a couple of pain pills down you. You were groaning in your sleep, so I figured you were hurting."

"Well, whatever it was, it worked." He flexed his shoulder and, except for a mild twinge, it felt fine. "Can I bum a ride?"

She frowned. "I thought I promised I'd go with you today."

He did vaguely remember their discussion. "I won't hold you to it. I know you're busy and—"

Liza shook her head. "Nope. I cleared my calendar with Arnie yesterday so you're stuck with me. Mom's already made breakfast, and then we can take off. But first you have to sit next to Beth at the table. It's the only way I could keep her from coming to check on you every few minutes yesterday."

That had him smiling. "That's great, but I don't want to be any more trouble. I can rent a car and—"

"No, please. This intruder came on Courtland property and disabled your vehicle. I want to get to the bottom of things, too." Through a long, restless night during which she'd crept in several times to check on Sam, Liza had struggled with her thoughts, her feelings. This she felt she had to do. She wouldn't rest until she knew who was responsible and why. "Unless, of course, you don't want me along."

His eyes darkened as they lingered on her face, her lips. "That day will never come."

Reluctant to break the look, Liza swallowed. "Okay then, let's go eat."

Tom Novak reached a bony hand into the plastic cup on his bedside table, picked up his false teeth and shoved them in his mouth. His thin face relaxed as he looked up at his old friend's son. "You sure are a fine-looking man, Sammy. If Joe was here, he'd be proud."

Sam sincerely doubted that, for his father had never wasted his breath praising either of his sons. "I appreciate you seeing us." Shifting the visitor's chair near the hospital bed, he indicated that Liza should sit down while he positioned himself at the foot.

"Hell, son, it's not as if I get a ton of visitors." Tom punched at the two pillows behind his head. "Crank me up a mite, would you?"

Sam found the power switch and slowly eased the older man's bed up to a sitting position. Novak was in a six-bed ward in Veterans' Hospital near Toledo, with curtains partitioning them off for minimal privacy. Studying the thin, unshaven face of his father's friend, Sam couldn't help thinking that if Joe were alive, he'd probably resemble Tom—frail, wispy gray hair, nose and cheeks dotted with broken veins, the telltale signs of a lifelong drinker. "They treating you okay here, Tom?" he asked.

The old man shrugged. "Clean sheets and three squares a day. Hell of a lot better than the third-floor walk-up I had." He rubbed absently at his stub. "Since they cut off my leg, I don't get around so good anymore.'' He thrust his chin toward a pair of crutches leaning against the back wall. "Ever try walking up stairs with those?" He shook his head sadly.

It was hard not to feel sorry for the man, Liza thought, although he'd only made his diabetes worse by years of drinking. "Do you have family nearby?"

Tom shook his head. "Not no more. Wife left me years ago, but my daughter Audrey used to live in Port Henry. She let me live with her and her two kids for a while, but I messed that up." He ran a trembling hand over his sparse hair. "I stole from her, you know. First money, then I hocked some of her things. I planned to pay her back before she found out, but it didn't work out that way. She moved away." His watery eyes looked up at Sam. "It was the booze, you know. It changes you." He gave them a wobbly smile, revealing stained teeth. "But I haven't touched a drop in five months and four days."

Sadness swamped Liza, for the wasted life, for the old man left all alone. "That's good, Mr. Novak, that's very good."

"Yeah." He sighed heavily. "Too late, though."

"Tom," Sam began, deciding he'd better get to the point before the poor old guy started crying, "I came to ask you a couple of questions about the weekend Joe disappeared."

"Sure, what do you want to know? I was there, at the Watering Hole that night. Guess it was the last time anyone seen Joe, eh?"

"Tell us what happened at the bar, everything you can remember, will you please?"

In his halting, rambling way, Tom Novak recounted the evening at the Watering Hole, saying that Joe had come in half-loaded, mad as hell at being thrown off the job for drinking. He wouldn't eat, just drank more. "I was feelin' no pain myself, but I could handle my liquor better'n Joe. Anyway, he wanted to play pool so I took him on. Next thing you know, he accused me of cheating.'' His eyes narrowed. ''I may not be perfect, but I don't cheat at pool. I couldn't let that pass, so I hit him. Hell, Sammy, you know your old man. He hit me back, 'course. We was fighting pretty good when Zac tried to get us to stop on account of we fell into a couple of his chairs and broke 'em.''

''Only you wouldn't stop, right?''

''Yeah, right. Joe, he swung at Zac and that did it. Zac called the sheriff. Only, Hayes showed up instead. He's big, you know, and mean as hell. Pulled us apart and shoved us into chairs. I was ready to quit. My face was bleeding, my ankle hurt like hell. Zac offered everyone a drink on the house, and I took him up on it. Not Joe. He was fumin' and swearin' at Hayes.''

''What did Hayes do then?''

''Ordered Joe to leave. He went, cursin' all the way.''

''Did Hayes go after him?''

''Nah. He sat on a bar stool and had a beer, told me I'd have to pay for the broken chairs.'' Tom ran a hand along his whiskers. ''Weren't the first time. Joe and me, we got into it lots of times. Sometimes I think he said things just so one of us would start something, you know. He loved to fight, thought he was a champ.'' He made a grunting sound. ''Sure he is. Bet he's deader'n a door nail.''

Sam stared at him intently. ''What makes you say that?''

Again, Tom shrugged. '''Cause no one's heard from him all these years. Wherever he went, you know he didn't change none. By now, either the drink's got him, like me. Or someone killed him in a barroom fight. I'd put good money on it.''

* * *

"The sad truth is that I think he's probably right," Sam told Liza when they were back in her BMW.

"You think your father drank himself to death or died in a barroom brawl?"

"I don't know how he died, but I think he's probably dead. As Lyle explained to me, everyone leaves a paper trail, even the ones clever enough to change their identity. And Joe wasn't smart enough to do that." Sam hit the button and rolled down his window, breathed in deeply of the late-afternoon air. "So, since we can't find a trace of him, I have to believe he died sometime around that weekend. If he'd wandered off on foot somewhere and fallen because he was drunk and maybe hit his head fatally, someone would have run across his body by now. So the next logical step is that someone helped him get to his great reward. The question is, who and why." The why he wasn't sure about, but Sam had a feeling if they could learn the identity of the man that disabled his Explorer, they'd know who.

But Liza's thoughts were back in the hospital at the bedside of a sad old man. "I feel sorry for Tom Novak, despite the fact that he's the cause of most of his problems. What a sad way to end up, sick and alone, probably broke."

"I agree." Sam moved in his seat, turning toward her, trying not to wince as a pain reminded him of his shoulder injury.

"You're hurting. I should take you home." But she didn't want to go back, to leave him. Something had shifted for Liza over the past twenty-four hours. Finding out that Sam had been in a serious auto accident that could have killed him had forced her to face her feelings for him more seriously. The love that had been there from almost the first moment she'd laid eyes on him had resurfaced, stronger than ever.

And the visit to a helpless old man who'd wasted his life and would die alone had had a sobering impact on her as well. She was reminded that time was short and second chances didn't come along too often. Perhaps it would be a mistake giving in to her feelings for Sam a second time. And perhaps she'd be hurt again.

But the truth was that she'd been living her life in a sort of limbo, waiting for she knew not what. She'd tried to love another man when she'd first returned to Port Henry, thinking Beth needed a father. But she hadn't been able to be untrue to her feelings. And her feelings had always revolved around Sam Rivers.

He was here now, hers for the taking. It would be a risk, but then, life was full of risks. If she didn't reach out for him now, if she didn't allow herself the chance to know that kind of love again, she'd surely regret it the rest of her life.

He wouldn't stay. She knew that, knew he'd leave when the project was finished and the mystery surrounding his father's disappearance solved. She wasn't even sure they could work things out if he did stay. But she was sure of one thing: she didn't want to wind up like Tom Novak, lonely at the end, having caused her own loneliness by letting happiness pass her by.

"Is that what you want, to go home?" Sam asked quietly. He'd been watching her expressive face as a myriad of emotions washed over her lovely features. She was struggling with inner demons he couldn't even imagine, and he wondered if she would win.

"No. I want to be with you." Starting the powerful engine, she glanced around the hospital parking lot, then back at the man seated next to her. "I'd like to go somewhere private, a nice place, maybe on the water. One with room service."

Room service had to mean a hotel room, not a restaurant. Sam felt his body tighten in response but kept his features even. "Are you sure?"

"I've never been more sure." And she knew just the place. Slipping into gear, she drove out of the lot.

Chapter Eight

The trouble with making bold suggestions and impulsive decisions was that a nervous reaction often set in shortly after, Liza thought, as she followed Sam along the carpeted corridor to Room 212 at the Inn off the Park. She'd met a supplier for a dinner meeting at the lovely old inn several weeks ago. The landmark establishment was located on the opposite side of the bay from Port Henry, near the Bayside Yacht Club. She'd thought then that the quaint two-story brick building with ivy trailing up all four sides was charming. But she hadn't dreamed she'd be sharing a suite in it one day.

As Sam opened the door and stepped aside to allow her to enter, Liza was certain he could hear the thudding of her heart. Never in her entire life had she gone to a hotel room with a man. She and Sam had always met at the lake cottage, sparing her the embarrassment of the knowing look in the eyes of the clerk at the front desk, the slight twitch of his lips as he'd asked if they had any luggage. She hadn't been able to meet his eyes. So much for sophistication.

Of course a simple room wasn't good enough for the Sam Rivers of today. A suite, no less, with a spacious sitting area, a built-in bar and piped-in music. An archway led to a shadowy area she assumed was the bedroom itself.

Nervously, Liza walked to the three bay windows overlooking the sparkling water, shimmering in a late-afternoon sun. "Look at all the sailboats," she commented, pulling aside the sheer curtains. Colorful stripes, bright streaks of yellow and red, glittering white, they raced along, tilting in a westerly wind.

She heard Sam close and lock the door, the click sounding overly loud to her ears. Apparently he wasn't going to join her in admiring the view. Swallowing, she turned and spotted the room service menu on the table for two just in front of the windows. Snatching it up for something to do rather than because she was hungry, she quickly ran her eyes up and down both sides. "Mmm, they have escargots and caviar and champagne."

Sam tossed his keys onto a small end table before turning to study her. A shaft of sunlight from the windows backlit her hair, turning it a pale gold. There was a slight flush to her cheeks. The knitted top outlined her full breasts, gently moving with each breath she took. A heart on a gold chain dangled in the vee of her neckline, and on one slim wrist she wore a heavy gold bracelet. The navy slacks fit as if made for her, showing off her long, long legs. On her feet were white sandals, her toenails painted a pale pink.

Understated elegance, he thought. Her nerves were jumpy, he could tell, as were his own. He caught the trembling of her full lower lip as she worried it between her teeth. Liza Courtland, CEO, didn't fool him for a minute. She'd invited him here, chosen the place and set the scene.

But she was scared to death.

Eyes still on the menu, Liza tried to appear totally absorbed. "And look! They have truffles. Have you ever had truffles? The first time I saw them, I wondered what all the fuss was about. I mean we've all heard the stories. Supposedly, they only grow in special places, dark and moist. Truffle-sniffing pigs are the only ones who can locate them, usually at night. Probably at the full of the moon. A great story but—"

She felt the menu leave her hands. Sam tossed it aside and stepped close to her, tipping her chin up with one finger so she had to meet his eyes. "You're babbling, Liza. I remember you used to always run on like this when you were scared. You're scared now, aren't you?"

"Well, I..." She couldn't lie, not with him staring her down. "Yes." Her voice was whisper soft.

"Me, too."

"You are?" That had her fractionally relaxing. "Not of me, certainly." Men weren't the ones who got nervous. The first time they'd been together, Sam hadn't shown the slightest case of nerves, while she'd been a wreck.

"Yes, of you." His hands rested on her forearms, his thumbs caressing the sensitive skin there. "You always scared me to death. You were this lovely dream come true, someone I'd thought was out of bounds, out of my reach. I didn't think anyone had a right to be so beautiful, and you're even more so now."

She placed her hands at his waist, finally stepping closer. "You were the one out of reach. Did you know that I used to find excuses to drive to the building site where you were working, that I'd step behind the trees and watch you? You used to tie this red-checkered kerchief around your forehead to keep your hair out of your eyes, and you'd remove your shirt and toss it aside. I'd stand there praying I wouldn't be discovered, staring at your muscles while you measured and sawed and pounded nails. My mouth would be bone dry watching you.'' The memory had her licking her lips even now.

His crooked smile came then. ''You did all that?''

''Mmm-hmm. Once, I climbed out on the limb of this tree so I could see you better, and it snapped off. I went crashing down and the foreman came running over. I didn't care about him, but I was mortified at the thought that you might notice and laugh at me.''

His eyes darkened as he raised a hand to trail along one silken cheek. ''I wouldn't have laughed.''

''It took me three weeks of torture before I got up enough nerve to actually speak to you. I was sure you could read everything on my face, my every thought.'' He'd drawn her nearer until their lower bodies were slightly touching, lightly teasing. Liza felt the slow heating of her blood.

''And if I could have read those thoughts, what would I have learned?'' he asked.

No turning back, Liza told herself. She'd wanted to be alone like this with him, even though the dialogue wasn't one she'd have written. She might as well confess, for he could see the truth on her face. ''That I was nuts about you.'' She blinked, reaching for her nebulous courage. All or nothing, she decided. ''I tried, heaven knows, to forget you. I almost married someone else to prove to myself I was over you, that you no longer mattered. It didn't work.''

Was he really hearing those words from her, the ones he'd yearned to hear all those long, lonely years? ''For me, either. It was always you.'' Fiercely he gathered her close, his anger aimed at himself. ''I shouldn't have left you. I should have trusted you, confided in you. Things would be so different now.'' Beth would be his daughter instead of another man's child. And the woman he was holding would be his wife.

Liza rose on her toes to kiss his cheek, trying to soothe his troubled thoughts, to comfort, to kiss away the lingering bitterness. "Let's not do this. What's done is done and can't be changed. We both made mistakes, we both have regrets we have to live with."

Sam held her away so he could look deeply into her eyes. "I need you to know I never stopped wanting you. Not a day or night went by that you weren't on my mind."

Liza slid her arms around him as something stirred inside her. Was it the release of the resentment she'd built up over the years? Was it the reaffirmation of a love too strong to die? He hadn't said it in so many words, but she could feel the depth of his emotions. "There must have been at least an hour or so during those eight years when I didn't think of you at all, but I can't remember it." But he had to know the downside as well. "To be utterly honest, many times I thought of you with disappointment, with anger."

Sam nodded. "I know that, and I'm sorry I let you down, that I hurt you. I should have been stronger. The truth was, no one had ever really cared about me until you came into my life, and I was afraid to trust." He thought of the bleak, lost years of his wanderings, and wondered if she'd still care about him if she knew some of the things he'd done just to stay alive. "I have a lot of baggage still, Liza." For instance: the mystery of his father's disappearance; the troubled relationship with his brother; unresolved feelings for his mother and a town that had long ago labeled him a criminal. "Most of it's packed away, but occasionally something slips out."

She thought of the dark secret she'd kept from him, the one thing that could blow this tenuous reunion sky high, and knew she had her own fair share of baggage. She would have to deal with that soon, but not this day. "I know that while you were on the run, you probably did things you regret. Perhaps you even lived outside the law. But I don't care. Your past doesn't scare me. I'm still here, right where I want to be."

He couldn't take his eyes off her face, her beautiful face. The need for her was growing huge. "Do you know how very much I want you this minute? But I need you to be very, very sure. Tell me now if you've changed your mind, before we go any further. I don't want to hurt you again."

Slowly, with a smile forming, she shook her head. "I haven't changed my mind." Her breath tumbled through parted lips. "I never have had pride where you're concerned. Make love with me, Sam." Rising again on tiptoe, she brought her lips within a hairsbreadth of his. "Just love me, please."

The invitation he'd imagined in his restive dreams, the fantasy that had played over and over in his tortured mind, here at last. Gathering her up in his arms, Sam walked through the archway that connected the sitting room with the bedroom and set her on her feet.

The drapes were drawn against the heat of the day, and he left them that way. He turned on a low lamp with hands that shook slightly. He glanced up and saw she'd noticed, caught her gentle smile. When she held out her hand to show him that hers was trembling, too, he gave her his smile.

"It's all right," he said softly, cradling her face. "Don't be nervous and don't be scared. We'll go slowly, take our time."

To Liza, they weren't just two people who'd done without for too long, reaching out to the first available target. It wasn't that she wanted a man to satisfy this incessant craving. She wanted *this* man because only he seemed able to awaken her. "Yes, we have nothing but time." They had unresolved differences between them still, but at least here in the bedroom she knew she could trust Sam.

"I've thought about this so often, wanted this so badly." The first kiss was a tender meeting of lips, a gentle exploration. There was hesitancy and rebirth and finally an acknowledgment of the familiar. The gloriously familiar. Then his hands moved to unzip the opening of her striped top. "I want to see you. I want to watch your face when I touch you." He remembered how her eyes used to go hazy with passion as his hands had roamed over her flesh.

Ever a match for him, Liza fumbled with the buttons of his shirt. "I want to see you, too."

They were down to the bare essentials in a matter of seconds, then Sam pulled back the coverlet revealing pale blue sheets soft as down. Standing very still, they took their time looking, remembering, noting changes.

She saw the purplish bruise on his left shoulder and touched it with hesitant fingertips. "Does it hurt very much?"

"Not anymore." Then he eased her onto the bed crosswise and followed to lean over her. His heart was hammering in his chest, but he forced himself to take a deep breath, to go slowly. For her sake, and for his.

For if ever there was a woman made to savor, he was looking at her. Sam sent his hands threading through Liza's long, thick hair, letting the strands fall back in a cloud to frame her lovely face. Like a blind man might, his fingers traced the features of her face, as if memorizing them. They skimmed along a silken eyebrow, across the bridge of her small nose, along her cheeks and circled her stubborn chin. Then his lips followed the same path, pausing to plant warm, moist kisses on her closed eyelids and the corners of her mouth.

He heard a soft sigh escape from her, her body no longer able to lie still. He felt her fingers slide into his hair and grip his head, guiding his mouth back to hers. The kiss was slow and easy at first, but heated rapidly as he stroked along her shoulders, slipping off her bra. Breaking the kiss, he bent to flick his tongue over nipples hardening under his tender attention.

Everything was new, Liza thought, yet achingly familiar. The feel of his callused hands on her skin brought back a rush of memories, yet thrilled her even more than before. It was so easy to fall back into the ways of the past, as if they'd shared all the nights since, as if intimacy so intense was theirs alone. It was so thrilling to let him explore places untouched since the last time they'd been together. It was so wonderful to again feel her body come alive, her heart beat furiously, her breath catching in her throat as he worked his magic on her.

Her skin quivered as he took his mouth on a journey of her, taking his time, ignoring the impatient sounds she made. She felt his clever hands remove the last silken barrier and toss it aside, then she arched as his fingers moved inside her. So ready was she that in seconds she cried out as the first powerful wave took her. She forgot her own name as her eyes closed in acute pleasure.

Watching her incredibly expressive face as she let go, Sam fought back the need to bury himself deep inside and join her. Aroused beyond belief just looking at her, he held on to his control, needing to make this wondrous day perfect for Liza. Not once, but again and again, as he'd dreamed he would.

The softness of a woman had for too long been missing from his life—the silken hair, the gentle female touch, the soothing voice, the moist welcome of her body. He needed this, needed her, more than he could put into words.

She was a tall woman, yet with small bones, delicately built. She was tough when she needed to be, he knew, yet there was a fragility to her that slowed his moves and made him ever more tender. She'd always been so openly responsive, so trusting that he felt awed at the gift she gave him. He watched her blink to clear her vision, her every emotion visible on her lovely face.

She never held back, and that humbled him. There was a generosity to her that he'd never known in anyone else. That alone had him wanting to please her, to pleasure her in every way possible. And he would, but for now his control was slipping rapidly as he yanked off his briefs. When her seeking hands closed around him, he knew he had very little time left.

Shifting to the side, he paused to protect them both, then turned back to her. An expectant smile played on her lips, lips slightly swollen from his kisses. Their eyes locked as at last he slipped into her. He heard her sharp intake of breath as she adjusted to the shape and feel of him. Then her arms encircled him as she moved to take him deeper.

Home. Finally, he'd come home, Sam thought as he began an easy rhythm. Slowly, savoring the feel of her, he lowered his head and took her mouth. Exerting iron control, he didn't rush, not for long minutes. Not until he heard her breath catch and knew she was about to tumble over the edge. Only then did he give in and allow himself to follow her.

From somewhere out on the bay, the blast of a ship's horn could be heard, carried on the still summer air. Inside, two lovers peaked and collapsed, still in each other's arms.

Liza dipped her hands in the fingerbowl, wiped them on the linen napkin and sat back. "Do you know this is the very first time I've ever had room service?"

Sam looked up as he set down his champagne glass. "I'm surprised. You must do some traveling for Courtland Enterprises."

"Not much. I don't like to leave Beth. The few times I have gone, I plan a dinner meeting so I won't have to eat alone." She scrunched up her nose as she drew the folds of the thick, white terry cloth robe around her. "This feels positively sinful, eating lobster and drinking champagne when it's scarcely dark out."

Slipping into his Groucho Marx pose, Sam flipped ashes from an imaginary cigar. "Hey, lady, you ain't seen nothin' yet."

"Hmm, let me see." Liza put on an exaggerated frown. "Bogie? Or was that Cagney?"

"Cute." He reached across the table, took her small hand in his and gazed into eyes as green as the Caribbean. "I can't remember when I've felt this good."

Heat crept onto her cheeks as her mind flashed back to their lovers' bed, but she smiled. "Nor I."

"Will you stay the night?"

A whole night in his arms, something she'd longed for. But she had responsibilities, obligations. She had Beth. "I don't know." She glanced at her watch. Nearly eight. Her mother was probably beginning to worry already.

"Call your mom," Sam said, reading her expression clearly. "She won't mind keeping Beth. You said yourself you're rarely gone overnight."

On business. But what explanation could she give Elizabeth tonight?

A smile tugged at his lips. "You're a big girl, Liza. Surely your mother knows you're entitled to a personal life. Besides, it's not smart to drive after downing two glasses of champagne." Lazily, he rubbed his thumb along the delicate skin of her wrist. "Unless you don't want to stay."

She met his eyes. "I think you know better than that."
Rising, she walked to the desk and reached for the phone.
Her mother picked up on the second ring. "Hi, Mom. Is
everything all right?"

"Why, yes, dear. Of course. Are you back?"

"No, not exactly." How easy it had been to make vague
excuses when she'd been nineteen and rushing off to meet
Sam. But now… "The meeting lasted longer than I'd
thought. Would you mind if I stayed over?"

After a slight pause, Elizabeth recovered. "Stayed over
where?"

"We're at the Inn off the Park, just the other side of the
bay. We just had dinner and…" This was silly. She was a
grown woman who owed no explanations. "Mom, Sam and
I would like to spend the night here, if you don't mind
watching Beth." Her mother knew now how it was between her and Sam. Still, her nervous fingers twined the
telephone cord.

Elizabeth wondered if Liza could tell she was smiling.
For too long, she'd watched the sadness in her daughter's
eyes, seen the loneliness not even Beth nor she could completely erase. A young woman needed a man in her life,
and she'd learned recently that for Liza, that man had always been Sam Rivers. "You know I never mind keeping
Beth. We're playing checkers and she's beating me badly."

Relief flooded Liza, relaxing her tense shoulders.
"Thanks, Mom. I appreciate this."

"Certainly. I might mention that Ed Hayes came by
around noon with his niece in tow. He wanted to take you
and Beth on a picnic, since he'd checked with your office
and learned you were taking a day off."

Liza frowned. "What'd you tell him?"

"That you were away on a business trip. He tried to get

me to say more, but I wouldn't. I don't like that man nosing around every chance he gets.''

"Ed's not so bad, Mom. But he's barking up the wrong tree. Listen, we'll be back fairly early in the morning. I called Edith earlier, and things are calm at the office, but I do have to go in tomorrow.''

"All right, dear. And Liza? Do be careful.''

"I promise I will. Can I say good-night to Beth?'' In a moment, Beth came on the line. "How are you, sweetie?''

"Fine, Mom. Guess what? Grandma made chocolate pudding with whipped cream and *three* cherries on top for dessert. I ate all my dinner except the peas. Mom, I *hate* peas.''

"You know you have to eat vegetables, too. And only one dessert, Beth. I mean it.''

"Okay. Is Sam there? Can I talk to him?''

Surprised, Liza swung around, her eyes wide. Of course they'd all had breakfast together and Beth had seen her mother leave with Sam. But Liza hadn't been expecting this. "Just a minute.'' She held the phone out to him. "Beth wants to talk with you.''

A man who prided himself on not revealing his emotions, Sam utterly lost it as a wide smile split his face. He walked over to take the phone. "How's my girl?''

"Good. Sam, do you know how to play checkers?''

"Do I know how to play checkers? You're talking to the third-grade champion checker player, I'll have you know.''

Beth giggled. "When you come over next time, maybe we can play a game. Grandma says I just beat her pants off.''

Sam grinned. "You're on. You sleep well, sweetheart. Here's your mom.''

"Okay, Beth, now you listen to Grandma. Brush your teeth and go to bed when she tells you. No arguing.''

"I will. I love you, Mom."

"I love you, too, sweetie. Sleep tight." She replaced the phone slowly.

Sam waited until she turned around. "Did I hear you mention Ed's name? Not Ed Hayes, I hope."

Liza sighed. "The one and only." She told him what her mother had said. "Sometimes he doesn't come around for weeks, then suddenly he gets pesky."

He tried to ignore the jealousy that sparked so swiftly, but it didn't work. "Is he coming to see you and using his niece as an opening to get his big foot in the door?"

"Probably." She hadn't thought so for a long while, but lately Ed's suggestions and comments had gotten more personal. She didn't want to hurt his feelings, but she'd have to straighten him out. Liza returned to the table to finish her iced tea. "I've told him I don't date, but he's obtuse."

Yeah, like a fox. "How does Beth feel about him?"

Liza shrugged. "She mostly ignores him. She likes to play with Debbie, Ed's niece. Beth doesn't have a lot of friends so I put up with Ed for her sake."

Perhaps it was time he had a talk with Ed, Sam thought. Without Liza's knowledge, of course. He reached for her hand and walked them both over to the couch. He tugged her down onto his lap. "Beth's a mighty lucky little girl to have you. You've done a great job with her. She's charming, bright and funny. Like you."

She slanted a surprised look in his direction. "Thank you."

"It can't be easy, raising a child without a father and running Courtland Enterprises. You should be proud of yourself."

Cautiously she dropped her guard. "It's not the path I would have chosen, but I wouldn't trade a moment with Beth for any other life."

Sam stared off into middle distance a moment. "I wonder how many of us ever wind up on a path we would have chosen." He brought his eyes back to hers. "At any rate, whether you adopted Beth or you're her birth mother, it's obvious how much you love her."

Liza tried to keep her expression even as her heart thumped in her chest. "Is that the scuttlebutt around town?" she asked, hoping she sounded mildly curious.

"Yup." He wound his arms around her, loving the feel of her, the just bathed fragrance of her. After the first time, they'd stepped into the shower and made love again, then put on the matching robes the inn provided before ordering dinner. His hands toyed with the belt of her robe, thinking it was time to ease it from her. His body told him he was ready for a rematch. "You going to tell me which it is, adopted or natural?"

Swallowing, Liza shook her head. "I never respond to rumors." She searched for a change of subject, desperate to drop this one. "Aren't you going to call your mother? I'm sure she'll wonder, if you don't show up sooner or later, especially after yesterday's accident."

He smiled. "No one's tracked my comings and goings for a lot of years now." He moved his shoulder and arm. "Besides, I'm fine and I've told her so."

"But mothers worry, anyway, no matter how old you are."

Nuzzling her neck, he shifted her hair aside to give him better access. "It's different with my mother. She's not like yours."

"What do you mean?"

He let out a huff of air, reluctant to get into this now. "Did your mother love your father?"

"Worshiped him. As far as Mom was concerned, Dad walked on water." She'd heard the stories about Joe Rivers, had seen him about town, drunk and disorderly, and she'd seen Ann Rivers with empty, downcast eyes. "I don't imagine your folks had the love match of the century."

"Ha!" The sound he made said it all. "I never could figure why she stayed with him, why any woman puts up with all that."

"Perhaps he was different once, and she loved him in the beginning."

"Oh, I don't think so. They *had* to get married because I was on the way. I ruined both their lives, so they both told me often enough. Joe wanted to be a prizefighter, but he had to get a job instead. Mom wanted to be a nurse. Bingo! I botched up both their dreams." He wondered if he sounded as bitter as he still felt.

Liza shifted on his lap, touched his face. Had both parents made him feel so unwanted, so unloved? "None of that was your fault. No child asks to be born. It's the responsibility of each parent to take care of that little person, to love him." They were wandering into quicksand here, Liza thought. Still, he looked so angry, so filled with buried resentment. "Maybe she couldn't give you the best life, but I'm sure your mother loved you."

The welcome he'd received from his mother when he'd returned had seemed genuine enough. Now. But back then, Ann Rivers had been stern-faced and devoid of affection and humor. "She was too unhappy, too frightened to pay much attention to Jim or me. If she did care, she kept it to herself, to this day."

Her heart went out to the boy who'd never been told he was loved. "She's obviously led a sad life, Sam. I'm sure she has many regrets. Apparently you've forgiven her for any lack you felt as a boy, since you've taken care of her all these years." He cared, even if he couldn't admit it.

"Who else did she have?" He captured her hand in his.

"Look, let's not talk anymore about your parents or mine. It's too crowded in this room. We don't need them in here with us. We came here to be alone, just the two of us." He pressed his lips to her palm in a soft, tender kiss.

There was much unsettled between them, Liza thought again. But oh, Lord, how she loved him. Loved his dark head that she now caressed, his strong face, his hard body.

She watched his hands open her robe, freeing her breasts. His eyes darkened as he looked, then touched, finally tasted. Squeezing her eyes closed, Liza forgot about everyone, everything else.

Headlights bouncing as a car came into view over the hill had Ed Hayes awakening from his slouched position in his sheriff's vehicle. Dawn hadn't yet broken over the horizon. He glanced at his watch and saw that it was half past five in the morning. No wonder he'd dozed off. Squinting out the windshield as he shifted in his seat, he recognized Liza's white BMW turning into the drive and circling around back.

Ed had parked on a little-known dirt path in a wooded section alongside the Courtland Mansion so he could keep both entrances in view. He hadn't believed for a moment Liza's mother's terse explanation about her business trip. He'd had a chat earlier with Edith, Liza's secretary, and learned she'd taken a personal day. So where had she gone?

Rolling down the window, he leaned out and saw the BMW pause at the back stairs, not pull into the parking space she usually used when she didn't garage her car. Growing ever more suspicious, he waited until he saw the driver's door open. But it wasn't Liza who stepped out.

Ed Hayes watched Sam Rivers walk around and open the passenger door. He helped Liza out, then, arms around each other, they walked to the edge of the steps. There, just as the first sliver of sun could be seen rising in the east, Liza slipped her arms around Sam and kissed him. Long and lingeringly.

Damn! Ed's two beefy hands slammed against the steering wheel as angry frustration burst from him. He heard a sharp crack and wondered if he'd broken the column. He didn't much care one way or the other.

What was wrong with Liza? What was she doing with that renegade? How had Rivers coaxed her right back into his arms after all these years? His vision blurred as Ed watched them separate, then kiss once more before she ran up the stairs and Sam climbed back into the BMW. Bold as you please, now he was driving her car, seemingly with her happy permission.

All right. He'd done what he could to hint at what kind of man Sam was, what kind of family he came from, and still, the finest woman in all of Port Henry chose to ignore his warnings. He would have to find out more about Sam so he would be discredited further in Liza's eyes. Or—and this was a last measure, one he didn't want to use—about *her* so Sam would turn from Liza.

Because if Ed couldn't have her, he sure as hell wasn't going to allow that shady drifter to have Liza Courtland.

Turning on his engine, the sheriff gunned the motor and shot out of his hiding place.

Chapter Nine

It was a glorious morning, Liza decided as she parked her BMW in her designated spot at the Courtland Building. Somehow, Sam had had it returned to her while she'd been showering and dressing. Although she hadn't had much sleep during the wondrous night she'd spent in Sam's arms at the Inn off the Park, she felt rested and ready to tackle the world.

Amazing what a few hours of loving could do for a body, she thought, breaking into a smile.

Leaving the elevator, she walked down the carpeted corridor to her office, trying to focus on what she had to do today instead of reliving the past twenty-four hours. It wasn't easy. Lingering memories heated her face and put a spring in her stride. Nothing between them had been settled, yet today, she felt anything was possible.

Digging in her shoulder bag for her daily calendar, she glanced at Edith seated at her secretarial desk. But the greeting she'd been about to give died on her lips as she noticed that the older woman's face was tearstained, her eyes red from weeping, her glasses resting on the desktop. "Edith, what's wrong?"

"Everything," Edith sobbed around a soggy tissue.

"Come, now. It can't be that bad. Let's go into my office and talk about it." Liza dropped her things onto her desk and walked to the sideboard where Edith had a pot of coffee brewing. She poured two cups and carried them over to the conversation area in the far corner of the room. "Sit down and drink this." Liza settled in the chair while her secretary perched on the edge of the love seat, dabbing at her eyes.

Liza waited until Edith had taken a few sips and seemed more composed. "Now, tell me what happened."

"It's Kristen," Edith blurted out as she put on her black-rimmed glasses. "She's pregnant."

Liza's first reaction was pure emotion, a rush of déjà vu. At seventeen, Kristen was two years younger than Liza had been when she'd faced the same problem. It was almost as chilling. "Is she certain? Has she been tested?"

"Oh, yes. She'd taken a home pregnancy test before she told me. I simply couldn't believe it, so I had her take another right in front of me. They were both positive." Edith closed her eyes and shook her head. "After all the talks we've had about sex and about using protection, about diseases."

All the talking in the world sometimes isn't enough, Liza was well aware. "Did she tell you who the father is?"

On a shuddering breath, Edith nodded. "The boy she's been seeing for some time, Jim Rivers. You remember, I told you a while back that they were dating and I wasn't too pleased." She sniffled into her tissue. "Turns out I was right. That boy seduced my baby."

A bit dramatic, Liza thought, and a seduction that had

yet to be proven. She'd met Kristen and had found her to be very attractive and amazingly self-confident for someone so young. Recalling her own situation, she knew there'd been no seduction, just two very willing people, each equally responsible. That could very well be the case here.

However, she couldn't help wondering if Jim Rivers would run back to school, leaving Kristen all alone to cope. Would history repeat itself from brother to brother?

"Are you sure Jim's the only boy Kristen's been seeing?" Liza asked, her sense of fairness demanding she give Sam's brother the benefit of the doubt.

"Oh, absolutely." Edith was shocked to be asked. "My daughter may have given herself to this one boy, but she's not a tramp."

"I wasn't suggesting that, Edith, but you have to be very sure if you're going to make accusations. Has Kristen told Jim yet?"

"No, but I'm very sure he's the father," Edith stated emphatically. "My daughter doesn't lie to me."

Except about her sex life. There were ways to establish paternity, the most reliable being DNA testing, but Liza thought it best to wait to see what Jim Rivers would say when confronted.

"I don't know what to do, Liza," Edith groaned. "Now that that boy's brother's back and everyone says he's got lots of money, is Sam Rivers going to use his clout so Jim will walk away from my Kristen?"

Not if Jim proves to be the father. Not if I have anything to say about this. "I'm sure Sam will persuade Jim to do the right thing if the boy's reluctant. You need to do several things here, Edith. Kristen needs to go in and be tested for AIDS." She watched her secretary's eyes widen in shock behind her glasses. "Just a precaution, but you know what unprotected sex can lead to today, and pregnancy isn't the worst of it.''

Edith had paled, but she nodded. "You're right, of course. I'll do that today."

"You also need to find out just what Kristen wants. I mean, is she in love with Jim? Is she thinking marriage here, at seventeen?''

"Well, what else? I'm certainly not going to raise that child. I've done all the child rearing I intend to. And Kristen can't do it on her own, not as young as she is." Again, Edith sniffled. "She's not like you, educated and from a family with a business background, and all.''

A monied family was what she meant, Liza thought, and couldn't blame the woman. Children did cost money. "I understand. Of course, I'm not sure how equipped Jim Rivers is to support a wife and baby. He can't be more than nineteen or twenty. He'd have to quit college and—"

"Let that rich brother of his help out. Kristen didn't get pregnant alone, that I know."

Apparently this was getting nowhere. "Why don't you take the morning off and go with Kristen for her tests? Afterward perhaps you and Kristen can set up a meeting to talk with Jim about this. If there's anything I can do…''

"There is. I hate to ask, but you know the family, Liza. Could you sort of run interference here? Would you mention this to the older brother and ask him to talk to Jim? It would be so much better coming from you. You must think me a coward, but I don't honestly think Sam Rivers will listen to me.''

"I believe Sam would, but I'll call him for you, if you like." Liza stood. "Take your time and let me know how things go." Feeling the happy mood she'd walked in with dissipate, Liza sat down at her desk and picked up her phone. She was frankly curious herself how Sam would handle the situation.

Seated at his desk in the site trailer, Sam leaned back in his chair, listening to Liza on the phone. He'd been pleased to hear her voice until he'd learned the reason for her call.

"So that's the situation," Liza stated. "Do you know anything about Jim's relationship with Kristen Hanks?"

"This is the first I've heard her name. But then, I haven't been around until recently." And even after he'd returned, he hadn't really discussed Jim's friends with him. Perhaps he should have. "How long did you say your secretary claims they've been dating?" Seventeen. Jailbait. He fervently hoped Jim wasn't the father. This could be serious.

Claims? "She doesn't claim, she *knows* they've been seeing each other, since your brother blew off his last semester and came home."

He heard the hint of accusation in her voice and wondered why Liza was so testy. "Exclusively? Kristen dates no one else?"

"So Edith *claims.*" She'd expected him to be somewhat defensive. But she also expected Sam to be fair. "Can you help with this?"

Sam let out a frustrated sigh. He certainly didn't need a new problem this morning. The site had been cleaned up by the men yesterday, and most of the storm damage repaired, but the two days off had put them behind schedule, and he had a ton of work to do. "I'll get Jim in here and ask him about Kristen." Even if Jim was the father, surely he wasn't the first boy to find himself in this situation. Why was Liza so cranked up?

"Let me know what you find out. I expect your brother to do the right thing by this girl, Sam."

Frowning, he stood. "So do I, Liza. I'll get back to you."

Damn, but she was a volatile woman. It took him but a few minutes to raise Jeff on his cell phone and ask him to send Jim to the trailer. Sam was standing looking out the window, his mood thoughtful, when Jim walked in carrying his hard hat.

"You wanted to see me?"

Sam turned and indicated the chair. "Yeah. Have a seat. Do you know Kristen Hanks?"

Jim slumped into the chair, wiping his damp forehead with a red bandana. "Yeah, sure. We've dated a couple of times. Why?"

Carefully watching Jim's face, Sam tried to read his expression. "I just found out she's pregnant, and she says you're the father."

Jim almost rose up out of the chair. "What? Well, she's dead wrong."

Sam leaned against the counter. "You've had sex with her?"

"Yeah, sure, me and half the guys in town. But I *always* use protection. I may have screwed up my grades, but I'm not stupid. I swear, that kid *can't* be mine. There's a whole string of guys I know who've been with Kristen."

Sam was the first to admit he didn't know his brother well. But he felt he was a fair judge of people. He studied Jim a long moment. "You'd swear that, even willingly submit to a blood test?"

"Damn right I would." Jim's young face was earnest and very adamant. More than Kristen's baby was at stake here. He badly wanted his brother to believe him.

Finally, Sam nodded. "All right. I'll let you know if a blood test will be necessary."

Slowly, Jim got up. "Do you believe me?"

"Yes, I do."

Relief had Jim's shoulders relaxing. "Thanks. That means a lot to me."

Watching his brother leave, Sam found himself frowning. He did believe Jim. But would Liza? Probably not, if he were to judge by the tone of their last conversation. He'd only met Edith Hanks briefly that one day and wondered how close Liza was to her secretary to be so obviously upset by this whole thing.

He sat for a few minutes, wondering how best to approach Liza, then picked up the phone. She answered her own line after several rings and sounded like she was distracted. "Hi. I'm calling back on that matter we discussed earlier."

How businesslike he was, Liza thought. So calm and collected. "Yes, how'd it go?"

"Jim says he's not the father."

"Why am I not surprised?"

It was Sam's turn to get annoyed, and he didn't bother to hide it. "Do you know my brother at all?"

"Not personally. I know he's had a recent DUI, that he dropped out of college and that he runs around town at all hours."

Sam's grip on the phone tightened. "I guess you've been listening to our illustrious sheriff. Since you've made up your mind that Jim's guilty, I see no point in defending him to you. Funny, I remember you as being less judgmental and having more of an open mind, someone willing to hear both sides."

Chagrined, Liza sighed. She was taking this too seriously, her own past situation coloring her responses. "You're right. I'm sorry. Tell me what Jim said."

He waited a moment, then decided there was no point in being as stubborn as she. "He said that it's a pretty well-known fact that Kristen has been with *several* young men, something her mother may not be aware of.''

Liza had wondered about that, but Edith had been so sure her daughter was anything but promiscuous. The other thing that bothered Liza was that Edith seemed hell-bent on these two kids getting married. Even if Jim proved to be the father, would marriage at such a young age be best for them, or the baby? ''Her mother claims that Kristen's only been with Jim. Yes, yes, I know. There's that word *claims* again.''

''Yeah, it works both ways.''

''Listen, I'm on my way to the hospital. Edith is there with Kristen, and she just called, asking me to join them. They've run into some sort of problem in arranging the DNA test. Will Jim come in and be tested?''

''Yes, of course. Jim will do the right thing. Despite what you may have heard from Ed Hayes, Jim's a good kid.''

''Maybe so, but my experience has been that the Rivers men aren't exactly reliable. I'll talk with you later.'' Liza hung up and dashed out the door.

Staring at the silent phone still in his hand, Sam swore. Now what in hell did she mean by the last crack?

Dr. Douglas Bremer, chief of obstetrics at Port Henry General, was a short, portly man with thick hair dyed an awesome shade of black. Seated in a secluded alcove, he adjusted his rimless glasses as he shook his head. ''Mrs. Hanks, I told you, before you called Liza Courtland over, that I will not risk the life of the fetus by doing a totally unnecessary DNA test at this time. You will have to wait until the child is born.''

Seated alongside Liza in a matching green plastic chair, Edith twisted her hands nervously. ''Liza...I thought, you being on the hospital board and all, that you could persuade Dr. Bremer to bend the rules this time.''

"Edith," Liza said softly, "we can't endanger the life of the baby. You wouldn't want that, would you?" She glanced over at Kristen, sitting on the couch against the wall, and saw her sullen expression suddenly change to one of relief. Was it the procedure the girl had been worried about, or something else?

"But then, how can we establish paternity? The baby's not due till after the first of the year. Jim will be back in college by then. We might not be able to get him to return. Or that brother of his will send him away to some remote school where we'll never find him." Edith's lower lip trembled noticeably as she remembered a confident Sam Rivers arriving at Liza's office that first morning.

"Now, that's not going to happen. Wherever Jim is when the baby's born, we'll get a blood sample from him."

"Yes, Mrs. Hanks, that's definitely the route to take," Dr. Bremer added. He rose, checking his watch. "All in good time, my dear. I have to make rounds, so please excuse me. Young lady, you follow the instructions I gave you. Liza, good to see you again." He hurried off, white coattails flapping.

"This isn't good, Liza," Edith went on. "What about the wedding? How can we force Jim Rivers to get married when we can't prove he's the father? By the time that happens, the baby will already be here and...and what will people think?" Pulling out another tissue, Edith's tears began again.

"Edith, if there's one thing I've learned in this town it's that people will think what they want, no matter what we do. Or don't do. Let them. The important thing now is that Kristen has a healthy baby." She swung toward the young girl. "Did you already have the AIDS test?"

Kristen's huge blue eyes got bigger. "Yes, but they won't have the results for a couple of weeks. You don't think that...I mean, I can't have that, can I?"

So young, Liza thought. And so stupid to think she was invincible. "Let's hope not, but we need to know for sure." She leaned closer, lowering her voice. "Kristen, is there any chance at all that you've been intimate with anyone other than Jim Rivers?"

Kristen's eyes slid to her mother, then very quickly back to Liza. "He denied being with me, didn't he? I knew it. You don't believe him, do you? I don't care what he says. He's the one."

She was pretty enough, Liza thought, slender with long, dark hair and lovely skin. But she had a pouty mouth and wore far too much makeup. Liza well remembered being in the same boat, and she'd been petrified out of her mind. Kristen seemed more defiant than frightened, which worried Liza. "He doesn't deny being with you, but he maintains that he's not the father."

Suddenly Edith jumped up, angry now. "Well, we'll just prove him wrong, won't we, Kristen? Then we'll see what tune he sings. Come on, I've got to drive you home so I can get back to work. Thanks for meeting us here, Liza, and for trying. These doctors are so rigid and unbending."

Liza watched them walk toward the elevators, wondering why neither seemed concerned for the safety of the baby. She remembered how fearful she'd been during her pregnancy, so afraid she would inadvertently harm her child. Perhaps Edith was just too upset and Kristen too young to realize the enormity of the situation yet.

They would learn, all too soon.

Just as she rose, she spotted Ed Hayes sauntering over to chat with Edith at the elevators. He was the last person she wanted to see today. Turning on her heel, she headed in the opposite direction.

The men were catching up, Sam was pleased to note. The Oakview project was once more back on track time-wise. It had taken them a full week after the storm, but there was noticeable progress. The first model was being carpeted and would soon be ready for the Realtor, the second was framed in and the third had the cement base drying. The streets were going in next week. He and the men had put in back-breaking hours, but things were moving along nicely, he thought as he slipped off his work boots.

It was late, about nine, the men long gone. He'd finished up some paperwork, then eaten the sandwich he'd bought earlier for lunch and hadn't had time to get to. It went down real well with a cold beer. He simply didn't feel like driving to Woods Lane, so he'd called his mother and told her he was spending the night in the trailer.

Sam stretched out on the wide bunk, glad that he'd had a bathroom with shower added to his customized trailer office, as well as a closet for a change of clothes for nights like this. Tomorrow morning maybe he'd take a couple of hours off and drive to Sandusky to talk with Mike Ruggero, yet another friend of Joe's. It was a long shot, but maybe Mike could tell him something that would help in his investigation.

His Explorer was repaired and back, parked right outside the trailer. The cyclone gate was locked, for all the good that would do someone wanting to get in. But there'd been no further incident since the brake line damage. Still, Sam wasn't about to drop his guard. Someone wanted him to stop looking for his father, he was certain. That someone was lying low just now, but Sam had a feeling he'd show up again.

Raising his arms, he planted his hands under his head and stared up at the shadowy ceiling. He'd left on only the four small floor guide lights. He wished that Liza was here, curled up against him.

He hadn't seen her since before their phone conversation about Jim and Kristen Hanks. They'd talked a couple of times, mostly about the project. He'd asked about Beth, and Liza had confessed that the little girl was hoping he'd come by. Sam fully intended to, but he'd decided to give Liza some cooling-off time. He'd spent more than one restless hour trying to figure out why she'd gotten so defensive with him about the Hanks kid.

Was it just her maternal instincts on overtime, projecting how she'd feel if a teenage Beth were in that situation? Had that crack about the Rivers men being unreliable been aimed at him, because he'd left her eight years ago without giving her a reason? She didn't know Jim, so she couldn't have been referring to his brother.

A hard woman to figure, but then he supposed he wasn't all that simple himself. Still, he missed her. So much so that he swung his legs from the bed and reached to pick up the phone. She answered on the first ring. "Hi," he said, his voice low.

Taken aback because she hadn't been expecting his call, not at home nor at this hour, Liza sounded hesitant. "Hi, yourself."

"I was lying here missing you, and I thought I'd call and tell you so."

Didn't he always know just the thing to say that would get to her? "Are you in bed?" she asked. And her mind conjured up the night they'd spent together, the hooded look of those dark blue eyes as he'd studied her face, the scent and feel of him. Liza swallowed around a suddenly thick throat.

"Not exactly. I'm sitting on the edge of the trailer bunk thinking about you. It's dark and windy out there, and I wish you were here."

She set down the glue applicator she'd been using and leaned back in the kitchen chair. "Why are you still there?"

"Too lazy to drive back to Mom's. I decided to spend the night. I don't suppose I could coax you out?"

"Mmm, I'm afraid not. Beth's almost asleep."

"Your mom would watch her," he persuaded.

He was temptation personified, but she decided to pass. Things had been a little strained between them since the incident with Edith's daughter. She wasn't exactly angry at Sam. Perhaps she was angry at herself. "How about a rain check?"

"Sure, anytime. What'd I catch you doing?"

Liza gazed at the white-and-gold angel that she'd brought home from her office, at the two perfect pieces she'd been trying to glue back together. She wasn't sure why, but somehow she needed to know if she could make it whole again. "Oh, just working on an old project."

"Mending? You mentioned you like to sew."

"Something like mending. Do you do this often, spend the night in the trailer?" She thought the whole idea a bit spooky, especially alone. "Are you sure that's wise after someone messed with your brakes?"

"The trailer's solid and locked up tight. I test my brakes very carefully these days before starting out."

"They might think of some other way to hurt you."

"Hey, let's not get paranoid. Life's a risk, you know. Are you all right?"

Liza sighed. Was she? "I suppose."

He paused for just a heartbeat. "Liza, are *we* all right?"

She took her time answering. "I don't know, Sam. You tell me."

"I have no quarrel with you. Can we get together maybe tomorrow, talk some?"

Talk. What about? Their daughter, the one in the next room who'd been asking daily why Sam hadn't come around? She didn't like the way things were between them. But she didn't know how to mend them, either. "Yes, why don't we try?"

"I'll call you in the morning. Good night, Liza."

"Good night, Sam." Slowly she replaced the receiver and struggled with a rush of longing so strong as to be physical.

"Mommy," came a sleepy voice from the doorway, "was that Sam? Didn't he want to talk to me?"

There it was again, that reaching out. "He loves talking with you, sweetheart, but it's past your bedtime." She smiled at her daughter looking adorably rumpled in a Winnie the Pooh nightie, autographs all over her walking cast. "Can't sleep?"

"Uh-uh." Beth limped over to the table to check out the angel drying on newspaper. "What's that? I've never seen it before."

Liza's sigh was audible. "A broken angel, a gift someone gave me long ago. I'm trying to mend it, but I'm not sure I can."

Beth's trusting young face turned up to look at her. "You'll fix it, Mommy. You're good at fixing things."

"Some things, baby. But not everything can be fixed." Taking her hand, Liza led her daughter back to bed.

The night wind swirled around outside the trailer, drifting in through the one small window left open above the bed. It carried the misty flavor of the bay and a hint of dust from the work site being cleared. And there was the unmistakable smell of smoke, dark and pungent.

Sam stirred in his sleep, restless as usual. Eyes closed, he punched the pillow then tried to resettle. Drawing in a deep breath, he squirmed to get more comfortable.

Suddenly his eyes popped open as his brain registered what his nose had smelled. Smoke!

His feet hit the floor and his hands reached for his jeans. He saw wispy trails of black smoke whirling around the ceiling up near the window he'd left open, the acrid scent spreading. Hurriedly, he yanked on his boots, then grabbed his shirt.

Sam pulled open the trailer door and stepped out. What he saw had him swearing ripely. Flames shot high from the completed model as well as the frame of the second one. The dry wood had undoubtedly caught immediately, and the wind had busily spread the fire quickly. The sound of breaking glass and scorched lumber falling filled the air. Then he saw something that had his blood running cold.

Fingers of flame were dancing along a definite path heading for the trailer. Only one thing could make fire run uphill like that: gasoline had been poured in a direct line to the target. He could smell it, almost taste it.

Like a mad man, he ran to the water truck parked several yards over and yanked free the hose line. Racing against time, his eye on that crackling dance of fire moving closer and closer to the trailer, he got the rig going and rushed over.

Water spurted furiously, diluting the gasoline and dousing the fire. Struggling with the heavy hose used for dust control, he drenched the line back to its source about a hundred yards over the rocky incline. The sound of more wood splintering and falling had him looking up in time to see a part of the roof of their model home slam down onto the ground as the support beams gave way.

Pure white rage had Sam clenching his teeth as he cut off the hose and ran toward the trailer to call the fire department. It was then that he heard the sirens in the distance, coming closer. Apparently someone else had seen the blaze and phoned it in. But until they arrived, he'd do what he could.

Quickly he reattached the hose to the water truck, then climbed in and drove it closer to the model, yet back out of harm's way. Scrambling out, he grabbed the hose again, released the lock and aimed the flow at the back of the building. Sam knew he was too late to save the house, but at least he could keep the fire from spreading.

As he fought to contain the blaze, his angry thoughts had him grinding his teeth. Who had deliberately done this? And why?

Liza lay in her bed, feeling warm and restless. She'd read for a while, then finally turned out the light. But still, sleep wouldn't come. Now she threw back the covers and got up. Some nights, there was no use struggling.

In bare feet, she padded over to check on Beth who was sound asleep. Liza adjusted the covers over her sleeping child, then walked to her small kitchen and poured herself a glass of milk. Maybe the age-old remedy would work.

Glass in hand, she strolled to the double doors leading out to her porch. She unlocked one and stepped out. It was then that she heard the sirens screaming their frightening song off in the distance. It sounded as if there were several. Not ambulances, then, but probably fire trucks. Frowning, she walked to the far end, turned the corner and gasped out loud.

The Courtland Mansion was sitting on the highest hill in

Port Henry, offering a panoramic view from the wrap-around porch. Above the treetops, Liza saw flames whirling skyward and a dark, billowing cloud of smoke perfectly outlined in a moonlit sky. Squinting, she tried to determine the location of the fire. East of the center of town would be…oh, God!

She almost dropped the glass of milk. The fire had to be at Oakview Estates. Sam was spending the night in the site trailer. Rushing back inside, Liza snapped on the light and picked up the phone. With shaky fingers, she dialed the trailer. Her heart beat wildly as she counted six, seven, eight rings.

Where was he? Racing back to her bedroom, Liza knew what she had to do. Quickly she dressed and hurried to wake her mother and ask her to come stay with Beth so her daughter wouldn't be frightened if she awoke and found no one there.

Then she ran down the stairs and climbed behind the wheel of her BMW, only one thought on her mind. Sam. Sam had to be all right. Dear God, he just had to be.

Chapter Ten

Clement C. Brown had been the fire chief in Port Henry since the town had been a village over thirty years ago, when it had only a volunteer fire department. Now in his mid-sixties, he was an imposing figure, six feet tall and well over two hundred pounds with a full head of white hair and a long, curling mustache to match. Despite his years, he always went along on the big ones.

And, by Port Henry's standards, a fire that devoured two houses in various forms of completion, several stacks of new lumber and caused considerable damage to an important building site was a biggie.

Chewing on his unlit cigar, Chief Brown stomped his boots through a stream of water and made his way over to the trailer where Sam Rivers was sitting on the front stoop staring at the ruins of his model homes. "The boys are about through, Sam," the chief said, stopping in front of him. "Everything's soaked enough so you shouldn't get any flare-ups, even with this damn wind still blowing. We're lucky we contained it before it spread to the homes beyond that hill.''

Wearily Sam got to his feet. "You're right. Thanks, Chief.''

"I radioed for the sheriff on my way over. Hayes said he was at a break-in on the west side. He should be along any minute.'' Brown tossed away his cigar, took a white handkerchief from his pocket and wiped his sweaty face.

Sam's mouth was a thin, angry line. "Don't bet on it. Hayes and I aren't exactly best friends.''

The sound of a car coming through the gate had Sam turning, thinking the sheriff had finally made it after all, but it was Liza's BMW that slowed to a stop by the trailer door. Almost before she cut the engine, she was out and rushing over.

Eyes green and worried ignored the older man as she hurried over. Her thudding heart caused her words to tremble. "Are you all right? I heard the sirens and saw the flames from my porch. What happened?''

"Arson," Chief Brown answered. "Hello, Miz Courtland.''

Sam had forgotten that everyone in town knew Liza and her family. He wished that the chief hadn't been so blunt as he watched Liza's face turn pale in the trailer's spotlight.

"Arson?'' Liza wondered why that shocked her, considering the tampering done on Sam's vehicle a week ago. "Are you sure?''

Brown pointed to the blackened trail coming up over the rise and stopping perhaps six feet from the corner of the trailer. "See that? Hell, you can still smell the fumes. My guess is someone tossed an open can of gas in through the downstairs window of the model, then threw in a match. That's all he had to do over there, 'cause fire spreads like crazy in a wind. Afterward he came over this way and dribbled some more from the trailer to the other side of that rocky hill, then lit it from over there. That way, he had enough time to get the hell out of here before it got too bad."

"Oh, my God," Liza said, her voice a whisper.

Brown turned back to Sam. "I suppose it's lucky you were here in a way 'cause you managed to save the trailer. But if you hadn't awakened, you'd be a goner. Looks like someone's trying to send you a message, son. Doesn't seem like they want you building these houses. You got any enemies around here?"

"It looks that way." Sam rubbed a sooty hand along his beard, his expression fiercely angry.

Liza felt a shiver race up her spine despite the lingering heat from the fire. She felt impotent, angry, frightened. Who was doing this and why? Her eyes moved back to Sam.

He stood tall and straight, his eyes mere slits as he took in the devastation. His damp shirt hung open, his jeans were wet, his boots muddy, his face streaked with soot. But his shoulders were back and his head was held high, like a warrior planning the rebuttal attack. She knew deep inside that he wasn't going to give up in defeat and leave, the way the arsonist undoubtedly intended. No, not Sam Rivers.

Silently she stepped closer to him, slipping her hand into his. She was relieved when, after a moment, he returned the pressure of her fingers, as if accepting her support that they were in this together. And they were in it for the long haul.

"Chief Brown," she said, setting her emotions aside, "we'll need your report on this. I've got insurance on this property and they'll want that."

"Sure thing. Have it to you tomorrow. I've got to report

this to the arson investigation division. They'll likely send a man out early morning.''

Liza glanced around, noticing that the fire truck was packed up and the men climbing on board, ready to pull away. But one person was conspicuous by his absence. ''Where's the sheriff? Did anyone call him?''

Sam let out a heavy breath. ''Yes, some time ago. You know Hayes. Once he heard my place was on fire, he probably decided the whole thing could wait until tomorrow.''

''Now, Sam,'' Liza said quietly, even as she wondered if he might not be right.

''I may have to call him again,'' the chief said, frowning. ''He should be here to rope off the crime scene.''

''You can use the phone in the trailer,'' Sam offered. But as he finished, a car came through the gate. He recognized it as Jeff's and waited for the young job boss to get out.

''Man, what a mess!'' Hands on his hips, Jeff looked around. ''What happened?''

''I'll call Hayes from my car,'' the chief said as he waved at his engine departing through the gate. ''I'll be in touch, Miz Courtland.'' Walking somewhat stiffly, he made his way to his car parked near the gate.

''No use in you hanging around, Liza,'' Sam told her as Jeff walked around a puddle toward the remains of the model house he'd worked so hard on. ''We can talk tomorrow.''

''Are you going home?'' she asked.

He rubbed along the back of his neck. ''No, I'm staying right here tonight. I'm taking no more chances. We're going to clean this up and rebuild, but I'm putting a man on guard duty night and day. That bastard's not putting us out of business.''

She agreed with everything he said, except the first part.

"Have Jeff stay tonight. You're wiped out." She stepped closer, touched her palm to his face. "Please?"

"I'll be fine. I'll call you in the morning."

Stepping back, she nodded. "All right, if you're staying, so am I. I'm too revved up to sleep, anyhow."

"Now listen…"

"No. You listen. This is my investment, too." And she didn't necessarily mean the project. She waved a hand toward Jeff gingerly stepping around debris, checking out the damage. "You go talk to Jeff. I'll be inside." She walked up the stairs, put her hand on the doorknob.

"Damn stubborn woman." Grumbling, Sam turned away.

"Damn bossy man." Liza went inside.

She'd called and updated her mother, put on a pot of coffee and made up the bed with sheets she found in a drawer beneath the bunk by the time he returned. Apparently when he stayed overnight in the trailer, he didn't bother with bedding. Liza heard Jeff drive off as Sam stepped inside.

"Did Ed finally show?" She hadn't heard his car.

"Nope. Jeff talked to him on his remote. Seems he's tied up with a break-in at a hardware store on the west side. Since the blaze is out, he said he'd be over in the morning." He toed his boots off, thinking Hayes had behaved just as he'd predicted. The good sheriff was probably vastly disappointed Sam hadn't gone up in flames along with the houses.

Liza didn't want to think about Hayes tonight. She went to Sam, thinking to soothe, to comfort him after the shock, the disappointment. "I'll bet you're beat."

"Not really." He'd asked her to come to him earlier when they'd talked on the phone. He'd been in a loving, mellow mood then. But the fire had changed that, changed him. Without taking his eyes from her, he turned the lock on the door.

His blood thundered through his veins, perhaps fueled by the knowledge that yet again, he'd come too damn close to death's doorway. Needs hammered at him, making him hungry, ravenous. His eyes darkened as he reached for her, pulled her hard up against his chest. "Maybe you should have gone home. Maybe I scare you."

There was an intense look about him, a wild predatory gleam she hadn't seen before. She'd read that harrowing escapes from danger, near misses, often sent men back to elemental basics. It affected women, too. "No, I made the right decision. And you don't scare me."

Perhaps to prove her wrong or perhaps because he couldn't wait another second, he crushed her mouth with his, thrusting his tongue inside, demanding a response as his arms wound around her.

Liza tasted heat and need and frustration as his hands kneaded her flesh through the cotton blouse she'd hastily put on. He tugged the thin material free of her waistband and burrowed beneath. His fingers were callused, rough, exploring naked skin, his touch, as always, causing her knees to buckle.

Her head was spinning with dazed pleasure as her body movements urged him on. She moaned softly, overcome by the need to get closer to him, and closer still.

"I want you," he whispered against her lips, "like I've never wanted another woman." Unwilling to break the kiss, he walked her backward toward the bed.

"I want you more. Oh, God, Sam, when I saw the fire, I thought I'd lost you again." She clung to him, her nails digging into his back. "I can't bear the thought of losing you."

"You never will."

Nearly in a frenzy, she shoved his open shirt over his shoulders and dropped it to the floor.

Good sense prevailed for an instant. "I'm all dirty and…"

"I don't care." She ran her hands over his chest, her fingers tunneling into the dark hair that covered the firm muscles. Then her hands arrowed down to tug at his belt.

Breathing hard, Sam stopped walking when he felt the backs of her legs touch the edge of the bunk. His fingers fumbled with the blouse's tiny buttons, but he was too impatient. With one swift yank, he ripped it open. Buttons flew every which way as her breasts were revealed to his eager eyes.

"You're not wearing a bra."

"I was in a hurry to get here." And then she felt his hands cover her sensitive flesh. On a soft sigh, she let her head fall back as he dipped his head to sample, to taste. With unfamiliar abandon, she arched against his mouth, inviting him to have his fill. In seconds she was flying, desire raw and primitive making her ache, making her groan. "Now, Sam. *Now!*"

Her passionate demand had him half-crazy. They tumbled onto the wide bunk bed, still wearing too many clothes, struggling to free each other of every reluctant item. His mouth returned to hers, needing the contact as he bucked and strained to be skin to skin with her. Everywhere he touched seemed on fire. He sucked in air, breathing in the womanly scent of her, letting it drive him to the edge.

She responded with such fervor, such wholehearted participation, that she took his breath away. Her hands thrust into his hair, then skimmed down his rib cage only to wiggle between them and move lower. He wondered fleetingly how she knew just how to touch, how to make him feel so much. Then he gave himself up to the sensual pleasure of her mouth relearning him.

Liza's body was as hot as the fire she'd witnessed tonight. She searched for words to say, to explain how he moved her, how he was the only one who could; yet no words seemed right. So instead, she spoke to him with her mouth, with her fingertips, with the gift of herself. She knew she'd never wanted like this, never needed anyone so thoroughly, never loved another soul so deeply.

Finally Sam pushed her onto her back and leaned down to look at her lovely face. Her hands guided him inside her and he watched her eyes grow cloudy as he filled her. The night had been building toward this from the moment he'd seen her drive up. He'd tried to send her home, but knew in his heart he never wanted her to leave.

Liza felt the ache building and building. Her hands circled his back as she tried to keep her gaze on his. He pushed her higher, harder until there was nowhere else to go. At last she called out his name just before he sent her into a shuddering climax. Moments later she felt the peak subside, but he moved just so and sent her spiraling upward again.

In the dim lamplight, he studied her flushed face, the sheen on her satiny skin, the stunned surprise in her eyes. Her golden hair was fanned out on the coarse white sheet of the bunk. The love he'd always felt for her threatened to overflow his heart. Knowing he could never get enough of this one woman, he began to move again.

In seconds she was racing like a runaway freight train, arching upward just enough to send him catapulting off the edge. Clinging to each other, hot, damp and reaching, they flew together and met in a place only the two of them had ever known.

* * *

Standing outside the locked cyclone fence, Sheriff Ed Hayes took note of the Explorer and BMW parked side by side alongside the trailer. Then he looked at the window and saw the light go off. He stared a moment longer before slowly turning and walking back to his vehicle.

Sam drove along Highway 6, heading back to Port Henry, annoyed that he'd wasted an entire morning. He'd driven to Sandusky to talk with Mike Ruggero, Joe's old friend, hoping the older man could shed some light on his father's disappearance. Retired and widowed, Mike had moved to his daughter's home two years ago, but he'd been very willing to talk with Sam. As long as Sam kept buying drinks.

Mike had insisted they meet at the neighborhood bar around the corner from his daughter's house. With shaky hands, the old man had tossed back several straight shots while reminiscing about Joe Rivers. However, after two hours, Sam still had learned nothing new.

Irritated, he put on his signal light and eased over into the left lane to pass a Greyhound bus. He could have been back at the construction site helping with the cleanup work. But he'd thought it more important to try to trace down the person who had something to do with his father's disappearance, more than ever certain that the same man was the one causing all his current problems. The accident with the Explorer and the fire had both been deliberate acts not only meant to drive Sam out of Port Henry, but quite possibly meant to kill him as well.

Shifting back to the right lane, Sam mentally reviewed Mike's last words. No way would Joe have voluntarily left town, his old friend had stated emphatically. He didn't have the money or the guts, Mike felt. Sam agreed. Like most men who took their frustrations out on their hapless wives and children, deep down inside Joe had been a coward. Unable to adjust to life's problems, he'd blamed the world in general and his family in particular for his bad luck. But when his grown-up son had threatened him, he'd backed off immediately.

If that were true, it had to mean someone had gotten to him. For the life of him, Sam couldn't think why. Robbery certainly couldn't have been a motive, for Joe rarely had more than loose change on him, and he'd disappeared the night before payday. While it's true he was a quarrelsome individual, what kind of fool would have argued with a drunk walking home? And even so, why kill the guy? It made no sense.

If Joe had gotten hit accidentally by a car as he'd walked along the side of the road, might the driver have panicked and maybe gotten out and buried the body? But why go to all that trouble when they could just as easily have driven off? No scenario he could come up with made sense. No one Sam knew had a serious quarrel with his father back then, just general annoyances often lodged against a chronic drunk. Joe inspired annoyance and pity more than hatred.

Exiting off the highway to the road leading into town, Sam felt at a total loss to explain any of it. He probably should have stayed and helped his work crew rather than make this trip today, but he couldn't abandon his search for information. Someone had to know something, and until he found some answers, he had a feeling the incidents would continue.

And maybe next time he wouldn't be lucky enough to escape with his life.

He'd also wanted to leave today before Hayes arrived. He'd made sure that Liza left before dawn, but he didn't want to tangle with the sheriff just now, either. He'd asked Jeff the night before to come in early, and as soon as he had, Sam had taken off. It was nearly noon now, and he hoped that Ed would have taken his perfunctory stroll around the crime scene and walked away saying he'd look into the matter. Sure he would.

Sam had left instructions with Jeff to inform the men that nothing was to be touched until the insurance examiner had stopped by and the arson investigator had cleared the scene. Liza had said she would contact her insurance company first thing. With the clout of the Courtland name, he was sure the guy had been there and gone by now. It would take several days probably before the guys would be loading debris on trucks to haul away, salvaging what they could and making preparations to rebuild. He'd have to call Dirk in Akron and let him know about the latest interruption.

Perhaps he should have let his partner come to Port Henry, while he stayed away from this town that had never really hung out the welcome mat to him. But then he wouldn't have had the chance to pick things up with Liza again, or to meet Beth. Unbidden, a smile formed as he thought of the blond little girl. The last time he'd talked with Beth on the phone, she'd reminded him that she was waiting to beat him at checkers. He found himself looking forward to the match simply to watch her excited face as she played. So much like her mother.

Just the thought of Liza brought about a change in his breathing. If ever a man had met his match, he had with Liza Courtland. They'd made love on that three-quarter bunk bed so often last night that he'd scarcely had the energy to get up and shower. Nor had she. And she'd had to go home wearing one of his shirts after he'd ripped her blouse from her. He couldn't help wondering if she'd made it inside her apartment before her mother awakened and noticed.

Turning onto the road that led to Oakview Estates, Sam scrubbed a hand across his bearded face. He'd had several cups of coffee while Mike had been slamming back the booze, so you'd think he'd be wired. Instead, he felt like he could sleep a week. Probably the shock of the fire, the activity in bed last night and very little sleep. Sam grinned. It'd been worth it.

But the smile slipped as he spotted the sheriff's vehicle inside the fencing as he drove through Oakview's gate and stopped by the yellow crime scene tape. How was it that that so-called lawman was still here? Setting his teeth, he got out just as Ed came into sight from around the far side of the trailer. "So you finally decided to stop by," Sam said with barely concealed hostility. "About time. Too busy yesterday for a little case of arson?"

"I was here at seven this morning, but your foreman told me you'd taken off on an important errand." Ed removed his sunglasses slowly. "What exactly is more important than getting to the bottom of this?" He waved a beefy hand toward the ruined model home, the drenched stack of lumber, the blackened second frame.

"My errands are none of your business, Sheriff. And getting to the bottom of this fire is your job, not mine. I wonder what the people who elected you would say if they knew you don't bother to show up at a major crime scene until hours after the last spark is out. Nothing like looking at fresh clues, is there?"

Ed kept his reaction from showing. "I was busy last night. Your little problems aren't the only ones my department has to contend with, you know."

"Just do your job and then we'll judge how well your department does." Wanting to escape the sight of him, Sam walked up the steps and put his hand on the doorknob.

"Heard tell one of your men's got himself in a peck of trouble," Ed said, watching him closely.

Reaching for a remnant of patience, Sam swung back toward him. "Who would that be?"

"Why, your little brother, bigshot. Word around town is he's gotten a girl pregnant—sweet young thing under legal age. They say he's trying to wiggle out of papahood." Seeing that he had Sam's undivided attention, Ed allowed himself a sneer. "Not surprising. We've known all along that *all* the Rivers men are irresponsible."

Slowly Sam let go of the doorknob and curled both fists loosely at his side, wishing he could rip that uniform off the meaty sheriff and grind his fists into his fat face. How in hell had Hayes found out about Jim? "You'd better explain that last remark."

Ed narrowed his small eyes, enjoying himself immensely. "What's good for one brother is good for the other, eh?"

His face a mask of fury, Sam stepped down, stepped closer. "What exactly do you mean by that?"

"I see I managed to surprise you, hotshot. Thought you ought to know I've been to Ann Arbor to check up on your lady friend. Seems that Liza Courtland gave birth to a baby girl in an Ann Arbor hospital seven years ago, father listed as unknown. But we know who that baby girl's daddy is, don't we, Sammy? 'Cause that was six months *after* you left Port Henry. Do you by any chance know the name of a guy Liza was taking to her bed back in those days?"

Stunned, Sam just stared for several seconds. "You're lying."

"Hell if I am. Go check it out for yourself." Triumphant that his news has knocked Rivers off center, Ed laughed out loud. "Looks like our little Liza sure put one over on you, *Daddy.*"

Fists curled tightly, his face dark with rage, Sam took a step closer. "Get the hell out of here."

Ed moved back so quickly he nearly lost his footing. When he'd planned this little talk, he'd hoped Sam would throw a punch so he could arrest him for assaulting an officer. But the raw anger in the man's face at the moment told Hayes it would be suicidal to push just now.

Instead he turned toward his car. "Sure, I'll go. I know you have things to do." As he climbed behind the wheel, he let out a big victory laugh. Driving through the gate, he could see in his rearview mirror that Sam was still standing there immobilized by shock. At last he'd gotten the upper hand today. Sam would probably head right on over to Liza's and confront her. They'd have a big fight and Sam, with his fierce temper and hurt pride, would storm off. With no Liza and his project gone up in flames, he'd pack his bags and leave town.

It might take Liza a while to get over Sam, but she would. Ed would see to it. Chuckling, he drove toward his office, pleased with a good day's work.

It took Sam a full minute to be able to unclench his hands and go inside the trailer. Slumping into the nearest chair, he forced himself to calm down, to think rationally. His first instinct was to dismiss that clown's whole story, the second to pick up the phone and confront Liza so she could repudiate everything that insipid sheriff had said. Neither option seemed viable.

Swiveling the chair around, Sam braced his elbows on his desk and thrust both hands into his hair. Could Hayes be right?

Ed knew better than to make up something Sam could very easily check out for himself. He might be a clod, but he was a shrewd clod. Seven and a half years ago, six months after Sam had left Port Henry, Liza Courtland had given birth to a baby girl in Ann Arbor. He'd wondered ever since he'd heard the story about how she'd quit Ohio State so abruptly and moved to live with an aunt in Michigan. About why she'd walked away from the family she was so close to back then. About why she'd adopted a child at such a young age.

A child as blond as her mother and with eyes as blue as her father's.

Damn, but he should have seen it from the beginning. Look how quickly Beth had taken to him, a man who rarely paid attention to children, and he to her. He'd speculated that Beth was another man's child, but not his own. Yet it all added up.

Straightening, he frowned. But they'd always been so careful, always used protection. How could this have happened? Then again, nothing was foolproof except abstinence, and they hadn't abstained much during that long, hot summer.

As the shock wore off and acceptance moved in, anger took its place. Why hadn't Liza told him? How could she have a child without letting him know and… The letters, the ones he'd thrown away. Dear Lord, had she written him about her pregnancy, asked for his help, and he hadn't been there for her? That thought had him feeling like ten times the idiot.

From the beginning it had all been his fault. Five years older than teenage Liza, he should have been more careful about birth control. He should have gone to her before leaving, told her why he felt he had to go. He should have had the courage to read all of her letters. There was nowhere else to lay the blame but on his own shoulders.

But what about since his return? Was she planning never to tell him? Why? She'd wanted someone to love after he'd left, Liza had told him earlier. Wasn't she able to share that love with him, Beth's natural father? Just last night she'd said she'd been so afraid of losing him. Why hadn't she invited him into her life, into Beth's? So many questions needing answers. And only one person could give them to him.

He picked up the phone and dialed Liza's office. He hated storming around during business hours, but this couldn't wait. He wanted to tell her to wait there for him so they could talk.

"I'm afraid Ms. Courtland isn't in," Edith Hank's chilly voice said when Sam gave his name and asked for Liza.

Ah, yes, the mother of the girl who claimed Jim had gotten her pregnant. No wonder she was cool to him. "When will she be back?"

"Not until late. She's in Cleveland at a meeting."

Damn it, yes. Liza had told him yesterday that she was to leave early this morning for a meeting with a client. "What's late? What time, exactly, is she expected back?"

"Around eight this evening, I was told. She won't be coming to the office at all."

"Thanks." Sam hung up.

Eight hours. How was he going to make it through the rest of the day until then with all these questions churning in his brain? He jumped up and went outside. He'd have to do physical work so he wouldn't go stark, raving mad. It was the only answer.

Arriving at the Courtland Mansion and driving around back at eight-thirty, Sam saw that only Liza's car was in place. Of course, Elizabeth's could be in the garage. He parked and got out, brushing back his damp hair.

He'd worked like a wild man all day, then hurriedly showered and changed. He hadn't been able to put the situation out of his mind for more than a few minutes at a time. He'd sweated off some of his anger, though. Some, not all. But the burning questions remained.

Sam climbed the stairs like a man walking the last mile. He wanted to know, yet he dreaded knowing. His emotions were in a turmoil, his feelings suspended until he knew the truth. He knocked on the door and waited.

Liza snapped on the porch light before peering out around the blinds on the French door. Astonished pleasure registered on her face as she undid the lock. "What a nice surprise," she said, stepping back to invite him in.

But as he moved into the light, she got a good look at his face. Her heart fluttered. "What is it? What's wrong?"

"Liza, I asked you before, but you evaded my question. I need to know. What was in those letters I threw away?"

Chapter Eleven

"My letters?" Liza adjusted the folds of her robe more securely about herself, feeling the sudden need for its protection.

Sam closed the door and watched her turn aside, avoiding his eyes. "Yes. I get the feeling there was something important in them. What was it?"

Liza released a ragged sigh. Sometime, during the night she'd spent in his arms in the trailer, after the fire she'd feared might have taken him from her again, she'd decided she'd tell Sam about Beth. She felt he had a right to know, and she prayed he would understand. She'd been rehearsing, then discarding, several scenarios of how she would tell him. She wanted the moment to be just right. But not like this.

"What difference does it make after all these years?"

"Maybe a lot. I want to know."

She stood with her back to him, her arms wrapped

around herself in a defensive posture even she recognized. Gathering her courage, she turned and saw that his eyes were stormy and intense. "What makes you ask now?"

His patience, the little he had, had dribbled away over the long hours he'd waited to see her. "Humor me," he said through clenched teeth. "Tell me. What did you write?"

All her energy seeped from her as her shoulders sagged wearily. "I think you already know."

It took all of Sam's self-control to not grab her by the arms and shake her. "I want to hear it from you."

A wave of anger brought color to Liza's cheeks. "What right do you have coming in here after eight years and demanding answers from me?" Turning again, she walked to the couch and sat down in the far corner, struggling with her emotions.

Sam's temper rose to match hers as he marched over to her. "I believe I have every right!" he all but shouted.

"Lower your voice. Beth's asleep in the other room."

The anger he'd been nursing drained from him as he read the truth on her face. Slowly he sat down beside her. "I don't want to fight with you, Liza. I want some answers."

Blinking furiously, she looked at him. "How is it that it never once occurred to you that I might have been pregnant when you snuck out of town like a thief in the night? Eight long years and you never gave it a thought, never gave *me* a thought."

Sam let out a breath he'd scarcely been aware he'd been holding. Leaning forward, elbow on his knee, he bent his head into his hand and wrestled with an onslaught of emotions. It was one thing to hear the story from Hayes, to spend all day turning it over in his mind, and quite another to absorb the shock of reality. "Dear God, then it's true. I didn't know, didn't imagine."

He raised dark, troubled eyes to her face and saw the tears slowly falling like gentle rain. The quiet weeping was far more devastating than if she'd been sobbing. "I'm so sorry. I didn't know." He groped for words, to explain, to let her know. "We'd always used protection. How…?"

"How!" The one word was spoken harshly, defensively. "Sure we used protection, most of the time. But remember when we were out on the lake at the cottage in Dad's sailboat? You didn't have anything with you, so we… improvised. And another time when we were swimming and…" She waved a dismissive hand. "Why am I reminding you of this? Obviously you've forgotten that entire summer."

He grabbed her hand. "I've forgotten *nothing*. All those years I was gone, the memory of you and our summer together was all that I had to keep from going completely crazy." He released her abruptly. "Sure I remember the sailboat and swimming. And even once in the shower. I guess I thought that one time, maybe two, wouldn't matter. We were together three months and you never indicated anything."

"Because I didn't know until after you'd left. When I found out for sure, I got scared. You'd already been gone two weeks. There'd been no call, no letter. Finally I steeled myself and asked your mother for your address. I don't know what she must have thought, but she gave it to me without question." She remembered driving off from that terrible shack, looking back and seeing Ann Rivers watching from that rickety porch. Like now, she'd struggled with tears.

Liza didn't look at him as she groped for a tissue in the robe's pocket, then wiped her cheeks. "At first I didn't mention the pregnancy. I…I didn't know how you'd feel or if you were ever coming back. I didn't want to scare you away. But finally, one night in the dorm at Ohio State, I couldn't sleep I was so worried, so I wrote you a long letter telling you everything and asking for your help, then I mailed the letter before I could change my mind.''

"And I threw it away unopened.'' Sam couldn't recall ever feeling worse, not even when he'd left town and been suddenly so alone. He'd let down the one person he'd loved more than life itself. "If I could turn back the clock..."

"By Thanksgiving,'' she went on as if he hadn't spoken, needing, now that she'd begun to tell it all, to get it out as she never had before, "my clothes were getting tight, even though I could scarcely keep food down. My roommate guessed, but she was the only one who knew. I felt trapped—nineteen years old, pregnant, no money of my own and the man I'd thought loved me gone. I had no other choice but to tell my parents.''

She heard Sam suck in a deep breath, but she wasn't in the mood to be sympathetic. "Well,'' she said, sighing herself, "that's a scene I've never forgotten. My mother cried, of course, but it was my father's show. He demanded to know who the baby's father was and I refused to tell him. So he told me I was a little tramp just like my sister and ordered me out of the house.''

"Oh, God, Liza.'' Beyond risking rejection, Sam reached over and took her hand in his. She wasn't exactly receptive, but she didn't push him away, either. "I'm so damn sorry.''

"So am I, because he never spoke to me again, nor could I have stayed here knowing how he felt. Mom arranged to have me move in with my aunt Margaret in Ann Arbor. She'd never married and I was her favorite, thank God. She lived above this little florist shop she owned. I worked in it with her until Beth was born.''

She was aware of Sam swallowing hard, squirming on the seat, but the memories were too real, the pain too strong for her to respond to his. "I'd had to quit Ohio State, of course, but after I stopped nursing Beth, Aunt Margaret insisted I enroll at the University of Michigan not far from her shop while she watched Beth. She was wonderful. I don't know what I'd have done without her. She found an attorney and arranged a formal adoption so no one would be the wiser, so no one could ever take Beth from me."

And that's the information Hayes had somehow unearthed on his visit to Ann Arbor, undoubtedly by flashing his badge around. "Your mother and father never came around?" Having met Elizabeth, seeing her devotion to Beth, he could hardly imagine such a thing.

"Mother showed up one day when Beth was almost a year old. I knew she wasn't strong enough to stand up to Dad, so I told her the adoption story I planned to tell anyone who asked. She didn't ask any more questions. Then, when Beth was two, Dad had his first stroke and Mom called me. Cindy was long gone and probably wouldn't have been much help at any rate. Mom was alone and frightened. So I came home."

Sam had been listening hard and had some questions he wondered if she'd answer. "You said your father never spoke to you again?"

"When he was sent home from the hospital, Mom had to hire nurses to care for him, around the clock at first. He was paralyzed and couldn't speak." Liza's compassionate nature came to the fore. "Sometimes he'd look at me with tears in his eyes. I think he was sorry for the things he'd said to me, but we'll never know for sure. He'd sit in his wheelchair and watch Beth play, and at times I thought I caught him smiling. I think he died with a few regrets."

"And so, at twenty-two, you took over the running of Courtland Enterprises." His voice carried a hint of incredulity.

"What else could I have done? I hadn't even majored in business. However, Dad's right-hand man, Zeke Turner, was still alive back then and he taught me from the ground up. And I had Arnie West who's a godsend and still with me. Nothing like on-the-job training."

"About then was when you got engaged, if I remember my mother's letters correctly." Could he blame her? She'd been far too young to shoulder such responsibilities.

"Yes. I got so tired of handling everything alone. Matt's a nice guy. His father was CPA at Courtland and Matt came to work for us. I had all this *stuff* going on—Cindy popping up every little while with another mess to straighten out, Mother falling apart over Dad's illness, Dad looking worse daily, not seeing Beth enough, this huge corporation to run. I felt I needed some help, someone to work alongside me at home and at work." She paused to look up, look into his eyes. "And I hoped Matt could make me forget you. It didn't work."

For long seconds Sam gazed into the green depths of her eyes, thinking he could drown in them. "You've been through so much, and I'm responsible for most of the terrible things. I want badly to make it up to you."

That wasn't what she wanted to hear. "No, no. Let it go. All that's over and done with. Nothing can change the past."

"As usual, I'm saying this badly. Let me start over." Holding her hand, he cleared his throat and plunged in. "I've already told you why I felt it necessary to leave. Had I known about the baby, I'd have come back for you, and to hell with Hayes and what the town thought of me. But I can't rewrite the past, as you said. I have to admit that earlier today when I found out you hadn't told me I had a daughter, my first reaction was anger. Then I remembered the letters and realized it was my fault. I want to fix things, Liza.''

It appeared as if all he wanted was to ease his conscience. "I'm not asking you for anything."

"No, *I'm* asking *you*. Please, Liza, let me be a part of Beth's life.''

Cold fear ran down her spine, and she jerked her hand free. "No! Beth's mine. I gave birth to her, I'm the one who's always been there for her. You can't take her away from me.''

Puzzled, Sam stopped the nervous fumbling of her hands with his own. "Hold on here. I don't want to take her away. I want to become a part of her life—and yours. I want to marry you, Liza. I've always wanted that. I love you, more than I ever thought it possible to love someone.''

Stunned, she searched his eyes, afraid to trust him. The words she'd longed to hear since her first date with Sam were finally said, but could she allow herself to believe? "Are you sure? Do you mean it?''

For the first time since this long, long day had begun, Sam smiled. "I've never been more sure of anything in my life. I love you, Liza Courtland. But I guess I should ask, do you still care for me, after all you've been through because of me?''

Liza felt the tension of the last hour slip away. "There were days, too many to count, when I wished I could forget you, when I prayed never to think of you again. But nothing worked. And I always came back to this thought, that you gave me that beautiful child sleeping in there. I'd look into Beth's eyes and see yours, and I'd be lost all over again. Do I care for you? More than for my next breath.''

With more tenderness than he'd known he possessed, Sam took her into his arms and kissed her. It was a slow, smoldering kiss, filled with promise, with passion; a sleeping giant yet to awaken. Then he lifted his head and pulled her into a fierce embrace. "When I think of the years we've wasted because of my stupidity."

"Don't," Liza whispered, her mouth at his ear, "think only of the years ahead of us." Holding him close, for the first time since she'd learned Sam had left town so long ago, she drew in a cleansing breath. "No more secrets, no more evasions," she told him as again she met his eyes. "Only the truth between us from now on, I swear."

"Amen to that." He glanced over his shoulder, through the archway that led into her bedroom. "Would it shock your mother if I stayed the night? That is, if you want me?"

If she wanted him, indeed. Smiling, Liza got up and walked to the door that led to the hallway, the door that locked her apartment off from the rest of the mansion, and she slid the bolt home. "Mother knows how I feel about you. She guessed the first night she saw us together at the hospital when Beth broke her leg." Strolling back to him, she held out her hand. "I don't think she'll be shocked at all. I think she'll be pleased to find you here for breakfast. I know Beth will."

Walking with her toward her bedroom, Sam spotted something on the bookcase shelf. "Isn't that the angel I gave you that last day? I thought you said it was broken?"

"It was, but I fixed it." Liza stroked the figurine lightly, lovingly. It was whole once more, like their love.

Sam glanced at the door to Beth's room. "Do you think I could go in, just look at her for a minute?"

Liza felt warmth flood her heart. "Let's go in together, *Daddy*."

Sam couldn't help smiling at the word. "When can we tell her?"

"All in good time," Liza said, opening Beth's door.

* * *

Ed Hayes had always been a patient man. Until recently. The situation between Liza Courtland and Sam Rivers had sorely tried his patience. He'd done everything he could think of to pry them apart, to discredit Sam in Liza's eyes, to drive Sam out of town again. Yesterday he'd delivered the final little bombshell that he'd felt would undoubtedly do the trick. Now as he drove toward the building site at nine in the morning, he couldn't resist stopping by to catch Sam packing up before leaving for good.

Chewing on a toothpick, he turned into the drive and saw the gate was open. Jeff's car was by the trailer, but Sam's Explorer wasn't. Gleefully, Ed got out, anticipation putting a bounce to his step. Rivers was probably already on the highway headed back to Akron.

He poked his head into the trailer and found it empty. As he closed the door, Jeff came walking up. "Hey, there. Is Sam around?" Ed asked.

"Not yet."

Ed crunched down on his toothpick. "Oh? Is he coming in soon?"

"Yeah. He called, said he was running late, not to look for him before ten or so."

He had to be at Ann's house packing up his belongings before saying goodbye to Jeff and the crew. "Where was he calling from?"

Jeff shrugged. "He didn't say. Can I help you with something, Sheriff?"

"No, that's all right. See you later." Ed made his way back to his cruiser. Curiosity ate at him as he swung out onto the road. He'd just ease on over to Woods Lane and see if Sam's car was there.

Fifteen minutes later he pulled up in front of Sam's mother's home. No cars in sight. Tamping down on his jumpy nerves, he walked up to the door and rang the bell.

"Good morning, Mrs. Rivers," he said, smiling at Ann as she opened the door. "I was wondering if Sam's here."

"Why, no, Sheriff," Ann said, hesitant as always, facing the law. "He might be at work by now."

"By now? Did he just leave here?" Had he passed him en route?

"No, he didn't come home last night. But he called and said not to worry."

Ed frowned. "Do you know where he spent the night?" Maybe in the trailer. Hayes knew Sam often slept there. But then, Jeff would have said so, wouldn't he?

Ann knew, but she didn't think it was her place to say. Instinctively she knew Sam wouldn't like her revealing anything to Ed Hayes. "I can't really say," she answered. "You want me to tell him you're looking for him when I hear from him again?"

Ed's teeth snapped the toothpick in half. "No. Never mind." Scowling, he headed back to his cruiser.

He didn't want to think it—didn't want to discover all his efforts had been in vain. But he had to know for sure. Turning around, he headed over to Liza's.

His dark eyes narrowed to slits, his beefy hands gripping the steering wheel, Ed looked at the two vehicles parked at the back of the Courtland Mansion, Liza's BMW and Sam's Explorer, cozily side by side. How in the hell could this be? Could his plan have backfired? Hidden in the trees, he waited, his anger mounting.

It didn't take long. At ten to ten, the back door to Liza's apartment opened and three people stepped out onto the porch. Ed lifted the binoculars he'd finally thought to bring along.

Beth was smiling up at Sam, then she gave him a big hug around the waist before hobbling back inside. Next he turned to Liza who was wearing only a robe. For God's sake, had the woman lost her mind? Had she jumped from the frying pan into the fire?

What he saw next, had Ed's blood boiling. Liza wound her arms around Sam's neck and kissed him. The kiss went on and on while Ed's blood pressure climbed. Finally they pulled apart and Sam said something that had Liza laughing, then he kissed her again and hurried down the steps and into his Explorer. Liza stood gazing after him for some time after he'd turned the corner, then she went inside.

Damn! Ed flung his binoculars aside. What in hell did it take to get that woman to wake up? Well, this did it for him. He was sick and tired of trying to save her from the likes of Sam Rivers. He'd given her endless chances to see the light, and instead, she was shacked up with that no-account drifter again.

Fine. He'd fix her wagon, and Sam's, too. And Ed knew just how to do it. The editor of the *Port Henry Gazette* owed him a few favors, as did most everyone in town. The minister of the church the high-and-mighty Courtlands attended. Some of the firms Courtland Enterprises did business with. He'd get to all of them, let them know about Liza's bastard child, fathered by the son of the town drunk whose mysterious disappearance had never been solved. He'd dredge all that up again, planting careful hints and gossip here and there. He'd spill the beans about Jim Rivers getting a girl pregnant and refusing to acknowledge it. He'd see what he could learn about Sam's business operation in Akron, go through his records, see if he could find something that could hurt him. Man like that had to be operating on the shady side of the street.

Gritting his teeth, Ed shifted into gear and gunned it, shooting out of the cover of the trees, no longer caring who saw him. When he got through with the Courtland women and the Rivers men, they wouldn't be able to hold their heads up in this town.

Hands on his hips, Sam stood looking up as several of his men hoisted high the new side frame of the rebuilt model home just four days after the arson clearance. As the men at the roof line grabbed on, locking the side into place, he gave them all a thumbs-up sign. "Good work, fellas." Wiping his damp brow on his shirtsleeve, he left the area, waving to the day guard who was patrolling the fence line. Things had been quiet since he'd hired the watchmen, and he wanted to keep it like that.

"Hey, Sam," Jeff yelled across the yard. "Couple of people to see you in the office. Jim's already there."

Sam raised his arm to indicate he'd heard the message, and made his way to the trailer, wondering who wanted to see both him and his brother. Noticing Liza's car parked next to his, he smiled. He hadn't seen her in two days, but they were supposed to have dinner together tonight. He stepped out of the June heat into air-conditioned coolness, then raised a brow when he saw that Liza and Jim weren't the only ones present.

"Sam." Liza got up from the desk and met him at the door. "I hate to interrupt your workday, but Kristen and her mother have something important to say to you and to Jim." She glanced over at the young man standing at the far end of the trailer, his face wary, then to Edith. "Do you want to begin?"

Edith shook her head, her face registering embarrassment and anger just beneath the surface. "No, I believe Kristen should." Pointedly she stared at her daughter.

The defiance was gone from Kristen Hanks as she glanced over at Jim, then his brother. Her pale cheeks were blotchy, as if she'd been crying. "I made a mistake. Jim's not the baby's father."

But Edith wasn't satisfied. "Tell all of it."

The girl looked pained as she drew in a shuddering breath. "This boy I go to school with, Eric Rogers, he's the one. I know it was wrong, but I thought, well, Jim's family has a lot of money. I mean his brother does. And Eric, he can't even afford a car. I...I didn't mean any harm." She looked down as the tears started. "I'm sorry, Jim," she said to the floor. "Please forgive me."

"And *I'm* sorry, Mr. Rivers," Edith said to Sam. "I began to have my doubts so I kept hammering away at Kristen. I told her there was no point in lying, if she was, because eventually the DNA test would prove paternity. So last night she told me the truth." Looking older and very tired, Edith turned to Jim. "Please accept my apology for putting you through this."

Enormously relieved not to have all this hanging over his head, Jim could be generous. "Sure," he told her. He pushed away from the wall and walked over to Sam, keeping his voice low. "Thanks for believing me before you knew for sure."

Sam clapped his brother on the shoulder and watched him leave, then turned back to the room. After learning of his own carelessness, he was no one to judge another. "If there's anything we can do to help, Mrs. Hanks," he told Edith, "please let me know."

Edith closed her eyes a moment to get herself under control, then nodded. "Thank you," she whispered. Taking Kristen's hand, she walked to the door. "We'll wait in the car, Liza."

After they left, Sam slid his hands up and down her bare arms and smiled into eyes darkly green today. "Thanks. That made my day."

"Mine, too. I guess you know now why I felt compelled to help Edith. But I'm glad everything worked out the way it did." Rising on tiptoes, she kissed him lightly. "Are we still on for dinner tonight?"

Sam screwed up his face thoughtfully. "Could we meet somewhere later, after dinner? I think, in light of all that's happened, I need to bring my family in on *my* new family."

"Sure. How do you think your mother will react?"

"I think she's going to love her newly discovered granddaughter." His expression bordered on sad. "She never seemed able to relax enough when I was young to pay much attention to me, always afraid of the old man. She did a little better with Jim, but perhaps in getting to know Beth, she can make up for some mistakes she made with us. If you'll let Beth come over, that is."

"Of course. But I'd like to wait to tell Beth until after you find the person who messed with your car and set the fire. I don't want Beth in any danger. If he finds out Beth's *your* daughter, he might turn on her."

That thought was enough to curdle his blood. "You're right. I've waited this long. I can wait a bit longer." But as he pulled her into a slow, thorough kiss, he couldn't help wondering just how long they'd have to wait before the man he was seeking would be found.

Sam finished his lengthy story, then sat back in his mother's kitchen chair and looked across the table at both of them. "I know this must come as a real shock."

"Not to me," Ann stated. "I knew you were seeing someone that summer, but as usual I didn't ask. Then when Liza Courtland, of all people, called me that fall to ask for your address, I was certain she was the one." Leaning forward, she laid her hand on her oldest son's arm. "Sammy, I know I didn't do right by you all your growing-up years.

I...I have no excuse to offer, except that I was so cowed, so under Joe's spell, so afraid of him, that I guess I stepped back from life. I couldn't cope with thinking about anything except not getting him mad so he wouldn't beat on me.'' She looked down, shaking her head. ''I'm so ashamed.''

Sam took her small, work-roughened hand in his much larger one and felt a ray of hope spring alive inside him. Maybe she had loved him all along. Who was he to judge how someone in her shoes should act? ''Don't, Mom. You did the best you could. Jim and I both know that.''

Sam turned to face his brother. ''I guess maybe my best hope is that the mistakes I made in my life might keep you from avoiding the same things. I ran away when I should have stayed, and I learned you can never run away from your problems. I tore up letters from a girl I loved with all my heart, because they reminded me of all I'd walked away from. I never dreamed she was writing because she needed me. I missed out on over seven years of my daughter's life because of those mistakes. Don't mess up like I did.''

Jim nodded. ''I'm going to try not to. I want you to know I appreciate you telling me all this. I had you on this pedestal, you know. You could do no wrong, and it seemed, by comparison, I could do nothing right. Today I found out that you're human, just like me. I think I like it better this way.''

''I don't belong on a pedestal. I've learned something important through all this, that it isn't the mistakes we make so much as how we handle ourselves afterward that matters. Whether we learn from them and try to make amends to people we might have hurt.'' He smiled at Jim. ''You're all right, kid.''

Jim smiled back. ''You're all right, too.''

But Ann was thinking ahead. ''Sammy, what about the

future? Are you going to marry Liza Courtland? When do we get to meet my granddaughter?''

"I'm working on it, Mom." Sam pushed back his chair and stood. "Great dinner. I've got to make a call. See you later."

Afterglow. It was one of the most beautiful sensations known to man. And woman, Liza thought with a devilish smile. Settling against her lover's bare chest, she sighed in contentment. "I'm so glad you called me." Lazily she gazed out the window overlooking the bay from their suite at the Inn off the Park and watched the stars twinkling in a night sky. "This is my current favorite spot in the whole wide world."

"Mmm," Sam murmured in agreement. "Let's stay here forever. No work to distract us, no people to annoy us. Just you and me and room service."

"Works for me." Shifting, she studied his face, then reached up to stroke his wonderful beard. "Do you know, because of this fuzz, every time I'm with you, my face is red for hours, and everyone knows exactly what I've been doing."

"Well, looks like we have two choices. You get used to people staring at your red face or I shave off my beard. 'Cause, lady, we aren't going to stop cuddling in the foreseeable future."

"Good conclusion. I choose Door Number One since I love your beard. Frankly, I think all those stares and back-of-the-hand remarks are because folks are plain jealous that *I'm* the one you're nuzzling."

"You do, eh? I seriously doubt that. Especially the sheriff who'd like to throw me on the nearest freight train to nowhere."

Thoughtfully, Liza traced lazy paths along his chin and

throat and chest with one finger. "He's the one who somehow discovered you were Beth's father, right?"

"You guessed it. He went all the way to Ann Arbor and dug deep. I don't know whether to thank the creep or smack him upside the head. He's got the hots for you, you know. Always has had. That's yet another reason he wants to color me gone."

"I don't believe that." Liza scooted back onto her own pillow. "He doesn't think of me that way." But a little voice told her that Ed Hayes had made a few overtures that couldn't be interpreted any other way.

"Don't kid yourself." Sam shifted until he was leaning over her, brushing back her golden hair with one hand. "Old Beefy would like nothing better than to change places with me right now." He trailed his hand down until his fingertips were caressing her breast, which seemed to come to attention for him.

She watched his movements, watched her own flesh so recently satisfied grow aroused again. "That will never happen. No one but you has ever touched me. No other man ever will."

His eyes very serious, Sam looked into hers. "I do love you so very much, Liza. I want nothing more than to marry you, to live with you and Beth. But I have to clear up my past first. I hope you understand."

"I do."

"I hope you'll be saying those same two words in front of a minister very soon." And he lowered his head to kiss her.

Chapter Twelve

Seated at his desk in the trailer, Sam switched the phone to his other ear. "Don't worry, Dirk, we're pretty much back on track now, but it has been an interesting couple of weeks."

"Are you sure you don't want me to drive over?" Dirk asked. "Between a sabotaged car and arson on the site, it sounds like you could use a little help."

"No, things are under control." At least for now, Sam thought. "I've got round-the-clock armed watchmen patrolling with a guard dog. I doubt he'll try anything around here anytime soon."

"What about off site? Sounds like he's after you, not the project." Dirk sounded genuinely worried. "I think you're still in danger."

"I can take care of myself." Sam swiveled in his chair as he heard footsteps coming up the steps. "Matter of fact, here comes a sheriff's deputy now. We'll be fine. I'll call you later." Hanging up, he stood. "How's it going, Keith?"

"I've got some interesting news for you." Keith entered and walked over to lean against the counter. "I wanted to tell you in person. Thought you might like to know that we may have found your father."

Stunned, Sam sat back down. "No kidding! Where? When?"

"Last night a couple of teenagers were taking a short cut through the woods near where your old house used to stand. They ran across something large sticking up out of the ground under this big evergreen. They got curious, dug around a little and found some more when suddenly it occurred to them their find might be human bones. Scared the hell out of them, so they ran for help and called our office.

"I took a couple of guys over and we dug up the rest. It's a male skeleton, all right. I sent the remains over to the police lab in Toledo for analysis."

"After all these years." Sam shook his head. "Finally, it may be over. Did you find some sort of ID, his wallet maybe?"

"Everything's pretty rotted away, including what might have been a cheap wallet. There's a plastic envelope that might have held a driver's license, but water seeped in and obliterated all the writing. We didn't find any jewelry that you might be able to identify."

"Joe didn't wear jewelry, not even a wedding ring. How good are these labs in identifying old skeletons?"

"Shouldn't be too hard in this case because we have a full set of false teeth to work with. That's another reason I came over. Did Joe have dentures?"

"Yes, he did."

"Do you know what dentist he used?"

"Far as I know, all of us went to Dr. Miller on Main. I believe Mom still goes to him."

"I know Miller. I think I'll pay him a visit. Sure hope he keeps good records." Keith pushed away from the counter, his brown eyes serious. "There's one more thing."

"What's that?"

"We dug a .38 caliber bullet out of the skull. Whoever he is, he was most likely shot in the back of the head."

"Whew!" Sam released a rush of air. He'd wanted the old man gone, out of their lives. But shot in the back of the head?

"I sent that to ballistics. I hope you know I have to ask this, Sam. Did you have a gun back then?"

"No, and there wasn't one in the house, either. With Joe drinking so heavily, I made sure there were no weapons around. I didn't want him to get high and decide punching wasn't satisfying enough, that shooting might be more fun." He rose again, rubbing a hand along the back of his neck. "You seem pretty certain those remains belong to Joe?"

Keith nodded. "It fits. I did a quick measuring, and the guy wasn't more than five-eight or nine. The false teeth. The location of the burial site. What do you think?"

"Seems likely, but I'd heard that Hayes had half of Port Henry dug up after I left. How'd he miss that spot?"

"I don't know."

"Listen, I don't want my mother told any of this until we're certain. She gets pretty emotional these days."

"I'd like to keep this between the two of us, actually." Keith looked hesitant, then apparently decided to speak his mind. "I haven't even told the sheriff. He went out of town yesterday, said he was going to Ann Arbor on business and probably wouldn't be back for a couple of days, but he calls in."

Sam's nod was appreciative. "It's a stroke of luck that he's gone and you were on duty. I'm not sure what Hayes would have done. I don't trust him."

Keith felt the same, but he hesitated to say so out loud.

Sam walked out with the deputy into the bright sunshine of a summer morning. Too nice a day to be finding buried bodies. "Thanks for coming by, Keith."

"I'll be in touch." The deputy headed for his cruiser.

"Oh, by the way—" Sam waited until Keith turned "—what caliber gun do you and the sheriff carry?"

The look on Keith's face seemed to say he'd been expecting the question. "Thirty-eights." With that he climbed behind the wheel and drove out of the compound.

Of course, Keith hadn't been in law enforcement back then, but Hayes had been in charge of the investigation. Interesting, Sam thought, going back inside. Meanwhile there was someone else he needed to see, the man who'd been Joe's best friend. Waldo Franks had been in Florida and had just returned, according to his wife. Perhaps Liza would like to go with him. He picked up the phone.

"So, are we going to play good cop, bad cop with old Waldo?" Liza asked from the passenger seat of Sam's Explorer.

Sam raised an eyebrow as he glanced over at her. "What do you know about detectives?"

"Hey, I've got Kinsey Milhone's MO down to a T. I also watch that cop show set in Manhattan. I kind of go for those tall, lean, serious detectives." She gave him a teasing smile.

"Oh, you do, eh?" He reached for her hand, threading his fingers with hers. He'd reached her at the teen center where she'd been checking on the renovation's progress. He'd been enormously pleased when she'd quickly agreed to go with him. "You know what I'm going to do real soon?"

"What's that?"

"Get a vehicle that doesn't have a center console between the driver and passenger. I want you to sit much closer than this. Much, much closer."

"My, my, and it's barely ten in the morning. Mr. Rivers, you appear to need a cold shower."

"Already took one." He placed their clasped hands on his thigh and turned back to concentrate on the road.

Liza got serious. "Do you really think the body they found belonged to your father?"

"It's the best lead we've got so far. Keith picked up all of Joe's dental records and is driving them over to forensics personally. We're trying to keep this hush-hush until we know more." Reaching the pier, Sam swung off the road and angle parked in front of Bill's Bait & Tackle Shop, a low building at the near end of the fishing dock. "I haven't been in this place since I was a teenager. Waldo's wife told me he works here part-time."

"I think I'll let you do the talking since I'm not even sure what it is you want to learn from Waldo." Liza stepped down from the high seat, glad she'd worn slacks today. "Don't you just love that name? Waldo."

Sam came around and took her hand. "Then you'd love his wife's name even more. Myrtle Franks." Grinning, he opened the door to the bait shop.

The short, thin man behind the counter wore one-piece denim coveralls and had a cigarette dangling from the corner of his mouth. "Can I help you folks? Thinking of doing some fishing? Great day out there."

Sam led the way into the dim shop. "I'm looking for Waldo Franks."

"You found him." The man smiled, friendly like.

"My name's Sam Rivers, Waldo, and this is Liza Courtland."

Waldo reached into his pocket, pulled out a pair of horn-rimmed glasses and shoved them on, wrinkling his face as he looked them over. "Sure, I recognize Ms. Courtland." His rheumy gaze slid to Sam. "By God, you're Joe's son. When'd you come back?"

"Several weeks ago. I called, but your wife said you were in Florida."

"Yep. Just got back. My brother lives in the Keys. We like to fish, but Myrtle, she hates the water." He chuckled at what must have been an inside joke. "So, what brings you back, son?"

"I'm looking into Joe's disappearance, trying to find out what happened that night at the Watering Hole. I understand you were there, Waldo."

"Sure was." Waldo spoke through smoke curling up from the cigarette still in his mouth. "What'd you want to know?"

"Everything, starting with the fight."

Waldo scratched at his sparse gray hair with fingers very tanned and slightly crooked. "Well, sir, Tom Novak and Joe, they got into it. Weren't the first time. Both of them pretty far gone. Punching each other, knocking into people. Zac let 'em be until they busted up a chair and broke a table. Then he tried to stop 'em, but your dad, he shoved old Zac a good one. So Zac called the sheriff."

"But Deputy Hayes came instead, right?"

"Yeah, that's right. Got there in one hell of a hurry, too. He got the boys to stop, but Joe, he was pretty drunk and he didn't want to quit. He almost threw a punch at Hayes, swearing at him, calling him names. Man, that wasn't smart."

This differed slightly from Zac's version. "What did Hayes do?"

"Weren't nice, what he done. He's a big guy, you know, and Joe, hell, he's a lightweight. Hayes picked Joe up like a sack of potatoes and tossed him right through the swinging doors. I heard him land hard." The old man ran a hand over his unshaven chin, regret plain on his face. "I always felt bad I never stood up to Hayes over that. I shoulda gone out right then, helped Joe up and taken him home. He was my friend and I let him down." He shook his head, still disappointed in himself after all this time.

"What happened then?"

"Zac bought a round, like he always does if there's a scuffle. Everyone settled down. You know how that goes."

"And Hayes stayed and had a beer, too?"

Waldo removed his glasses and rubbed at his eyes. "Zac served him one at the bar, I seem to remember. But Hayes only took one swallow, then he left right away. Never said nothing to no one, just walked out. After a spell, I got to worrying about Joe, walking along the road home, 'cause he was really drunk. I hadn't had but two beers so I got into my van and drove along Joe's usual route. I couldn't spot him, even though I know he couldn't have made it home that fast. Took about thirty minutes to walk from the Watering Hole to Joe's place. All these years, I been wondering what happened to him, 'cause I never saw Joe again."

"So you're saying that Hayes threw Joe out of the bar, then left himself a few minutes later?" Zac had thought Hayes had stayed to finish his beer.

"Yes, sir. Nobody thought he'd stay. He never sat around drinking with us. He thinks he's better than us, you know. Better than most folks 'cause of his old man. The Hayes family's from Cleveland, you know. Shaker Heights, uppity. Takes more'n money to give a man class, you know what I mean?''

"I guess you don't think much of Hayes, then?''

Waldo grunted. "Port Henry ain't big enough to hold all the people who hate Ed's guts, 'specially since he went from deputy to sheriff. That man loves to strut his stuff."

"But he upholds the law in Port Henry." Sam led him on, trying to learn more.

"What's to uphold? Coupla speeders, a gas station robbery, some kids vandalizing the high school. Big deal. Your old man's disappearance was the biggest thing Hayes ever had to chew on. Made him feel important to strut around town saying he was 'conducting an investigation.' And it gave him a chance to get folks all worked up about how you might have done Joe in. Now that really had Hayes droolin'. Son, I don't know what you ever did to that man, but he sure hates you."

"So I've noticed."

Finished with his tale, Waldo shifted his interest to Liza. "You're sure pretty as a picture, Ms. Courtland."

Liza smiled at the old man. "Thank you."

"I appreciate you talking to us, Waldo," Sam told him.

"Sure, sure. You ever want to go fishin', you come on back. I'll rent you a nice boat and fix you up with some fresh bait."

"We might take you up on that." With a wave, Sam led Liza outside, blinking in the bright sun.

"That was interesting," Liza said. "I wonder how many others in town feel that way about our sheriff."

"More than like him, I'd guess." Sam opened the passenger door for her.

"Then how'd he get elected sheriff?" she asked as she climbed in.

"I think he's been methodically intimidating people

around here for a long time. They're afraid of him." Sam got behind the wheel.

"But we vote in private, secretly. Who'd know if you voted for…oh, wait a minute. As I remember, he ran unopposed last election."

"See what I mean?" Sam started the engine, his expression thoughtful. "There's something I didn't tell you yet. They found a .38 bullet in the skull. Hayes carries a .38 police issue gun."

"Oh, now, wait a minute." Liza looked shocked. "You can't seriously believe Ed Hayes is a killer. He's an officer of the law, has been for over ten years. I admit he's beginning to sound like not a terribly nice guy, but a murderer? No." She shook her head, wanting to deny the things she was hearing, her convictions slipping. "Besides, what possible motive would he have for killing your father?"

"You heard what Waldo said. Joe cursed him out in public. That's more than enough to set off some people. And then there's the other reason."

"What would that be?"

"So he could make people believe I did it."

"Oh, God, Sam." She thought about all the times Ed had suddenly shown up at the house with his niece, or at the park, or at a kids' movie where she'd taken Beth. He'd been so good with the girls, funny, kind. He did seem to hover over her overly much. Then she remembered Sam's words from the other night. *He's got the hots for you. Always has had.* Surely not. Could she have misjudged him so? "Do you honestly think Ed's capable of trying to frame you?"

Sam shrugged. "Look at the facts. Who else was involved in the so-called investigation after I left town, spreading rumors about me, telling lies? Who came to my mother's house and all but ordered me out of town less than an hour after I returned? Who's been sitting in his cruiser spying on Oakview Estates, watching my comings and goings, hoping I'll make a mistake so he can throw me in jail?''

"He's been spying on you?"

"Sure has, almost daily. Capable of murder? Hell, yes, I think he is. The trouble with a certain type of man drawn to law enforcement is that he gets a taste of power and begins to think he's above the very laws he's sworn to uphold. Who else can come and go in Port Henry and no one questions his presence anywhere at any hour?''

"You're beginning to scare me."

He reached over and took her hand. "I don't mean to do that. But I do think we should go have a talk with Lyle. Maybe he can do a little checking behind the scenes. I think Keith's an all-right deputy, but he does still answer to the sheriff. Ed could very well come back and order Keith off the case, then conveniently lose evidence the same way he's somehow disposed of the entire file on Joe Rivers.''

"Where is Ed, anyway? He never goes out of town."

Sam started the engine. "In Ann Arbor."

Liza's eyes grew wide. "Oh, no. Is he hoping to dig up more information on my past? There isn't anything else."

"But he doesn't know that." He shifted into gear and pulled out. "Let's go see Lyle."

Lyle Stewart said goodbye, hung up the phone and looked across his desk at the two people seated there. "All right, I've got the prosecutor interested. He's ordering a copy of the autopsy on the remains found yesterday and of the ballistics report on the bullet. He also is sending someone to pick up all weapons in the sheriff's department to have them tested.''

"That's going to go over like a lead balloon with Hayes," Sam commented.

"Do we care, at this point?" Liza asked. "Better to be safe than sorry, don't you think, Lyle?"

"Absolutely." When his line rang, he hit the button that connected him with his secretary out front. "Yes, Amanda." Lyle listened for several seconds. "Fine, put him through." He spoke aside to Sam and Liza. "Deputy Nickles calling. This may be connected."

Liza threw Sam a questioning look, but he just shook his head.

"Hello, Keith. How's it going?" Lyle listened for a moment. "Yes, he's here. You want to talk with him?" He paused. "Oh, all right, then tell me." For some time, Lyle listened, inserting only an occasional word of agreement. Finally he nodded. "I see. That is interesting. Yes, I'll tell him. You should probably know that I've brought the prosecutor in on things, and he's ordering copies of everything so his office can look things over, then he'll get back to me. Meantime, you be careful, you hear? And call me the minute you know anything, please." Lyle paused a final time. "All right, and thanks."

The attorney hung up and removed his gold-rimmed glasses before leaning back in his chair. "It seems the sheriff came back into town, found out about the discovery of the bones and is furious at the way Keith handled things. Apparently, he ranted and raved at his deputy, screaming that Keith should have notified Hayes immediately."

"Keith deliberately *didn't* call him," Sam said. "I believe he was worried that something like this might happen."

"I thought as much. Keith's trying to get a rush on the tests."

"Where's Ed now?" Liza wanted to know.

"Keith says he stormed out of there like a bat out of hell, but he doesn't know where he's headed."

"And the prosecutor's rep hasn't confiscated Ed's gun yet for testing," Sam said. "Actually, he doesn't know it's gone that far."

"No," Lyle agreed, "which is good because if he were forewarned, he'd probably get rid of the gun, if in fact he still carries the same gun, and if it's the one that killed your father."

Liza sighed. "A lot of loose ends yet. I just can't believe all this. If you'd have asked me a week ago if Ed Hayes could be involved in not only a murder but an eight-year coverup, I'd have thought you'd lost your mind. But now I'm not so sure."

"Nor am I," Lyle admitted. "The fact that I've never liked him is beside the point. We shouldn't convict the man mentally until we know for certain. So let's keep all this between us for now, all right?"

"Absolutely." Sam stood and reached to shake Lyle's hand. "Thanks for seeing us so unexpectedly."

"No problem." Lyle smiled at Liza. "Good to see you again." His eyes moved from her to Sam and back again. "Both of you."

Liza caught the speculative look, but didn't comment. "You, too, Lyle. Say hello to Sue for me. I haven't seen her in a while." She hadn't had time for the fitness center lately.

"Right, I will." Stewart watched them leave, his expression thoughtful. Sam Rivers and Liza Courtland. Now there was a pair.

"Why don't you take the rest of the day off, too?" Liza asked Sam as he pulled the Explorer up to the back stairs of the Courtland Mansion. "You don't have that much waiting for you, do you? We could do something with Beth.''

"Mmm, it's tempting. But I'd better take a rain check. We're two men short today, so I told Jeff I'd help out when I got back. I'd like to bring this project in somewhere close to deadline.''

"All right, if you must, but Beth will be disappointed.''

She knew just how to get to him. "Tell you what. Don't say anything to her and I'll see how the afternoon goes. If I can get away, I'll come back.''

"That's a deal.'' She leaned across the console and kissed him warmly, then her eyes got serious. "Be careful. Now that I know Hayes is involved, I worry about him coming after you again. If he's responsible for your father's death, there's something not quite right in his head.''

"I'll be careful. And you, too.''

Liza stepped out and closed the door. "I think I'll bake some cookies with Beth. Maybe that'll take my mind off this chilling morning.''

"Good idea.'' He watched until she ran up the stairs and disappeared inside, then drove off. An afternoon with Liza and Beth doing homey things held a lot of appeal. Maybe, if he was lucky, there wasn't much needing doing at Oakview for now.

Liza stacked cooled cookies in her big jar, humming as she worked. Two batches, a good afternoon's work. There was enough for Mom and some to take to Edith and, of course, Sam. She glanced at the clock and saw it was nearly four. It appeared as if Sam hadn't been able to break away early after all.

She glanced out onto the back porch to check on Beth who'd hobbled out to play after their baking session. Her daughter was busily talking to her dolls, one in a miniature high chair, another in a crib and a third she carried in the crook of her elbow. Playing house. Liza used to do it by the hour at Beth's age and older. She'd never much cared for the "pretty" dolls, the dress-up grown-up dolls, but rather the ones that resembled actual babies. Apparently Beth had inherited her mothering instincts.

Wiping the cookie sheets, Liza allowed herself to dream a little. In a perfect world, this mess with Sam's father would end, and they could finally be married. Beth would have a dad of her own and the three of them could be a family. Maybe there'd be more children. Perhaps she could give more authority to Arnie West and spend less time at the office.

Ah, yes, but whoever promised anyone a perfect world? Still she could dream, couldn't she?

The phone rang just as she put away the last tin. She walked into her sitting area and picked it up. "Hello?"

"I'm glad I found you, Liza," Lyle Stewart said. "I tried reaching Sam, but his foreman told me he's en route to your place. Keith just called. I've got some interesting news for you."

Sitting down, Liza felt herself tense up. "What is it?"

Sheriff Ed Hayes had been driving around for hours, trying to calm down, trying to think what to do. Damn those kids for finding Joe's remains and damn Keith Nickles for acting without contacting him when he'd known how to reach him in Ann Arbor. And that had proven a dead end, as well, for he'd learned nothing new on Liza.

Sweating heavily, Ed saw that his gas gauge was nearly on empty. He'd have to stop soon. But where would he go? It was all falling apart, his carefully constructed house of cards falling in around his head. He had to figure out a way to salvage his good name, his career, maybe even his life.

The bullet had still been in the skull, Keith had told him, and he'd eyed Ed suspiciously. Just his luck. After all these years, how had that body surfaced? He'd buried it pretty deep. But the woods had protected the area, keeping out the sun and keeping the earth wet from countless rains. Erosion had done the rest. Damn!

He swiped at his forehead with the back of his hand, he vacillated back and forth, wondering what to do. He dare not go to his family. He couldn't bear to see disappointment in his mother's eyes. He needed someone, a voice of reason, one who believed in him.

Liza. She probably didn't know he'd been trying to discredit her in Sam's eyes. She'd always been nice to him, kind and decent, even back when others had teased him because of his size. She'd treated him the same as everyone else.

All right, so she had a little lapse of judgment when it came to Sam. But if he went to her now, told her how much he cared for her, that everything he'd done had been for her, so she wouldn't get mixed up with trash like Rivers, she'd have to listen. She needed someone like Ed Hayes who came from a good family, who held a responsible job, who'd take care of her. She'd never be alone, never need be afraid as long as he watched over her.

Swinging his vehicle in an illegal U-turn, he headed up the hill toward her house. He'd driven by earlier and had seen her car parked around back, which meant she was home. She probably didn't know that his own deputy was having him checked out. He would talk to her and she'd understand. Liza was the most understanding woman he knew. Even if she'd heard about the body being found, she'd realize that ridding the world of Joe Rivers wasn't a crime, but rather he'd done everyone in town a favor. Still, if she didn't want to stay in Port Henry, he would take her away. Anywhere. So long as they were together. Beth liked him, too. They'd be a family.

He spat the toothpick he'd been chewing onto the floor and swung into the Courtland drive, following it around back, then stopping. He didn't want to park too near the stairs. He wanted to surprise her, so she couldn't think up an excuse not to see him if she noticed his approach. Stealthily, he got out and didn't slam shut the car door. He climbed the stairs slowly, mindful of any sound.

His heart started pounding heavily in his chest as he spotted Beth playing at the far end of the porch, her back to him. He'd forgotten that she'd be here. As he reached the top, he heard Liza's voice coming through the open window.

Ed froze. Was someone with her, perhaps her mother? He didn't know if he could convince her to leave with him if Elizabeth Courtland was there. The very proper older woman always made him feel like a clumsy fool. Cautiously he leaned closer to the window. Through the slanted blinds, he could see Liza seated on the couch across the room holding the phone. Thank goodness. He'd wait until she finished her call and then go in. Curious, he cocked his head, listening.

"I can't believe it," Liza said into the phone. "I know Joe Rivers wasn't well thought of, but to be shot in the back of the head, and at point-blank range—it's horrible. Is the medical examiner certain, Lyle?"

"Yes, he is. They're also fairly certain the bullet is from a police issue gun. Keith took in all the weapons they had at the sheriff's office, including his own, even though he wasn't a deputy at the time. No matches."

Liza rubbed at a spot over her forehead. This whole thing was enough to give her a headache. "So then Ed's gun is the only one they haven't checked yet?"

"That's right. I'm not a betting man, but I'd put money on this one. Ed Hayes is the only one who holds a serious grudge against Sam and his entire family."

"A grudge against Sam is no reason to kill his father. This is terrible. Do you think Ed had something to do with Sam's brake line being cut and maybe even the fire at Oakview?"

"That's what they're thinking, yes."

"To think he used to come over here, bring his niece to play with Beth. He seemed so nice. What happened?"

"Perhaps when we find him, we'll get some answers."

"Where is he, do you suppose?"

Scarcely breathing alongside the window on the porch, Ed felt tears form as he sucked in a shaky breath. They knew everything, all of them. And Liza thought he was horrible, dreadful, terrible. It was all over.

Frantically Ed looked around. There was no escape. But he wasn't going to make things easy for them, not even for Liza. She believed those awful things about him without letting him explain, letting him tell her that he'd done it all for her, for their future together.

His mouth a grim line, Ed crept to the far end of the porch.

Beth looked up, surprised. "Oh, hi. Is Debbie with you?"

"No," Ed told her. "But Mommy said it was all right if I take you to see Debbie." With that, he slid a beefy arm around Beth and picked her up, cast and all.

"Wait!" Beth said. "I have to ask Mommy."

"No, you don't." Ed rushed toward the stairs with his squirming bundle. "Just be quiet and I won't hurt you." He would make Liza pay for not giving him a chance. Her daughter was the most important thing in her life. And *he* had her. So who was so high and mighty now?

"Put me down!" Beth yelled. "Mommy!" Then Ed's hand clamped over her mouth.

Inside, Liza heard Beth's shout, recognizing the urgency in it. "Lyle, just a minute. Something's wrong. Beth's in trouble." She dropped the phone and rushed onto the porch. Before she could swing her eyes to the left where Beth had been playing moments before, a movement to the right caught her eye. Her heart leaped to her throat as she saw Ed Hayes carrying her daughter down the last few steps. "Hey! Ed, what are you doing? Put her down!"

Hayes paused at the door of his vehicle long enough to give Liza a chilling smile. "You're going to regret turning me down." He yanked open the car door, nearly dropping Beth in his haste. But as he tried to stuff the child into his cruiser, he heard the sound of a car turning into the Courtland drive.

He saw Liza dashing down the stairs, almost on him. Ed grabbed his gun and pressed the barrel to Beth's head. "Don't come any closer or your daughter's dead."

Liza came to a frantic stop on the bottom step. "Don't hurt her, Ed, please." In her peripheral vision, she saw a vehicle swing into the back, praying it was Sam. Lyle had mentioned that Sam was heading this way. "She hasn't done anything. Please, Ed, let Beth go. Take me instead."

Eyes darting to the Explorer and back to Liza, Ed backed away from his cruiser, dragging Beth with him. "Stay back. I'm warning you. Don't come any closer." He dared chance a look behind him and saw the woods where he'd often sat in his car watching the Courtland Mansion doors. If he could make it there, he knew a way out on the other side. He could still get away. As long as he had Beth, they wouldn't dare follow him.

Liza saw Sam jump out and come forward, then halt, one

hand behind him and the other outstretched as he assessed the situation.

"Put her down, Hayes," Sam said. "It's all over. Give up now before someone else gets hurt."

Sweat poured off Ed, mingling with his frustrated tears as he walked backward, dragging his young victim. "I've got nothing to lose. One killing or two, I can only die once. Stay back!"

Slowly Sam circled both vehicles, signaling Liza to stay where she was as he inched toward Ed. "I'll talk to them about going easy on you if you let her go now, Ed. Don't make things worse."

Ed made a disgusted sound deep in his throat. "Sure, you'll help me, all right. You come swaggering back into town, move in on the woman I love, worm your way into her good graces again. That shouldn't have happened!" His voice was edgy with strain. "*I* was the one here after you ran away. *I'm* the one she should turn to, not you. But no, she wants you. Always you."

Liza had a fist clamped tightly to her lips to keep herself from screaming out loud. Then she saw that Sam was holding a gun in the hand he had behind his back as he crept slowly closer to the madman holding her daughter. She began to pray.

"Let Beth go, Ed," Sam said quietly, trying for a reasonable tone, "and we'll talk. It doesn't have to end like this. If you hurt Beth, this town will hang you in the town square."

"They will anyhow." Again he glanced behind to the woods, closer now, then back at Sam. "Stop right there!" He shifted the gun from Beth's head and aimed it at the man who'd ruined all his dreams, ruined his life. Sam was the one Ed really wanted dead, not Beth. "You never should have come back, Rivers." Ed took careful aim.

But he hadn't counted on Beth dipping her head and sinking her teeth into his fleshy hand. Yelping in pain, Ed let go of her and she slid to the ground.

It was all Sam needed. He shot only once and hit Hayes in his right upper thigh. Screaming, Ed spun around and dropped the gun as he fell backward.

Sam ran to Beth and picked her up, then turned and handed her to Liza who'd run up behind him. Swinging about, Sam picked up Ed's gun as the sheriff lay gripping his bloody leg and moaning. Sirens coming closer almost drowned out Liza's grateful sobs as she held her daughter close in her arms.

Sam walked over and put his arms around the two of them. "Are you all right, Beth?" Only when she nodded did he begin to relax.

"Thank God you arrived in time," Liza whispered.

Sam kissed her head, then touched his lips to his daughter's cheek. "Finally, it's all over."

It was much later the same evening, and Lyle had come over to try to explain to them what had happened.

He set down his coffee cup and raised his eyes to Sam and Liza on the couch in her sitting room. "In answer to your question, Liza, I don't think you should blame yourself. Ed Hayes became obsessed with you. I don't even think it was a sexual thing. You came to represent all he couldn't have and yet was determined to win over."

"But I never encouraged him, not romantically. Only insofar as his niece's friendship with Beth was concerned."

Lyle nodded. "I believe you. Lots of people become obsessed with people they've never spoken a word to, or even seen in person, like the celebrity stalkers we read about. You don't have to beat yourself up thinking you led him on. All of this was a fantasy he'd built up in his mind."

"I guess I'm as confused as Liza," Sam admitted. "What would his obsession with her have to do with killing my father?"

"I talked with Keith after he took Ed's statement in lockup. Oddly enough, he seemed eager to tell his side of the story. It seems that Ed began to hate you, Sam, back in high school. He couldn't handle a guy with obvious home life disadvantages getting scholarships and football trophies and the prettiest girls, when he, who'd come from a prominent family, couldn't get any of those things. Through the years, he'd stockpiled all those resentments. He'd even spied on the two of you and followed you up to Crane Lake that summer."

"Oh, that's sick," Liza said, cringing at the thought that their privacy had been invaded.

"He is sick," Lyle agreed. "The night he killed Joe, Ed really lost it. He was furious that the town drunk had sworn at him in front of people, embarrassing him, undermining his authority. So he followed Joe, thinking he'd scare him a little, demand a bit of respect. But apparently your father taunted him with all your achievements and accomplishments, then he turned his back and walked away. That sent Hayes over the edge and he shot him in the back of the head. Afterward, he coolly buried the body and made sure everyone suspected you. He felt certain no one would ever find Joe because Ed directed the digging operation himself."

Sam was baffled. "My father actually praised me to someone? You've got to be kidding."

Lyle shrugged. "That's what Hayes said. Maybe your father was proud of you in his own way and just couldn't show it or say it. Maybe he was also a little envious that you were becoming what he never had been able to be." The lawyer shook his head. "We'll never know."

"Did Ed sabotage Sam's car and set the fire?" Liza asked.

Lyle finished his coffee, then nodded. "Oddly enough, he even bragged to Keith about what a slick job he'd done, sneaking in and punching a hole in your brake line while you and Liza were in the trailer, and next time pouring gasoline all over Oakview, knowing you were asleep inside that same trailer."

"So they've got him on attempted murder, murder and arson." Liza sighed. "He may never get out."

"That's all right by me," Sam said emphatically.

Lyle agreed. "Keith found Joe's file when they searched Ed's place. He kept it in a locked drawer. And he had newspaper articles and pictures of himself conducting the search for Joe pinned up on a bulletin board."

"His fifteen minutes of fame," Liza commented.

"Right." Lyle glanced at his watch and got up. "I've got to run along."

They both walked him to the door. "I can't thank you enough for all you've done," Sam told him as Liza gave the attorney a quick hug.

"I'm just glad everything worked out so well," Lyle said. "Talk with you soon." He walked outside and down the stairs.

On a huge sigh, Liza closed and locked the door after him, then turned to face Sam. "He's not half as glad as I am that all this has ended well."

"Or me." Sam took her into his arms, gazing into her wonderful green eyes. "Are you ready to start over, to make us a family finally?"

"I've been ready for a mighty long time." Winding her arms around his neck, she leaned into his kiss. It was long and very thorough and might have gone on much longer except for a sleepy voice interrupting from the doorway.

"Does this mean I'm going to have a daddy pretty soon?" Beth asked as she rubbed her eyes.

Breaking the kiss, Liza went to her. "What are you doing out of bed, young lady? Seems like I tucked you in over an hour ago."

"Well, does it, Sam?" Beth asked, peering around her mother and looking up at the tall man.

Sam smiled at her, glad it wasn't a nightmare that had awakened his daughter, but rather their conversation. He hoped in time she'd forget the harrowing events of the afternoon. "Have I told you how brave I think you were, biting the sheriff's hand like that?" he asked, stooping down to her.

"I was awful scared he was going to shoot us." But her eyes were clear as both of them slid their arms around her. "Nobody answered my question. Mom, are you going to marry Sam?"

"Yes, honey," Liza said, her heart full to overflowing. "But first, there's something Sam and I have to tell you."

With that, the three of them sat down to discuss the past so they could begin their future.

* * * * *

Return to the Towers!

In March
New York Times bestselling author

NORA ROBERTS

brings us to the Calhouns' fabulous
Maine coast mansion and reveals the
tragic secrets hidden there for generations.

For all his degrees, Professor Max Quartermain has a
lot to learn about love—and luscious Lilah Calhoun is
just the woman to teach him. Ex-cop Holt Bradford is
as prickly as a thornbush—until Suzanna Calhoun's
special touch makes love blossom in his heart.
And all of them are caught in the race to solve
the generations-old mystery of a priceless
lost necklace…and a timeless love.

Lilah and Suzanna
THE
Calhoun Women

**A special 2-in-1 edition containing
FOR THE LOVE OF LILAH and
SUZANNA'S SURRENDER**

Available at your favorite retail outlet.

Take 4 bestselling love stories FREE

Plus get a FREE surprise gift!

**Make a Valentine's date
for the premiere of**

◆ HARLEQUIN® **Movies**

starting February 14, 1998 with

Debbie Macomber's

This Matter of

Marriage

on **the movie
channel**

Just tune in to **The Movie Channel** the **second Saturday night** of every month at 9:00 p.m. EST to join us, and be swept away by the sheer thrill of romance brought to life. Watch for details of upcoming movies—in books, in your television viewing guide and in stores.

If you are not currently a subscriber to The Movie Channel, simply call your local cable or satellite provider for more details. Call today, and don't miss out on the romance!

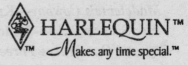

**the movie ⓜ
channel**
*100% pure movies.
100% pure fun.*

◆ HARLEQUIN™
Makes any time special.™

SANDRA STEFFEN

Continues the
twelve-book series—
36 Hours—in February 1998
with Book Eight

MARRIAGE BY CONTRACT

Nurse Bethany Kent could think of only one man who could make her dream come true: Dr. Tony Petrocelli, the man who had helped her save the life of the infant she desperately wanted to adopt. As husband and wife, they could provide the abandoned baby with a loving home. But could they provide each other with more than just a convenient marriage?

For Tony and Bethany and *all* the residents of Grand Springs, Colorado, the storm-induced blackout was just the beginning of 36 Hours that changed *everything!* You won't want to miss a single book.

Available at your favorite retail outlet.

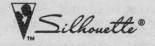

MONTANA Mavericks™

RETURN TO WHITEHORN

Silhouette's beloved **MONTANA MAVERICKS** returns with brand-new stories from your favorite authors! Welcome back to Whitehorn, Montana—a place where rich tales of passion and adventure are unfolding under the Big Sky. The new generation of Mavericks will leave you breathless!

Coming from Silhouette Special Edition®:

February 98: LETTER TO A LONESOME COWBOY by Jackie Merritt

March 98: WIFE MOST WANTED by Joan Elliott Pickart

May 98: A FATHER'S VOW by Myrna Temte

June 98: A HERO'S HOMECOMING by Laurie Paige

And don't miss these two very special additions to the Montana Mavericks saga:

MONTANA MAVERICKS WEDDINGS
by Diana Palmer, Ann Major and Susan Mallery
Short story collection available April 98

WILD WEST WIFE by Susan Mallery
Harlequin Historicals available July 98

Round up these great new stories
at your favorite retail outlet.

Silhouette®   Look us up on-line at: http://www.romance.net

SSEMMF-J